MONSTER CLUB

MONSTER CLUB

DARREN ARONOFSKY
AND
ARI HANDEL

ART BY RONALD KURNIAWAN

HARPER
An Imprint of HarperCollins Publishers

Library of Congress Cataloging-in-Publication Data

Names: Aronofsky, Darren, author. | Handel, Ari, author.

Title: Monster club / by Darren Aronofsky and Ari Handel.

Description: First edition. | New York, NY : Harper, 2022. |
Series: Monster club ; #1 | Audience: Ages 8-12 | Audience: Grades 4-6 |
Summary: Middle-schooler Eric, who lives near Coney Island, discovers a
magic ink that brings his monster drawings to life.

Identifiers: LCCN 2021061344 | ISBN 9780063136632 (hardcover)

Subjects: CYAC: Clubs--Fiction. | Magic--Fiction. | Monsters--Fiction.

Classification: LCC PZ7.1.A76326 Mo 2022 | DDC [Fic]--dc23

LC record available at https://lccn.loc.gov/2021061344

Book design by Alison Klapthor

22 23 24 25 26   PC/LSCH   10 9 8 7 6 5 4 3 2 1

❖

First Edition

Dedicated to the MBP

PROLOGUE

Coney Island, Brooklyn. July 1949.

This story starts a long time ago.

Like, more-than-one-hundred-years-in-the-past long time ago.

But, for our purposes, we won't go that far back. Not yet, anyway.

We'll start in the 1940s, which was a very different time from today, when no one had a smartphone and hot dogs only cost a nickel.

In Coney Island, Brooklyn—one of the best spots in the entire world—a twelve-year-old boy snuck out of his apartment so that he could finally go see King's Sideshow Extraordinaire. It was here that something happened that would change his life forever:

A tattoo winked at him.

It's true. This really happened.

But before we get to that, it's helpful if you understand a thing or two about Coney Island in 1949. Imagine a place that's all about fun, and weirdness, and excitement; a place that cultivates a childlike sense of wonder in every human being of every age. A place that's home to not just one amusement park but *several*, all clustered near each other so you could spend a day joyfully bouncing between them. A place with heart-pounding roller coasters with names like the Cyclone, and the Thunderbolt, and the Tornado. A place with other insane rides with names like the Flip-Flap, and the Razzle Dazzle, and the Hoodoo Room, and the Witching Waves, and the Steeplechase, where you'd ride a mechanical horse on a track while a little person chased you with a cattle prod. (Told you it was insane.) A place that stands right next to the beach, smack-dab in the center of five miles of boardwalk. A place like Disney World, except so much more fun and so much more weird and with no Mickey Mouse breathing down your neck all the time. When most immigrants came to America on ships back then, it wasn't the torch of the Statue of Liberty they saw first but the one hundred thousand electric lights of Coney Island.

And for the boy who starts our story, this place was everything. Once the summer season began, he went to

Coney with his parents at least once a month, but they were clear that one part was always off-limits: King's Sideshow Extraordinaire.

In case you're not familiar with what a sideshow is, it's where fascinating, unusual people get to show off their fascinating, unusual qualities. For example, you might see a bearded lady. Or a sword swallower. Or a man with a tiny head. Or a woman with no head! The boy and his parents would often walk past the barker in the black top hat and suspenders as he shouted about all the incredible-sounding people you could see at King's Sideshow—and for just twenty cents!—but the boy's father would always give the same justification when the boy begged to go.

"Because it's trash, that's why," he would say. "If I want to see some freaks, I'll just pick a street corner in front of one of my Lower East Side buildings, stand there, and look at who passes by."

The boy's father found a way to bring every conversation back to those stupid buildings he owned, and the boy was so tired of it.

And on this particular day, the boy was tired of being told no too.

So he grabbed fifteen hard-earned pennies and one nickel out of his piggy bank—a month's worth of allowance—and left his dull-looking row house in

Brighton Beach, telling his mom he needed to get something from the hardware store for a science experiment he'd heard about on the radio.

The boy was breathless in anticipation as he sat down in the warehouse bleachers of King's Sideshow Extraordinaire and the man in the black top hat and suspenders shouted that they were all about to see something incredible.

Even when the incredible something turned out to be identical-twin tattooed strongmen acrobats—not nearly as weird as the boy had been hoping for—he still felt euphoric. They were called the Spectacular Geilio Brothers, and they were the most muscular men the boy had ever seen in his life. Dressed in tight red jumpsuits with U-shaped collars that dipped halfway down their chests, the brothers performed truly astounding feats: walking on their hands, standing on each other's shoulders, *backflipping* off each other's shoulders, and—the boy's personal favorite—combining their bodies into a somersaulting human bowling ball and rolling themselves into giant-size bowling pins.

Just as mesmerizing as their feats, though, were the vivid and detailed tattoos on their chests, more like paintings in a museum than body art. The bottom halves of the tattoos were concealed by the jumpsuits, but as best as the boy could tell, one of the Geilio

Brothers had an image of a lion monster—green fur with black stripes, and two huge yellow dragon wings—and the other had King Neptune, the all-powerful god of the sea, complete with white beard, crown, trident, and explosively defined muscles.

After a final, extended sequence of tumbles, flips, and rolls, the strongmen raised their arms in the air for a bow. As the boy wildly applauded, he found himself staring in awe at the King Neptune tattoo, amazed by how real it looked, and that was when it happened:

The god of the sea *winked at him.*

The boy turned with his jaw dropped to the skinny bald man next to him, like *Wow, did you see that?* but the man just nodded politely and continued applauding as if he'd witnessed an acrobatic show and nothing more.

Perhaps it had just been a trick of the light, some kind of magician's illusion.

The boy didn't think so, though.

Dozens of sweaty people filed out of the warehouse, and the boy impulsively squeezed past a rowdy group of sailors and ducked under the bleachers. He had no real plan, but he needed to know if he'd actually seen what he thought he had. After every audience member had left and the warehouse had gone silent, the boy crept out from his hiding spot like he was the Spirit, the masked crime fighter from his favorite newspaper

comic. The boy tiptoed toward the back of the cavern-
ous room, passing the stage and the red curtain behind
it to find a half-open door that led into a dim, dingy
hallway.

Shouts and cheers from farther down the hall made
the boy hesitate.

But he summoned his bravery and walked forward,
the voices and laughter getting louder.

At the end of the hallway was another warehouse-style
space, smaller and darker than the one he'd just been in,
where a group of people was gathered in a loose circle,
surrounded by lit torches. They were yelling and cheering and swigging from bottles as two men stood in the
center of the circle.

"My money's on Neptune!" someone shouted.

"You kidding me?" someone shouted back. "This is
Leo's day!"

As the boy huddled in shadow in the door frame,
his eyes adjusted to the darkness, and he saw that the
two men in the center of the ring were the Spectacular
Geilio Brothers.

"Quiet! Quiet, please!" a man said from the side. "We
are about to begin." It was the barker, without his black
top hat but still in suspenders. He was holding a wad of
cash. Next to him was a man with a tiny head, and next
to *him* was a bearded lady. The boy quickly realized

with delight that everyone there was a performer in the sideshow.

Almost in spite of himself, he took a few steps closer.

"Are you ready?" the barker asked the Spectacular Geilio Brothers.

They nodded.

"UNLEASH!" he shouted.

The brothers pulled their shirt straps down from their shoulders, letting the top halves of their jumpsuits flop over their waists.

The boy gasped as their full tattoos were exposed to the light.

They were glorious.

But, more surprisingly, King Neptune had crab legs.

His bottom half, previously hidden by the Geilio Brother's jumpsuit, wasn't human at all, and that somehow made the image even more astonishing, like some kind of beautiful monster.

The boy couldn't help but stare at King Neptune's face again, hoping the tattoo would give him another wink.

Instead, King Neptune began to ripple on the Geilio Brother's skin, and both of the Spectacular Geilio Brothers began to scream out in pain. The skin around the tattoo seemed to be stretching, pulsing, leaving the god of the sea tattoo flopping down from the Geilio Brother's chest like his jumpsuit straps.

The boy watched in horror as the same thing happened to the lion monster, the chest skin pulling and undulating and loosening in a way that looked terribly unpleasant. Suddenly both tattoos flipped back up and folded inward, as if they were burrowing into each brother's rib cage. Through all this, the Spectacular Geilio Brothers gritted their teeth and tried not to scream, stanching their pain by taking a swig from a bottle passed to them by the bearded lady.

Just when the boy thought he couldn't watch a second longer, there were two loud *POP!* noises in quick succession. He wasn't sure what had just happened, but the brothers stopped screaming—now they were breathing fast and their chests were red and raw. It was then that the boy realized:

The tattoos were gone.

Again, he thought his eyes were playing tricks on him, but no—the Geilio Brothers' chests were blank.

"Come on, Neptune!" the tiny-headed man shouted. Soon everyone was yelling and cheering again, and the boy had no idea why.

He followed the crowd's gaze down to the floor, shifting himself slightly to see in between people. Then he understood.

Standing in the circle were a couple of creatures, each of them about one and a half feet high.

One was a yellow-winged green-and-black lion monster.

The other was King Neptune with crab legs.

The tattoos had leapt off the Geilio Brothers' chests and become real. From flat drawings to three-dimensional live creatures.

"All right!" the barker said, raising his voice over the din of the small group. "We are now moments away from witnessing the epic confrontation we have all been waiting for. Leo and King Neptune: Are you ready?"

The lion monster roared his approval.

King Neptune bowed his head.

The barker lifted an arm, and the room went silent.

He dropped the arm and shouted, "FIGHT!" and called out:

LEO VS. KING NEPTUNE!

The crowd exploded with cheers. King Neptune and the lion monster began to slowly circle each other as shadows from the torches flickered over them and shouts came from all sides.

"Tear him to pieces, Leo!"

"I believe in you, Neptune!"

The boy could barely process what he was seeing.

Leo the lion monster made the first attack, lunging

forward and swiping his claws at King Neptune. The
god of the sea skittered backward on his crab legs to
dodge the parry and then stabbed his trident into one of
the beast's hind legs.

Leo the lion howled in pain as the room filled with
cheers and boos.

"Don't let him do that to you, Leo!" the barker
shouted. "I drew you to be better than that!"

Almost as if he understood, the lion recovered,
righted himself, and flapped his large yellow wings. He
lifted a couple of feet into the air before dive-bombing
King Neptune, sending both of them hurtling along the
ground.

The fight went on like that, a constant back-and-forth between the monsters, the boy's heart racing for every second of it. Several times he had to restrain himself from shouting, "Holy moly!"

Then Leo the lion let out a roar as he hopped on top of King Neptune and chomped into his shoulder.

"There it is!" the barker shouted as the man with the tiny head groaned.

Leo's victory seemed imminent—the beast wasn't letting up, continuing to snarl and tear into King Neptune as the crab god screamed. After a few moments, Neptune went silent and slumped to the ground.

The boy watched for any sign of movement. There was nothing except for a stream of black dust flowing from the fallen monster's shoulder as if escaping a chimney. It was like King Neptune was bleeding puffs of floating black powder.

The boy was stunned. He was witnessing the death of a *tattoo*.

Leo roared triumphantly as his opponent's life force drifted away into the air, when suddenly what remained of King Neptune's dissolving body snapped back to life!

The boy grinned in the darkness, elated that he hadn't left after the show and missed all this.

With a majestic grunt, the god of the sea thrust his trident diagonally upward into Leo's chest. The lion monster howled, blindly slashing his claws across Neptune's torso.

The rest of King Neptune exploded into a large cloud of black dust, but not before giving his trident one last heave, bursting Leo into dust too. The two monsters disintegrated into the air, and everyone in the room went absolutely nuts—hooting, howling, and hollering.

Unfortunately, that also included the boy, who involuntarily made a joyful shrieking sound.

The barker's head snapped toward him.

"What the . . . ," he said.

The rest of the group's heads spun toward the boy too, and a chill ran through him as he realized that he'd somehow ended up right next to one of the torches, leaving him very much illuminated.

"He saw," one of the Spectacular Geilio Brothers said in a thick accent. "I can tell he saw."

The boy wanted to tell them how amazed he was by what he'd witnessed, how it was the best thing he'd ever seen in his entire life, how he could easily keep this secret if that's what they wanted from him.

But instead, the boy decided to run.

"Get him!" the barker shouted, even more passionately than during the tattoo fight. "He cannot give away our secret!"

The boy had never in his life swung so quickly from

ecstatic joy to full-flung terror. He'd also never been a particularly fast runner, but he had a couple of seconds' head start on his side. He hoofed it back down the grimy hallway, a stampede of sideshow performers behind him, at least a couple of them holding torches.

"Slow down, boy!" the Geilio Brother yelled. "We don't want to hurt you!"

"You have nothing to be afraid of!" the bearded lady shouted.

But the boy didn't listen. He certainly didn't believe them. Soon he was back in the semidarkness of the warehouse—it was lit by a single bulb on a stand in the center of the room—trying to cut as direct a path to the exit as possible.

Yes! There it was ahead of him. He was going to make it.

But then his path was blocked.

Conjoined twins—two women's heads on what was essentially one body—stepped in front of him, holding a torch in each hand.

"Stop!" the women's heads said at the same time.

The boy ducked low, charging forward into their stomach, evading the Geilio Brother and the rest of the sideshow performers just in time.

"Oof!" the twins said, heaving a few steps to the side, their torches clattering to the ground.

As the boy sprinted toward the exit door, he felt a heat grow alongside him, and he realized that their torch flames must have caught the bottom hem of the thick curtain hanging down the warehouse wall.

"Fire! Fire!" the bearded lady screamed.

And suddenly the boy realized the flames had somehow leapt up onto his hand.

His left hand was on fire.

He used his right one to push open the exit door. He dashed out across the boardwalk, through the throngs of tourists, down onto the sand, where he plunged his hand into the ocean tide and immediately fainted.

The boy never knew exactly who had called an ambulance, or who had gotten in touch with his parents, but he did know that he woke up the next day in the hospital, his left hand wrapped tightly in bandages.

It felt as if he'd dreamed the entire experience, but when he saw the front page of the newspaper his father was carrying, he knew he hadn't.

MASSIVE FIRE DESTROYS KING'S SIDESHOW

It was gone. The sideshow was gone. And it was his fault.

It was a headline the boy would never be able to forget, even when King's reopened several years later as an amusement park.

He would also never forget those tattoos.

Those wonderful, impossible tattoos.

They became something of an obsession for him.

They changed the boy. They helped him realize who he was.

He wanted nothing more than to experience that magic again.

And eventually, many years later, he would.

1

THAT HORRIBLE BOX

Coney Island, Brooklyn. Now.

I don't think Dad's going to be staying for dinner.

There are several reasons I have come to this conclusion, the main one being that he and Mom are shouting at each other so loudly, I can hear every word through my bedroom door.

"Other options?" Dad is saying. "What do you mean *other options*?"

I try to focus on my pen skimming the surface of my sketchbook.

"What do you mean *what do I mean*?" Mom says. "We've had this conversation four thousand times! You need a plan in case things don't go well with King's."

I outline one of Brickman's muscular arms, then the other.

"Oh wow, thanks so much for believing in me," Dad says.

Then Brickman's torso, one tightly packed brick after another.

"Ugh," Mom sighs. "It has nothing to do with believing in you; we got slammed by a hurricane!"

My pen slips and gives Brickman something resembling a tail.

Brickman doesn't have a tail.

I put the pen down.

The King's that Mom mentioned is King's Wonderland, the amusement park Dad owns and runs. The hurricane she referred to is Hurricane Zadie, who swooped in last fall and wreaked absolute havoc on our lives. Zadie hit King's hard. Very hard. Like, all-the-rides-were-damaged-and-some-were-completely-destroyed hard. The rest of the Coney Island boardwalk didn't fare too well either. In fact, at least a couple of the other amusement parks have already thrown in the towel, allowing themselves to be bought out in the off-season by "the Vultures" (as Dad calls them) to make way for luxury condos. Dad's not gonna let that happen to King's. "There's too much magic in Coney Island," he says, "for a measly hurricane and a couple of suits to end it."

Still, it's stressful—as Dad gears up for opening day on Friday, he's been so overwhelmed with the amount he has to do to get everything in working order that he's actually been sleeping in the shed at King's instead of at home. There's a bed in there—it's not like he's lying on a pile of tools or something—but still. He's done that a few times over the years, but never for a full month straight. These days I pretty much only see him when I visit him at King's, which is why I was so excited to hear he'd be stopping by tonight.

I should've known it would turn into an argument with Mom within two minutes of him walking in the door.

My parents are at it again, I text my best friend. *Super fun.*

Yoo-hoo replies with a GIF of a cartoon man whose face is melting off.

It's a pretty accurate depiction of how I'm feeling. Yoo-hoo is a GIF genius.

Sorry dude, he says. *That sux.*

Yoo-hoo (his name is Alan Yoo, but he's gone by Yoo-hoo almost the whole time I've known him, in no small part due to his obsession with said beverage, specifically when it's flavored vanilla) is no stranger to this sort of thing. His parents got divorced when we were in second grade.

I'm about to text back when I realize the kitchen has gone quiet, which either means Dad has left without saying bye (or hi) to me, or there's a temporary lull on the battlefield. I pocket my phone and step out of my room to find out.

Once I'm downstairs, I see Mom standing next to the counter staring at nothing while nibbling on a piece of grated cheese, still in her lawyer clothes. Our dog, Dr. Pepper, is lying underneath the kitchen table, head on her paws. Pepper doesn't like the fighting either.

"Oh, hi, sweetie," Mom says, looking sort of sheepish, as if I've caught her shoplifting or something. "Tacos will be ready in five."

"Did Dad leave?"

"Leave? No, not yet."

"Oh. Good." I'm glad he's still here, but the words *not yet* have all but confirmed he won't be sticking around for taco night.

"Yeah." Mom turns to the pan on the stove, shifting the sizzling seitan around with a wooden spoon.

"Hey, buddy," Dad says from behind me.

"Hey, Dad." I'm so glad to see him and his stubbly face, I don't realize there's a box in his hands until I go to hug him. Dad awkwardly shifts it to the side so he can kiss the top of my head.

"What's that?" I ask. "Stuff for King's?" I try to peer into the box, but it's closed.

"Uh, sort of, yeah," Dad says, suddenly seeming as

sheepish as Mom did a minute ago.

"Can I see?"

Dad looks at me for a long moment before saying, "Sure." He angles the box toward me and opens the flaps, almost losing his grip because the box is flimsy and sort of falling apart. Inside there's a sea of random junk and old photos.

"Why do you need that for work? Are you starting the museum?" I ask.

"No, not yet, it's, uh . . . ," Dad says, opening and closing his mouth a few times before turning to Mom for an answer.

"Don't look at me," she says. "Like I said, I'm happy for you to put it in the basement if you want to. As long as you get it out of our bedroom."

"You know I'm not putting it back down there," Dad says. "That's how it almost got ruined in the first place." The basement flooded in the fall, courtesy of Zadie. Most of the stuff down there was Dad's—all these random posters and artifacts and knickknacks from King's Wonderland over the decades, from when his parents and grandparents and great-grandparents ran it. Dad always says he wants to start a museum with all of it someday. So when the flooding happened, he salvaged whatever he could, brought it upstairs, and spread it out among all the rooms. Our house isn't that big, so I

21

have to agree with Mom here—it definitely clutters the place up.

"Well, I don't know what to tell you, then," Mom says. "We've been stepping over all your ancient junk for months now." She picks up an old tin sign from the corner of the living room that says King's Wonderland with a mermaid leaning on the *K*. "Months!" She tosses the sign back to the floor. "I'm not asking you to take all of it yet, just this one box from the bedroom."

Dad shakes his head, puffing air out of his nostrils. "Your mother's right, kiddo," he tells me. "This box is getting in the way in her bedroom—I mean, *our* bedroom—so I'm taking it to King's."

"Put it in my bedroom," I say. "That's fine with me."

Dad looks thrown by this, as if it's a brilliant idea and he doesn't know why he didn't think of it. I can't help but feel proud.

"No," Mom says. "Eric, that's not the point."

"Yeah, bud," Dad says, "I appreciate that, but—"

"Your room is a mess as it is, Eric," Mom says.

"That's why it's not a big deal," I say. "That box will blend right in with my—"

"Fine!" Mom rarely shouts at me, so it's always pretty shocking when she does. "You want to hold on to Dad's box for him, then fine, shove it in with the rest of the junk in your closet. Let's just have junk in every room, and I'll keep nagging both of you till the end of time to do something with it, and we can stop talking about this already now."

"Geez, okay," I say, looking at the floor.

Mom and Dad are silent, and for some reason that's the moment my brain decides to clue me in on what's been in front of my face this entire time.

"Wait," I say. "Is this . . . I mean . . . Once King's opens up and things get less stressful, will . . . Like, Dad's coming back then, right?"

I don't look up from the floor the whole time I say it.

"Uh," I hear Dad say. "Yeah, we're gonna . . . We're gonna see."

We're gonna see.

Not what I was expecting.

"It's complicated, Eric," Mom says with another sigh. "We're trying to figure it out. But that doesn't mean we're not both here for you as much as ever. More than ever. And you can talk to us about all of it."

"Yeah," Dad says, picking the worst possible moment of all time to pass that horrible box to me.

I feel so ridiculous. I thought Dad had been staying in the King's shed because of work and work alone. It didn't even occur to me that the fighting between him and Mom might also be part of it.

"Are you okay?" Mom asks.

I nod, even though I'm having trouble taking a deep breath.

"One second," I say, trying unsuccessfully to sound normal and relaxed, before walking back upstairs and into my room. I drop the flimsy, water-damaged box onto the carpet, then shut the door and face-plant into my bed, pushing aside my pathetic Brickman-with-a-tail so I don't cry on him.

2

YOO-HOO AND ME AND MONSTER CLUB

So my parents might be splitting up.

I can't stop thinking about it.

I had a totally restless night of sleep, an endless stream of questions bouncing through my brain: *How will this even look? Am I gonna live with just Mom? Or will I live part of the time with Dad in his weird shed?*

It's hard to believe it's real. And I can't help but think that if Dad is able to get King's up and running and doing well enough to stave off the luxury condo vultures, it will solve everything. If you took away that stress, he and Mom wouldn't fight anymore. Or, at least, not nearly as much.

Man, how I wish I'd never seen Dad holding that stupid box.

I almost trip on it when I get out of bed, and I'm angrily sliding it into the closet when I decide to peek inside first, to see for myself what all the fuss is about.

There are tons of photos, most of them bent, misshapen, faded, and really old. Like, so old that they're black and white, not in an IG filter way, but in a this-is-the-only-option-because-color-photos-don't-exist-yet way. One jumps out at me, an old picture of the Parachute Jump, this huge 250-foot-high structure on the Coney Island boardwalk that used to be a ride. Even though there are no longer twelve parachutes going up and down the sides, two people seated below each one, the Parachute Jump is still one of the most iconic symbols of Coney. It's kinda like what the Empire State Building is for Manhattan, or what the Taj Mahal is for India, or what the Golden Arches are for Mickey D's. Standing and smiling at the base of it in this photo are an older man and woman looking weirdly formal for Coney, the man in suspenders and a tie and—hilariously—a black top hat, the woman in a dark collared dress. Probably my relatives. I try to zoom in so I can see them better before remembering it's not on my phone.

I paw through the rest of the box's contents, and, much like the other stuff Dad's had spread all over the house since the fall, it really does seem like junk. There's a strange metal device with screws and coils and a long rod jutting out, like some kind of medical instrument.

There's also a green-tinted mason jar, filled with some kind of dark substance, that I struggle to open for an embarrassingly long time before I finally get it to budge. I immediately regret it. The black stuff in there smells so nasty it shuts my brain off for a second. It's like all the worst fishy smells from the ocean blended with a heaping pile of garbage that's been sitting out in the sun for a week. I put the lid back on and screw it closed as tight as possible, chuck it into the box with a thud.

Guess when you save some random black liquid for like a hundred years, it goes bad. No wonder Mom wanted it out of her bedroom.

I should put it in the trash, and that useless metal device along with it, but I know Dad feels nostalgic about and protective of all this stuff, probably wants to put it in his museum. Instead, I push the stupid box the rest of the way into my closet, balancing it awkwardly on top of dirty clothes and old sneakers, before shutting the door.

I'd prefer not to think about that box—and my parents' possible divorce—ever again, honestly. But that's easier said than done. I think about it all morning, as I shower, as I eat a waffle, and as I walk my bike out of the garage.

"Sup!" Yoo-hoo says as he comes out of his house across the street, wearing his usual cargo shorts and black Kylo Ren bike helmet and throwing both arms in the air excitedly, bouncing up and down, as if it's not seven in the morning. I can't help but grin for the first time in twelve hours. Yoo-hoo has that effect on me.

"Sup," I say, steering my bike around the lifeless tree still lying alongside the curb thanks to Zadie.

Yoo-hoo moved to Sea Gate in first grade. It's a community near Coney Island, with lots of little houses right next to each other. It's also surrounded by water on three sides, which is why Zadie beat us up so bad. Since he got here, Yoo-hoo and I have traveled to school together—in elementary school, our parents carpooled, but since middle school started, we've been taking our bikes. It's an easy ten-minute ride.

We go to Mark Twain Middle School for the Gifted and Talented. (I know it's kind of an embarrassing name, like I'm bragging or something, but it's just what it's called.) Even though it's a public school, you have to apply and get accepted for a specific talent, which was actually pretty nerve-racking because Yoo-hoo found out he got in a day before me. After twenty-four horrible hours where I had to imagine going to school without my best friend, I got in too. Thank god. I got in as art talent; Yoo-hoo is music talent. (He plays the drums. He's really good.)

"This feels like a Tuesday with potential," Yoo-hoo says, cutting across the lawn of mainly dead grass to the side of the house where he keeps his bike. "Don't you feel like that?"

"Uh," I say. "I mean, maybe? Not really."

"You're wrong, Doodles." Doodles is my nickname. Because I doodle a lot. Yoo-hoo unlocks his bike and walks it to the street. "I'm very tapped into these things, and I am feeling very powerful Tuesday vibes."

"Okay." I immediately know that I should have mustered more enthusiasm, as Yoo-hoo picks up on everything, and now he's going to ask if I'm okay.

"How are you, by the way?" he asks. Right on schedule. "Everything work out with your folks?"

"Oh yeah, definitely," I lie. "Just one of their usual stupid fights." It's rare that I hide things from Yoo-hoo, but I don't want to talk or think anymore about my parents' pending breakup. Especially since they might figure things out and not even break up at all.

"Okey dokey." Yoo-hoo hops on his bike, and we start pedaling toward school. "But you know I have lots of wisdom on this topic. If you ever want to talk."

"Thank you, oh wise one," I say.

Yoo-hoo bows his head. "Speaking of which, I was hoping to get *your* wisdom on something."

"Go for it."

"Well," Yoo-hoo says. "I'm kinda feeling like . . . maybe I want to start going by Yoo instead of Yoo-hoo?"

"What? Why?"

"Just, I don't know, to change things up. I don't even drink Yoo-hoo that much anymore."

"No way," I say. It's actually comforting to be posed with such an obvious no-brainer. "You're Yoo-hoo. That's, like, who you are. It's the best nickname ever."

"Yeah. Okay," Yoo-hoo says, nodding. "You're probably right. Thanks."

"Sure."

We pedal in silence for a few moments.

"You ready for tomorrow?" Yoo-hoo asks.

It takes me a minute to understand what he's even talking about, which is a testament to how much my parents' situation has thrown me. Tomorrow is the Monster Club Battle Royale Semifinals, and until last night, I'd been thinking about it nonstop. That's why I was drawing Brickman. My monster.

"I was born ready," I say. "Brickman's gonna crush."

Yoo-hoo hangs back to let a car pass us on the left. Mornings when we have more time, we take the scenic route to school—down the boardwalk, past the Parachute Jump, the Wonder Wheel, the Cyclone, the aquarium—but we're running a smidge late today, so it's just a straight shot down Neptune Avenue. Yoo-hoo shouts from behind me. "I hope he does crush! That way we can meet in the finals next week. There's no way I'm not taking down Hollywood in the semifinals. The BellyBeast I drew last weekend is truly something to behold. Possibly my best ever."

"You say that literally every time."

Yoo-hoo pedals back up next to me. "Yeah, but this time I really mean it."

"You say that every time too."

Yoo-hoo grins and rings the bell on his bike twice.

He and I formed Monster Club in fourth grade after we realized we were both obsessed with drawing monsters. We found ourselves constantly comparing our creations, talking for literally hours about whose would come out victorious in a battle, until finally it occurred to us that, duh, we could *actually* make them battle. Well, not *actually*, but pretty close.

Over the course of the next few weeks, we holed up every day after school in one of our bedrooms like a couple of rocket scientists—testing, adjusting, calibrating, perfecting, as we developed the coolest, smartest monster battle game of all time. Yes, it's true that most of the elements of the game are stolen from *other* games— in some cases literally, as our game relies on four-sided tetrahedral dice from Dungeons & Dragons, the spinner from Life, and the multisided letter die from my mom's all-time favorite game, Scattergories—but we've fused them into a Frankenstein's monster–like game that, as far as I'm concerned, is a work of art.

For a month or two, Yoo-hoo and I were the club's only members, and that was honestly fine by us. In fact, it was sort of our intention. We liked the idea that we'd founded a highly exclusive team, one where you had to prove yourself worthy of membership. Our classmates would see us battling at recess and want to get in on it, and we'd explain that first they'd have to put in at least one day of watching, after which we would see if they were ready for battle action. Obviously no one ever wanted to devote a full recess to watching other people have fun, so no one was ever worthy. Yeah. We were total snobs.

When we finally did admit someone else, it wasn't one of our classmates but Yoo-hoo's family friend Ahmed. "He wants in," Yoo-hoo told me.

"So what?" I said. "Lots of people want in. How does

he even know about it?"

"I told him."

"You *what*?"

"Dude, it's not like Monster Club is a secret. That is not a rule of Monster Club."

"Well, maybe it should be."

"This is a good thing, Doodles! I think Hollywood could be great."

"Hollywood?"

"Oh. That's Ahmed's nickname."

"Why?"

"'Cause he wants to be a movie star one day. But the point is, Hollywood has true potential. Also, we're gonna need more members if we want more epic battles."

"Fine," I said. He had a good point there, but I was skeptical that *anyone* other than us could be worthy of Monster Club. "We'll see."

Hollywood and his family were over at Yoo-hoo's house the next Sunday, so I went across the street to see what all the hype was about. And wouldn't you know it: Hollywood lived up to his name. He was way cooler than me and Yoo-hoo, with brand-new Air Jordans and zigzags shaved into the sides of his buzz cut. He was also passionate about movies, and funny, and—Yoo-hoo was right—he really did show membership potential. Not only did he have no problem with just watching for thirty minutes, but he easily picked up on the game rules once we allowed him to play. And he said nice things about Brickman.

"Your monster is dope."

"Oh, thanks," I said.

"What's that coming from his hand? Cement?"

"Yeah. He can shoot it out of the fingers of his left hand."

"But not his right?"

"No. Only the left."

"I like that," Hollywood said.

"BellyBeast is dope too, though, right?" Yoo-hoo asked.

"Yeah," Hollywood said. "Sure."

And thus, Ahmed "Hollywood" Wilson became the official third member of Monster Club, along with his creature, RoboKillz, a beautiful robot with shoulder missiles, all-terrain tank treads, and a saw-blade hand, inspired by Hollywood's love of sci-fi, especially the *Terminator* movies. Hollywood went to PS 206 in a different neighborhood, Sheepshead Bay, so he obviously couldn't play at recess, but after school and on the weekends, we battled every chance we could get. That's the way it went through fifth grade, and then, miracle of miracles, Hollywood got into Mark Twain too, as a drama talent, so when this school year started, Monster Club went full throttle. He brought on his elementary school friend Beanie (science talent), I pulled in Smash (art talent, like me), and suddenly we were doing full tournaments, with brackets and everything.

It's been the best part of my year by far.

Which is why I can't believe I forgot that semifinals for the Spring Battle Royale are *tomorrow*. I haven't even finished my new Brickman yet.

A car horn blares. I swing my handlebars wildly toward the curb as a Honda passes within inches of me, sending a gust of air whooshing past my nose. I was so lost in thought, I strayed into the line of traffic.

"You okay back there?" Yoo-hoo shouts from behind me.

I have no idea, I want to say. I'm not used to zoning out like that. I regain balance and stop wobbling. *Possibly not.*

Instead I shout back "All good" and we continue on our way.

3

SCHOOL MONSTERS

Brickman wasn't my first monster.

There were a few others before him. They were solid but ultimately failed attempts at creating the perfect battle beast.

There was Dust-Dragon, a huge purple dragon who, well . . . breathed dust instead of fire. There was The Hermit, a gigantic hermit crab who could ball up in her shell and steamroll her opponent. There was 5G, essentially a giant smartphone with claws who could blast Wi-Fi lasers at anyone in his way.

And then there was Brickman.

He's not as flashy as those other monsters, and he doesn't have nearly as many bells and whistles, yet something made me fall in love with him, made him become the faithful monster I've relied upon now for more than two years. Could be the insanely cool cement he blasts out of his left hand. Could be the equally killer demolition ball he swings from a chain in his right hand. Could be that he's trained in Krav Maga, this Israeli approach to fighting I learned about on YouTube that combines techniques from boxing, wrestling, karate, judo, and aikido. Or maybe it's the personal triumph I've felt in how I nailed the shading of the bricks that make up Brickman's rock-solid, nearly invincible body. But,

most likely, it's the humanity I've drawn into his eyes and features; he feels less like a creation and more like an actual friend.

I realize the ridiculous nerdiness of me talking this way about my own drawing, but I guess my point is, I didn't just randomly sketch Brickman one day and then commit to him forever. Like everything else Monster Club–related, it was a decision made over time and with great thought and care. It's the same great thought and care I'm currently channeling into my rendering of Brickman for the semifinals tomorrow. Since part of every battle is marking up your opponent's monster based on the damage you inflict, everyone needs a fresh drawing each round. Honestly, the quality of the drawing barely factors into winning the game, but it's, like, a side competition we have among ourselves. To take the tournament *and* have the sickest-drawn monster is the ultimate triumph. And I want it bad. I was ranked first during the spring season, so I got to skip quarterfinals last week and advance directly to semifinals, where I'll be facing off against Beanie and her monster, DecaSpyder. Deca's this incredible spider made of metal that shoots titanium silk webbing and also lasers. Considering my only loss this season was to them, I'm taking it really seriously. Not to mention that Beanie won the Winter Battle Royale in February, so she's the current holder of the Monster Club Crown of Glory (a tin crown I stole from my dad's collection of old King's junk). I'm excited to take it from her.

I was able to spend most of first period working on Brickman since Mrs. Franklin doesn't really care what we do while she lectures about weather patterns and cold fronts or whatever, but my world history teacher, Mr. Zendel, is more of a stickler for paying attention. So even though the second-period bell hasn't rung yet,

I'm still trying to hide the fact that I'm doing the detail work on Brick's mortar thighs.

"Ooh, nice." I realize Mr. Zendel is hovering over my shoulder. He's in the same blue polo shirt that he seems to wear every day, nodding appreciatively. "My six-year-old would go nuts for that."

For a second, I feel really good about myself, but then I hear a couple of snorts and giggles from my classmates. Like it's so hilarious that I'm art talent and I'm drawing something a little kid would love.

"Thanks," I say, sliding Brickman from the desk onto my lap before more people start laughing.

"We're about to get started, bud," Mr. Zendel says, patting me on the back, "so if you wouldn't mind putting that away . . ."

"Yep," I say. I can feel my face has gone red.

Mr. Zendel makes his way to the front of the room, and I assume the moment is over.

"Totally awesome drawing, though," he says, giving me a thumbs-up.

"Totally awesome, dude!" someone says in a mocking voice from behind me. "You draw like a six-year-old! Way to go!"

"Okay, okay," Mr. Zendel says. "Everyone quiet down. Let's return to where we left off in our discussion of the fall of Rome."

I sneak a peek over to Yoo-hoo, whose seat is diagonally behind me. He holds up a Post-it he's written on from the neon-green pad he always keeps in his pocket. It has a *U* on it. He flicks it down on the desk, then holds up another: *OK*. Then one more: a question mark. I don't respond, both because I'm nervous I'll draw more attention to myself and because I feel like I might cry.

When the bell finally rings, Yoo-hoo and I burn out of there.

"I'm sorry, Doods," Yoo-hoo says, putting one hand on my shoulder as we walk down the hallway. "Zendel's like a clueless dad sometimes."

"Do you think it's true?" I ask, and it takes all the effort in the world.

"Yeah! I mean, that thumbs-up he gave you was just—"

"No, I mean . . ." All class there was a thought I'd been trying desperately not to think, a thought I know I have to face head-on. "What they were laughing about." I stop in the hall and hold up my drawing of Brickman. "Is it true that this is, like, what a six-year-old would draw?"

"Hell no, Doodles!" Yoo-hoo says. "I mean, of course kids would love it because Brickman is, like, the coolest monster of all time, and you're an incredible artist. But a little kid couldn't *make* that. Unless they were a superprodigy or something. Those guys laughing were just being jerks."

I'm relieved to hear him say that, even though part of me wonders if it's actually true.

"It is really good," a voice says from next to us. "Subject matter's not my taste, but there's a nice attention to detail."

Much to my surprise, it's Jenni Balloqui, staring down at Brickman with that intense gaze she has.

"Uh, thanks, Jenni."

I don't know her that well, other than knowing she is a very active and passionate participant in class who gives off a general vibe of being very on top of everything.

"It's not a compliment," she says, turning her laser gaze onto me. "It's a fact. You're a really good artist."

"Oh," I say, my head expanding to twice its size. "Cool."

"Um, I'm gonna split," Yoo-hoo says, probably picking up on the weird intensity in the air. "See ya in a bit."

"Later, Yoo-hoo," I say as he gets swept up in the stream of kids heading to third period.

"The question is," Jenni continues on, as if Yoo-hoo were just a figment of my imagination, "can you draw something real? Something like . . . this?"

She pulls a purple folder out of her backpack, the

word *Research* meticulously Sharpie'd on its front, and then pulls from that an old black-and-white photo. I have to stare at it for a few seconds before I realize it's the Parachute Jump ride from Coney Island, the thing I was staring at earlier this morning in that photo from my dad's box.

Whoa.

I desperately want to say that I can draw it, especially because this feels like fate or something like that, but the truth is I have no idea. Drawing "real things" is pretty much my kryptonite. Monsters, creatures, aliens, super-heroes, supervillains? All in my wheelhouse. Everything else? Less so. Maybe it's the pressure of having to get the details right instead of just creating directly from my imagination. Like, people will have concrete proof that I haven't done a good enough job. But when I'm the one who thought it up in the first place? No one can correct my work! Mr. Solomon, the art teacher at Mark Twain, has been pushing me a lot lately to go outside my comfort zone, but with mixed results. Well, mainly bad results, to be honest. Like when I did a self-portrait that everyone thought was a picture of eggs and bacon. But here, now, with Jenni staring at me in that way she has, no way I'll admit I can't do it. So instead I say: "Yeah, sure, I probably can draw that."

Jenni picks up on my uncertainty and squints at me. "Probably?"

"I mean, definitely. It's, like, just a big piece of metal, really, so . . . I mean, yeah. That's a no-sweat kind of thing for me."

"Good." She starts walking down the hall, and I'm unsure if that's her way of saying bye, but then she looks back to me like *You coming?* so I follow. "Take a look at this," she says, before grabbing a green three-ring binder out of her bag, carefully unclicking it, and pulling out a piece of paper enshrined within one of those clear page protectors. Jenni Balloqui does not mess around. "Page one," she says, handing it to me.

"Of what? A comic?"

"Ew, no! It's a graphic novel." She sounds like that should be obvious from the large empty comic panels above freakishly neat handwriting. "It's on the history of Coney. From the Mesozoic dinosaur era through the indigenous people all the way up to the hurricane."

"Oh, I get it," I say. "So the drawings go in the big boxes." I sound like an idiot even to myself.

Jenni stares at me again, like she's regretting this entire interaction.

"Very cool," I say, trying to redeem myself. "I love history." That's a total lie. I think history is super boring; it's all dates and faraway places and old guys in awkward wigs.

"Okay, good. Because I want you to be my art talent."

"Huh?"

"Creative writing talent has to find art talent to collaborate with. For the seventh-grade project."

"Oh. Even though we're in . . . sixth grade?"

"Getting a head start," Jenni says, smiling for the first time that I've ever witnessed, revealing that she has dimples. Who knew? "You in or out?"

"Uh . . . in?"

"Superb," Jenni says. She takes the Parachute Jump photo and blank page out of my right hand, grabs Brickman out of my left, puts them all into the purple folder, then places the whole thing into my hand. "I'd love to see a sample page one by the end of the week."

"*This* week?"

Jenni stops walking. "I have a couple of other partners in mind. So if you don't think you're up for it, let me know. I only get A's, obviously, so speak now if this is too much for you."

"It's not," I say, holding up the folder in a way I hope will inspire confidence. "It's the perfect amount of much."

"Great. Excited to see what you do." And there's that smile again. And those dimples. I smile back as the one-minute-warning bell rings for third period. I can't believe we've been talking that long. Jenni heads into the classroom right next to us, which is when I realize that, in blindly following her, I've ended up at pretty much the opposite end of the school from where my third-period class is.

And that's when the purple folder gets snatched out of my hands.

"Hey!" I shout before realizing it's my least favorite person in the entire school, Darren Nuggio. The tall, redheaded seventh-grade monster who thinks he's hilarious and derives immense pleasure from others' pain. Especially mine.

"You think you'd ever have a chance with someone like Jenni?" Darren asks. "Dream on, Fart Talent."

That's what he's been calling me since he first saw me drawing in the cafeteria. It's his not-so-clever spin on "art talent."

His two henchmen, Cyril Sklar and Buzzy Hoffman, laugh, right on cue, as if Darren hasn't used that joke hundreds of times. Cyril has long black hair that he wears in a threatening man bun, while Buzzy has a shaved head and a long scar under his left eye. All three of them are athletics talent. (Yes, Mark Twain unfortunately recognizes many kinds of talent.) Which means they're scary. They all hit puberty in third grade.

"Okay, fine, whatever," I say. "Just give me the folder."

"Why?" Darren asks. "Is this where you keep all your fartwork?"

More cracking up from Cyril and Buzzy.

There are all sorts of rumors about why Darren is the way he is: that his dad is in prison for stealing a car, or that his mom is a drill sergeant and he's rebelling against her, or that his parents work for NASA and are ashamed of having a son who's athletics talent. Whatever the reason is, it's never made it suck any less to have him pick on me.

"I'm serious!" I say, trying to grab my folder back. "I'm gonna be late, and I need it for—"

"Okay, okay, fine." Darren holds the folder at a height I could never reach. He's aggressively tall. "You want it? Ready . . . . fetch!"

Darren throws the folder down the hall, and I start to run after it.

"Sucker," Darren says, cackling along with Cyril and Buzzy, and I realize it was a fake throw. You know, the kind of thing you do to trick a dog.

"Give him his folder back," a voice says, and I'm both relieved and embarrassed to see Mr. Solomon standing there, arms crossed, wearing one of his usual colorful, crisp button-down shirts.

Darren points to me as Cyril and Buzzy scatter like frightened mice. "He started i—"

"Come on, Darren," Mr. Solomon says. "I'm not an idiot."

Darren hands the folder back to me.

"If I catch you treating another student like this, I won't hesitate to write you up. You understand?"

"Yeah," Darren says, looking at the floor.

Mr. Solomon turns to me. "You okay, Eric?"

"All good," I say. Seems to be my go-to phrase today when I'm pretending to be okay.

"Good. Now y'all need to get to your next class."

Darren heads down the hall first, turning to shoot me a death stare once he's past Mr. Solomon.

"You sure you're all right, Eric?"

"Yeah. Thanks, Mr. Solomon." I'm so grateful he bailed me out, I could almost cry.

"If he does anything else, you let me know, okay?" He pats me on the shoulder and goes back into the art classroom.

Alone in the hallway, I take a deep breath. Then I head to math, holding the purple folder in one hand and praying the day won't get any worse.

4

MONSTER CLUB ASSEMBLE

"Monster Club assemble," Yoo-hoo says, appearing at my locker at the end of the day. It's literally music to my ears.

"You know it," I say, zipping up my backpack. We're having one last meetup / practice before tomorrow's semifinals, and I could not be more excited. I don't have to think so hard when I'm with them. I don't have to keep my guard up like I do against the Darren Nuggios of the world. Kind of ironic, I guess, that I love meeting up with Monster Club so I can avoid monsters. "We all out front?"

"Yeah," Yoo-hoo says, "except first we have to swing around back to get Beanie. She's doing Robotics Club."

"Traitor." I slam my locker shut for dramatic effect.

"If it were up to you, no one would be allowed to even *think* about anything except Monster Club."

"That is correct," I say. "Because it's the best and deserves everyone's full focus."

"I love you, Doodles," Yoo-hoo says, laughing. "You're so hard-core."

Behind Mark Twain, there's a set of steps kids hang out on after school, along with a bunch of handball courts and a big field, which is where Yoo-hoo and I immediately spot Beanie and Robotics Club. She's one of five nerds decked out in VR goggles (the tallest one and the only one with long, thin braids trailing down her back) and holding remote controls. Her attention is focused up on the five drones racing through the bright blue sky. Even as someone who resents this club for stealing Beanie's time, I can admit it's pretty cool.

"Oh yeah!" Yoo-hoo shouts as he gallops toward them. "Go, Beanie, go! You got this!"

"The racers need to concentrate, Alan," Mrs. Franklin, the club supervisor, says. "Please keep quiet."

"Yeah, otherwise I'll have to dive-bomb you with my drone later," Beanie adds, her attention focused on the sky.

"Geez, okay," Yoo-hoo says as he opens up a granola bar and takes a bite. "No need to make threats."

Beanie's real name is Yvette Ofege—her grandma

coined the nickname when Beanie grew six inches from third to fourth grade, said she "shot up like a beanpole"—and she was a September addition to the club, brought in by Hollywood. She's a genius in, like, everything, and it only took a month before she and DecaSpyder started totally dominating.

We watch in silence for a few moments, the drones buzzing and weaving complicated figure eights around each other, before Yoo-hoo can't help but speak again.

"So, like," he says, his mouth full of granola, "what are you seeing in your goggles? Like, is it seeing from the drone's point of view, or is it like that *plus* being in different virtual places and stuff?"

"Shhh," I say.

"What? I'm considering joining, I need all the deets!"

Something about the emphatic way Yoo-hoo pronounces the word *deets* startles Beanie. She accidentally flicks her joystick the wrong way, and her drone collides in the air with Michel Spanaros's.

"Watch it!" Michel says, leaning his whole body to the right along with his remote handle in an attempt at saving his drone.

"That was all Yoo!" Beanie says.

"Me? You straight-up crashed into my drone!" Michel shouts.

"Not *you*. *Yoo* as in *Yoo-hoo*. As in Alan Yoo, the clown standing to my right!"

"Uh," Yoo-hoo says, taking a few nervous steps backward in the grass. "I'm very sorry?"

Michel regains control of his drone, but it seems like that's not in the cards for Beanie. Hers bobs and twists erratically in the air.

"It might be broken, Yvette," Mrs. Franklin says, her voice the slightest bit worried. "Just try to land it if you can."

"I can't believe you messed me up, Yoo-hoo," Beanie says through gritted teeth, still trying to regain control. "These trajectories are all out of whack."

"I really am sorry!" Yoo-hoo says.

"He is," I say. "That's his for-real sorry voice."

"Stay out of this, Doodles. Hey, Yoo-hoo, remember what I promised I'd do?"

"What, the dive-bomb thing?" Yoo-hoo takes another dozen steps backward. "You were serious about that?"

"I'm always serious." Beanie is for the most part a calm and logical person, but if you cross her, she *will* get revenge. She seems to get some control over her drone, which is not good news for Yoo-hoo.

"I won!" Michel shouts as the other two robotics nerds groan, but at this point I've stopped paying attention to any drones except the one rapidly buzzing toward

Yoo-hoo, who is madly sprinting away and screaming.

"I said I'm sorry!" Yoo-hoo yells.

At the last second the drone veers to his right and lands in the grass with a few skips as Yoo-hoo does an unnecessary action-hero-escaping-an-exploding-building jump.

"You are nuts, Beanie," Yoo-hoo says, rolling onto his back, out of breath.

"I didn't actually let it hit you, did I?" she asks with a grin, raising her goggles on top of her head.

"Are you out of your mind?" Mrs. Franklin asks, the rest of Robotics Club watching.

"Sorry, Mrs. Franklin," Beanie says. "But once Yoo-hoo did me like that, it would have been inappropriate *not* to take some retaliatory action."

"If I can't trust you to use the drones the way they're intended, you're banned from using them."

"Banned?" Beanie says. "Definitively?"

"Yes," Mrs. Franklin says. "Definitively."

Beanie sighs. "Just have to build some more of my own, I guess." She hands Mrs. Franklin her goggles and remote. "See y'all later."

Not gonna lie, watching Beanie get banned from using drones, knowing that it likely means she'll now have more time for us, is a very joyful experience. She and I help Yoo-hoo up from the grass and head to the front of school to meet up with the rest of Monster Club.

5

BATTLES AT NATHAN'S

"Finally," Smash says, her skateboard flipping up into her hand as she leaps off it onto the sidewalk in front of Mark Twain. "I was texting. Didn't know where you guys were."

"Had some drone drama," Beanie says as we walk up from the side of the building, Yoo-hoo and me with our bikes and Beanie with the electric scooter she built herself.

"That's a new one." Smash pulls a kiwi out of her backpack and takes a bite. "Just glad you didn't ditch me."

I met Linda "Smash" Cartageña the first day of the school year, and for at least a month, I thought she hated me. She's one of those people who seem untouchably cool—the short pink hair, the smiling skulls in her ears, the skateboard that's like a fifth limb—and she is, but she's also, I learned later, unbearably shy. I'm shy too, so it was possible we might have gone all of middle school without speaking.

But then I saw her drawing a monster.

I happened to glance at her desk during Mr. Solomon's class, and it was as if she were already a member of Monster Club. She was doodling a badass winged skeleton on the page in front of her, with *SKELEGURL* written above it in bold, angular letters. Just like Smash, Skelegurl has pink punk hair, but unlike Smash, she carries two gleaming swords with bone handles. I was astonished.

"Ditch you?" Yoo-hoo says. "Never!"

"Word," Smash says, looking down with a small smile as she takes another bite of kiwi.

"Speaking of ditching," I say. "Where's Hollywood?"

"I saw him right after school," Smash says. "Said he was going to Nathan's for a dog."

"What? Now? He knew we had practice." By Nathan's she means the world-famous hot dog place on Surf Avenue by the amusement parks, and by dog she means . . . well, you get it. Point is, Hollywood knew we were meeting out front after school.

"True that," Smash says, her voice getting quiet.

"But he was with that girl Jamie."

"Wait, Jamie Posterman?" Yoo-hoo asks. "The seventh grader?"

Smash shrugs. "I dunno, I think so."

"Go, Hollywood!" Yoo-hoo throws a triumphant fist in the air. "Sixth graders hanging out with seventh graders. The dude is an inspiration to all of us."

"Shut up," Smash says. She punches Yoo-hoo's raised arm.

"Ow!" Yoo-hoo somehow grimaces and smiles at the same time, rubbing his triceps where she made contact. "Okay. Yeah. It's actually not inspiring at all."

"It's offensive, is what it is," I say. "He chose a date over Monster Club? I mean, come on. He knows semis are tomorrow."

Everyone's silent, like I'm thin ice and if someone speaks I might crack. I'm trying not to show how ticked off I am, but it's hard. Hollywood has been doing stuff like this a lot lately.

"All right," Beanie says after what feels like a full minute has passed. "I think we'll live without Hollywood for a day. And he can't ditch out of lunch tomorrow, so we know he'll be there for semis. Where do we wanna do this? Your place, Doodles?"

I'd been thinking we'd go to my house—it's our main practice spot since it's not too far from school—but now

I have a new idea.

"Let's do it at Nathan's," I say, as innocently as possible.

Yoo-hoo, Smash, and Beanie go silent again, exchanging skeptical looks even though I'm right here next to them.

"We can't . . . ," Yoo-hoo says. "We can't go to Nathan's just because Hollywood is there and you want to rope him into practice."

"That's not why I want to go," I say, even though of course it is. "Just hearing you say Nathan's made me realize how hungry I am. We can grab food and practice at one of the outside tables. Also I was planning on stopping by to see my dad anyway."

King's Wonderland is right near Nathan's. I definitely wasn't planning on seeing Dad today—when he's this stressed out, it stresses *me* out—but it makes for a more convincing argument.

"Fine," Beanie says, sounding more resigned than convinced. "As long as you leave Hollywood alone while we're there."

"I will," I say. "I promise."

We throw on our helmets and hit the pavement, our motley crew of two bikes, one skateboard, and one scooter sharing the side of the road as cars and trucks speed by. Beanie's scooter is surprisingly fast, rigged up with some sort of e-propulsion engine that sends her blasting ahead of us. Nathan's isn't far from Mark Twain, so we're there in like five minutes, the big neon letters welcoming us.

We pass the line of people waiting for dogs—there's always a line at Nathan's—and I immediately spot Hollywood sitting at a table talking with that Jamie girl, him making that face he makes when he wants to seem cool as he takes a bite of his hot dog. When we met in fourth grade, Hollywood was shorter than me and Yoo-hoo, and it pretty much stayed that way until sometime this year, when out of nowhere Hollywood turned giant. Now, compared to him, me and Yoo-hoo are the pip-squeaks, and Hollywood totally knows that. He's always acted cooler than us, but suddenly he's not the only one who thinks that. Before I'm even aware of what I'm doing, I'm standing next to Hollywood and Jamie's table and shoving some of his fries into my mouth.

"Oh. Hey," Hollywood says, clearly not pleased to see me. "Help yourself, I guess. What's up, Doo—Eric?" *Eric?* He never calls me Eric.

"Just saying hi," I say. "Thought you were coming to Monster Club today."

"Nah, I told Smash to tell you I couldn't make it. Because . . ." Hollywood gestures to Jamie.

"Hi," Jamie says.

"Hi," I say, one fry still sticking out of my mouth. I turn back to Hollywood. "So then I guess you're fine not being prepped for semifinals tomorrow?"

"Semifinals for what?" Jamie asks.

"Nothing," Hollywood says. That stings.

"Monster Club Battle Royale," I say.

Jamie smiles and looks to Hollywood, but it's more of an *I'm making fun of you* smile. "Which is what?"

"It's this game we play," I say.

"Used to play," Hollywood says. That does more than sting. It's a dagger to the heart.

"Used to?" I say, and my voice cracks a little. "What're you . . . Are you saying you're not coming to semifinals tomorrow? Does RoboKillz forfeit his match against BellyBeast?"

"RoboKillz, huh?" Jamie says, once again flashing that mocking smile at Hollywood.

"Long story," Hollywood says, on the verge of teetering from annoyance to anger. "Look, Doodles. I'm saying I'm chilling right now, so let's talk about this later. Okay?"

Used to play is still ringing in my head.

"Yeah, whatever." This isn't a battle I'm going to win. I turn around and walk toward Yoo-hoo, Smash, and Beanie, who are twenty feet away in a little clump, obviously having watched the whole thing.

"You promised, Doodles," Beanie says once I reach them. "You said you would leave Hollywood alone."

"It doesn't matter," I say. "Let's just find a table."

"You okay?" Yoo-hoo asks. Obviously, I'm not, and obviously he can tell. I don't want to let Hollywood ruin this practice, though. I don't want to give him that too.

"I'm all good," I say.

We grab a table as far away from Hollywood and Jamie as possible, and I open my backpack and start setting up the game. Yoo-hoo gets up to grab a dog, and Beanie does too, and then so does Smash. She's a vegan, so I know she only got up to avoid getting stuck here with me and my bad mood. "What do you want on your dog, Doodles?" Yoo-hoo asks.

"I'm not hungry anymore," I say. I hate myself right now—everything about me screams *five-year-old having a tantrum*—but it's out of my control. Monster Club was the one part of my crappy day I thought I could count on.

Yoo-hoo shrugs, and the three of them get in line without me.

I open my notebook to the battle royale bracket and take out the Brickman I finished during lunch. I place all the game gear—the four tetrahedral dice, the Scattergories letter die, and the Game of Life spinner—on the table, and I'm about to shoot another dirty look at

Hollywood when I notice two people who are far more deserving of stink eye.

The Vultures.

Dad's pointed them out to me before, two white guys in suits from an evil company called Pluto Properties. One of them is fat with a beard but no mustache, and the other is thin with a mustache but no beard—if you put their two facial hair configurations together, they'd probably fit perfectly. They're on the other side of the eating area, chowing down on fully loaded dogs and laughing as they look at a large map spread out on their table.

I walk over to the ketchup and mustard pumps, trying to seem real casual, so I can get closer. I still can't hear what they're saying, but it's obvious enough. They've got a black marker they're using to make X's all over their map—their Coney Island conquests, the private parks they've bought out. They keep cackling the whole time, in this way that makes them seem like grown-up versions of Darren Nuggio's henchmen, Cyril and Buzzy. If that's the case, I'd hate to meet their Darren.

I swear I see Beard mouth the words *King's Wonderland* as he points to the map, and I suddenly feel dizzy. I look over to my friends, hoping they're on their way back. They're still waiting for their food, Yoo-hoo laughing as

Smash punches him in the arm again.

When I look back, Mustache is grinning as he marks a fresh *X* on the map, right where Beard was just pointing.

I feel the sudden urge to run over there and shout in their faces like, "What are you talking about? You're never getting King's Wonderland!" but then Beard and Mustache are on their feet. They stuff the last chunks of dog into their mouths and walk away, leaving all their trash on the table.

I stumble back to our table just as my friends are returning.

"You're totally lying," Yoo-hoo says to Smash as the two of them and Beanie sit down around me, populating the table with dogs, fries, and sodas.

"I'm not," Smash says. "I wanted to experiment with some larger graffiti projects, so I figured it out on You-Tube."

"I'm very impressed," Beanie says.

"Doodles, check this out," Yoo-hoo says. "Smash found a way to fill a freaking fire extinguisher with spray paint, and then used it to—Whoa, you all right, Doods? You look like you need to barf."

"I . . . I just saw . . . It's . . ." I can't begin to get words out. If what I just saw is as bad as I think it is, it's very, very bad.

"Did Hollywood say something else to you?" Beanie asks. "I'd be happy to go get a drone, dive-bomb his butt too."

"No, it wasn't . . ." I need to tell Dad what I saw. "I actually, um, just found out I have to go." I get to my feet. "Because of my dad. My dad needs me. I'm sorry."

"Right now?" Yoo-hoo says. "Is everything okay? Do you want us to come with you?"

"I . . ." I can't think straight. But I know I don't have the time and energy required to explain what's happening. "I'm all good. Thanks, though. I'll see you tomorrow."

I'm hopping onto my bike when Yoo-hoo calls my name.

"You're good if we hold on to your notebook and the die? And the spinner?" he asks. "For practice?"

"Yeah, definitely."

"But don't you want to at least take Brickman?" He looks maybe more concerned than I've ever seen him.

I'm shocked too, actually. I never forget Brickman.

"Oh," I say. "Yeah. Sure. Thanks."

I grab my monster, hop back on my bike, and pedal away as fast as I possibly can.

6

KING NEPTUNE

I'm still speeding as I turn my bike off the street and up onto the alleyway of carnival games I've always thought of as the unofficial gateway to Coney Island.

"Hey, Eric!" a voice calls from my right. It's Amy Basis, the wrinkly-faced woman who's been running the Sirens Shooting Gallery forever. She's known me since I was a baby, so she's kind of like an aunt to me. "What's the rush?"

"Hey, Amy!" I say without slowing down. "Just gotta tell my dad something. Let's catch up later!"

"Look at this maniac!" I hear from my left. It's Freddie Eisenberg, who hasn't been around as long as Amy, but almost. He runs a bunch of different games along this strip, including my all-time favorite, Shoot the Red

Star. It's this game where you shoot BB pellets at a red star on a paper target—sixty pellets for a dollar—and if you completely eliminate the star, you win a giant stuffed panda. I'm too old to care about the prize at this point, but I'm determined to win anyway. I always give myself five tries a summer.

"Hi, Freddie!" I say.

He waves back with a wrench in his hand.

I pass the Spook-a-Rama ride, and the Wonder Wheel, and everywhere I look, there are people I recognize carrying things and fixing things, generally getting ready for the big opening day on Friday. Even in my panic, I can't help but feel a little calmer seeing this place come back to life. It's like my second home.

I won't let the Vultures take it away from me.

I pedal past the kiddie boat rides, and I'm turning onto the boardwalk for the last stretch to King's when I nearly collide with a human being. "Whoa!" I shout. I squeeze the brakes on my handlebar and come to a stop literally inches away from him. It's King Neptune.

"Take heed of where you steer that chariot, young man," he says, looking only slightly annoyed that he was almost run over.

I've never actually talked to King Neptune. I don't think that's his actual name. But everybody knows who he is. You see, he's this wiry old man in his seventies or

maybe eighties who wanders the beach with his metal detector. If you ask him, he introduces himself as King Neptune, god of the sea. He wears this weird, tattered wrap thing, like a toga, that has dried seaweed stapled to it, with these ratty old sandals, and a plastic crown in his long, knotty white hair. I'm not kidding. He also has a long, knotty white beard, and his exposed skin is covered with tattoos and is so sunburnt it looks like leather.

Hollywood and Yoo-hoo have occasionally been known to shout things at him like "Yo, Neptune, where's your trident at?" but I never do. I just feel bad for the guy.

And I *especially* feel bad now that I almost mowed him down.

"I'm really sorry," I say. "I didn't see you walkin—"

"Ah!" the old man says, a flash of recognition in his eyes. "Not just any young man, but the young prince himself! Is that your handiwork?" King Neptune points down at my left hand, which is gripping both the handlebar and my drawing of Brickman, now a little crumpled from the ride. I should have put it into my backpack, but I was too focused on getting to Dad.

"Oh, this? Yeah. It's . . . just a drawing."

I gasp as King Neptune grabs it from me with his grimy hand. I'm not judging him or anything (okay, I guess I am), but I don't necessarily want to mess up this latest Brickman. Too late for that.

Neptune stares down at my drawing, his eyes flicking all over the page, like he needs to devour every inch. "As if it were his own hand . . . ," he mumbles without looking up.

"What?"

"You're an echo of your forefather, young prince," he says again, this time lifting his head to look straight at me. I notice that tattooed on each side of his neck are these two ridged openings, almost like fish gills. The whole thing is undeniably creepy, and it is definitely time to go.

"Um, okay," I say, gingerly pulling Brickman out of his grip and steering my bike out of his path. "Cool. But I actually have to get going. Because I'm . . . Yeah." I start pedaling before he can drop any more weird on me.

I'm "an echo of my forefather"? What was that about?

Thankfully, I don't have much time to dwell on it before I'm pulling up to King's and reminded of my mission, the reason I ditched Monster Club for the first time in my life (well, I missed once for the flu, but that doesn't really count). I jump off my bike and let it topple to the ground next to the bumper cars as I race deeper into the park, leaping over random mechanical parts strewn all over the place.

"Dad!" I shout. "Dad!"

He's sitting on a step in the front of the shed, working on an engine and looking frustrated. When he hears my voice, he looks up and offers a strained but genuine smile.

"Hey, kid. I thought I wasn't seeing you till Friday."

"You weren't," I say, catching my breath. "But I was at Nathan's, and I saw the Vultures talking."

"Ya don't say?" Dad digs around in his massive tool-box, not as intrigued by this as I thought he might be. "The ones from Pluto Properties?"

"Exactly! They were putting black X's on a map, and it looked like they put one over King's—"

"They're dreamin'," Dad says, finding the screw or whatever that he was looking for and fitting it into the engine in front of him.

"But they were laughing. They seemed really confident—"

"That's what vultures do, kid. They talk a big game. You don't have to pay attention to it. They think the bank is gonna take this place from us, then they'll swoop in and buy it from the bank. But guess what? I have till Monday to make a payment to stop that from happening. So we'll get this place up and running and have a solid opening weekend like we always do, and we won't be going anywhere."

I want to believe Dad, I really do, but I can't help but hear Mom's voice in my head, the one saying that he needs to consider the possibility that King's might have to close down.

"Look," Dad says, gesturing to the engine he's been messing with. "I got the Beast Infinity ready to go." Out of the nine rides at King's, Beast Infinity is probably my favorite—you're in your own individual car suspended by one of eight long mechanical arms that move the cars in infinity loops, getting slower and faster at random, while loud, growling beast sound effects play on the speakers. It's the best. Well, one of the best.

Dad yanks the engine's starter and revs it up. Much

to my relief, it sputters to life. I can't help but smile. Only for a moment, though. The engine quickly chokes and dies, and, hate to say it, but some of my faith does too.

"Just gotta open 'er up a little," he says, diving back into his toolbox.

We're silent as Dad fiddles some more with the engine, and I'm reminded of the metal piece of junk that was in his box this morning. Is that what's going to happen to King's Wonderland, to all these rides? Forever banished to the basement, never to be seen again?

That can't happen. It just can't. King's is too important. It's been a part of my life forever, like school, or eating, or sleeping, or breathing. If there's no King's, is Coney Island even Coney Island anymore?

"All right, let's see if that did it," Dad says, putting down his screwdriver.

With a dramatic flourish, he tries to start the engine again, but guess what? Nothing happens.

7

SEMIFINALS

I release one of the four-sided dice, watching as the pyramid rolls across the cafeteria table.

It's a four.

"YES!" I shout, a fist in the air.

Monster Club Battle Royale Semifinals are in full effect during school lunch, and for the first time all week, I feel amazing. As I'd predicted, Brickman and I are in the process of absolutely crushing DecaSpyder and Beanie.

Rolling what I did means that, on this offensive attack, Brickman will get in four consecutive hits. In other words, I get to roll all four tetrahedral dice at once. I do—they come up with two 3's and two 4's. Fourteen hit points. Killer. I roll the Scattergories die, and it miraculously lands on exactly the letter I was hoping it would: *D*.

"That's a demolition ball attack, baby!" I say. I flick the Life spinner to determine Brickman's current energy level and thereby how much damage will be done—it lands on 8. "Boom! That's gonna be one hundred twelve hit points gone!" I spin the cardboard Wheel of Body Parts that Yoo-hoo and I crafted ourselves years ago to determine the point of contact: leg, arm, head, chest, or back. Once the spinner's arrow stops, I make the whooshing sound of Brickman's chain cutting through the air, followed by the devastating crunch of his wrecking ball colliding with DecaSpyder's titanium skeleton. I reach over with my pen and draw a deep dent on Deca's back. "That's gotta hurt."

"Yeah, all right," Beanie says, taking a bite of grilled cheese with one hand and marking up the score sheet with the other.

"Deca is on the verge of death, my friend," I say. "But don't be too depressed. Everything's just going Brick's way today."

Beanie looks at me, lifts one eyebrow. "I think I'll be okay, Doodles."

I can't tell if she's being sarcastic, but I take it as permission to gloat freely without fear of hurting any feelings. This is a lesson I learned the hard way after the Nail Polish Remover Incident. It happened last fall when we decided to hold our battle royale finals in the back room of Mermaid Nails, Smash's mom's nail salon. After a very intense battle, Brickman narrowly defeated Skelegurl to win the championship. I did some show-boating, dancing around, maybe even literally rubbing Brickman in Smash's face, which she understandably did not appreciate. Long story short, Smash grabbed a bottle of nail polish remover and poured it all over my tournament-winning Brickman. Nail polish remover and ink don't get along well—most of that Brickman vanished like it was never there. Suffice it to say, I've been much more respectful in victory since the Nail Polish Remover Incident.

"Hey, it's not over till it's over, right?" I pass Beanie the dice and the spinner. "Your turn."

Smash and Yoo-hoo are cracking up about something to our left, where they're in the midst of their own battle, Skelegurl vs. BellyBeast. Technically, Smash was eliminated by Hollywood in the quarterfinals, but once he officially forfeited this morning because he "didn't have time" to get RoboKillz ready, she took his spot. When I look over, though, Smash and Yoo-hoo have straws sticking up their noses, and they're making stupid faces at each other.

"Are you even battling right now?" I ask.

"We are, yeah," Yoo-hoo says, his face totally serious even though there's still a straw sticking out of one nostril. "This is just a short break."

"True that," Smash says, moving her nose straw around. "A tiny little break. There's not something on my face, is there?"

This gets Yoo-hoo laughing all over again, and Beanie joins in too.

I try to find the humor. I cannot. I'd been successfully ignoring all the annoying stuff in my life—for example, Hollywood currently sitting a few tables away with Jamie Fricking Posterman and her friends instead of with us—but now it all comes flooding back, decimating the joyful triumph of a minute ago.

"You need to finish your battle so that we know who's going to finals," I say. "Whoever wins is probably gonna face Brickman. No offense, Beanie."

Beanie shrugs.

"Don't worry, Doodles," Yoo-hoo says, now with a straw in his right nostril too. "We are very serious people, and our battle will be finished shortly."

"Come on!" I say, smacking the straws out of his nose.

"Ow!" Yoo-hoo rubs his face, and I feel a little bad. But not that bad.

"Sorry," I say. "Just want to make sure we can actually finish."

"Hey, at least we actually showed at semifinals," Smash says, looking down at the table.

A fresh wave of anger pulses through me, but she's right—they're not the ones I should be annoyed at.

"Hey, Hollywood!" I shout across three tables.

He's in the midst of saying something in his animated way—charming smile, wildly gesturing hands—and Jamie and her friends are totally captivated. Hollywood's eyes shoot toward me for half a second, so I know he heard, but he ignores me.

"HOLLYWOOD!" I call again, louder this time.

Jamie hears this one, and she puts a hand on Hollywood's shoulder, points over at us. Hollywood looks right at me, so I wave for him to come over.

"You know this isn't gonna end well," Beanie says as Hollywood stands up and walks toward us, shaking his head.

"Seriously, Doodles," Yoo-hoo says. "Just let him do his thing."

"If he's gonna ditch semis," I say, "he should at least tell us all to our faces."

"Why?" Smash asks.

Hollywood arrives at our table, towering over me even more than usual since I'm sitting. He couldn't look less happy to be here if he tried. "What?" he asks. "What do you want, Doodles?"

He seems so annoyed that it makes me question for a second if maybe I should have listened to Yoo-hoo, just left him alone. "We need you," I say. "We're going entirely without a ref today!"

Hollywood laughs a little, puts a hand on his chin, and shakes his head again. "Man, this has got to stop."

I look to Yoo-hoo, Beanie, and Smash, like *What the heck is this guy talking about?* before turning back to Hollywood. "What does?"

"You're acting like this is the most important event ever—like we didn't just do one of these three months ago. And you'll probably do another three months from now."

"Yeah," I say, "'cause that was the Winter Battle Royale. And next will be the Summer Battle Royale."

"Right, right, of course," Hollywood says, dripping with sarcasm. "My point is: We're kind of past this game, aren't we? I don't know . . . it's kind of like, embarrassing."

"Embarrassing?" I find myself pushing back my cafeteria chair and getting to my feet. After the way Hollywood acted at Nathan's yesterday, none of this should surprise me, and yet . . . I'm totally shocked.

"Yeah, man," Hollywood says. "Monsters fighting? Check yourself, we're over it."

I open and close my mouth a few times before I get words to come out. "What *we*? If *you're* over it, fine.

Don't have fun! See if I care."

Hollywood laughs again, and a panicky feeling blossoms in my chest. "Beanie?" he asks. "You still really into this?"

"I mean . . ." Beanie looks over to Hollywood, then to me, then back to Hollywood. "It's all right."

"Just *all right*?" I ask.

"Smash, how 'bout you?" Hollywood says. "Looking at your Skelegurl, I don't know . . ."

"What?" I say. "Smash put lots of . . ." But when I look down at the table, I see that Skelegurl is filled in with none of her usual detail. It's more like a sketch than a masterpiece. I can't believe I didn't notice.

"Uh," Smash says, directing her gaze everywhere except at me. "Yeah. That's . . . I was gonna finish her at practice yesterday, but then once Doodles left . . ."

"Wait, did you guys even have practice yesterday?" I ask, looking mainly at Yoo-hoo. I know for a fact he's still into Monster Club. "Or did you just skip it once I was gone?"

"No, we didn't skip—" Yoo-hoo says. "I mean, we were mainly eating food, I guess, but also I added some details to BellyBeast . . ."

"Told you," Hollywood says. "*We're* over it."

I don't even fully understand what's happening right now.

As I'm putting a hand on the table to keep myself from falling over, a voice cuts into our conversation.

"Oh look, it's Fart Talent and his fartsy friends."

Darren Nuggio. Impeccable timing.

"What is that?" He points down at my drawing of Brickman, his jerk buddies Cyril and Buzzy by his side peering down with him.

I can't begin to respond. It feels like we're under-water. Or maybe only I am.

"I said, what is that?" Darren takes a step closer to me.

"It's . . . It's Brickman," I stutter out.

"Brickman?" Darren laughs in my face, with Cyril and Buzzy joining in. He points to the other drawings on the table. "Do all these special creatures have names as cute as that one?"

"They're not creatures," Yoo-hoo says. "They're mon-sters. We fight them."

"Oh, I see," Darren says, snickering. "Is that before or after your mommy changes your diapers?" Cyril and Buzzy roar at that one, and I'm pretty sure I see some other kids one table over laughing too.

Hollywood shoots me the ultimate *told you so* look before walking back to Jamie's table. That snaps me out of it.

"It's not for babies," I say to Darren. "You probably

couldn't even keep up with our game. Too advanced for you."

His face goes slack for a moment. "Couldn't keep up, huh?" Darren asks. "How's this for keeping up?" I brace myself, expecting him to give me a dead arm or something, but what he does instead is far worse—he grabs my as-yet-untouched container of chicken noodle soup, pulls off the lid, and pours it all over Brickman.

"No!" I shout.

"Looks like my monster won," Darren says. "*Noodle* monster."

"Noodle monster!" Buzzy says, his huge mouth open wide as he laughs.

"That's genius," Cyril says.

Their cackles ring in my ears as I sweep the noodles off Brickman's face with the back of my hand. I look over to our ancient cafeteria aide Mrs. Ovadia, thinking she'll send Darren to the assistant principal's office, but as usual, she's asleep in her chair.

"It's not even a little genius," Beanie says to Cyril. "You're a bunch of jerks."

"Beanie," Smash says quietly.

Darren stops laughing. He puts his hands on the table and leans closer to Beanie. "I'd love to collect a whole army of noodle monsters. Enough to ruin all your cute little creatures."

Beanie shrugs, trying to seem chill even though I can tell she's seething as much as I am. "You do whatever you need to if it enables you to feel good about your sad life."

Another direct hit. Darren's eyes search the table for more food to use as a weapon, but all that's left is a banana lying near Yoo-hoo. "Wow," Darren says, breaking into an angry grin. "These nerds think *my* life is sad. Ha!"

Cyril and Buzzy try to muster a supportive laugh, but they seem to still be thinking about what Beanie said.

"Let's go," Darren says, strutting toward the other side of the cafeteria, Cyril and Buzzy right behind. "Stay out of my way, you little farts."

"You all right, Doodles?" Yoo-hoo asks, producing a paper towel from somewhere and soaking up soup from Brickman's legs.

"I hate those guys so much," Beanie says.

"Same," Smash says.

I can recognize that Yoo-hoo's being helpful, that all three of them had my back just now, but I'm still very angry.

"No," I say. "I'm not all right." My legs spring into action before my brain is even aware of what's happening, heading straight across the linoleum floor to where Hollywood is standing with Jamie.

"You seriously walked away in the middle of that?" I ask.

"Yeah, why?" Hollywood says. "You okay?"

"*Why?*" I say, my voice embarrassingly screechy. "You're asking why I'm surprised you abandoned your friends?"

"Look, I'm sorry, okay? I don't like that guy at all, but I mean . . . He did have some good points." Hollywood gives a little chuckle and looks over at Jamie, as if they're sharing some inside joke.

I shove Hollywood. "You're a terrible friend!"

After a brief moment of surprise, he charges back at me, gets right up in my face. "I know you didn't just do that."

I don't back away.

"Whoa, whoa!" Yoo-hoo says, appearing next to us. "Don't do this, Hollywood."

"Why shouldn't I?" Hollywood says, not taking his eyes off me. "He's being a clown. You see him push me just now?"

"I know, I know," Yoo-hoo says.

"Shut up!" I say, spinning toward Yoo-hoo, recognizing at this point that I'm out of control and out of line but unable to do anything about it.

"Stop picking on Yoo-hoo all the time!" Hollywood says.

"I don't pick on Yoo-hoo!"

"It's not a big deal," Yoo-hoo says. "I was like this when my parents—"

And before he can say another word, I shove Yoo-hoo.

He stumbles over the leg of a chair and falls to the floor. Before I can even check to see if Yoo-hoo's all right, to go apologize, Hollywood is shouting "Not cool!" and shoving me so hard that I fall to the ground too.

"Don't you get how stupid this is?" Hollywood asks as I rub my right knee where it made contact with the ground. "It's done, Doodles, okay? Monster Club is *over!*"

"No, it's not!" I rise to my feet and blindly charge at Hollywood, wrapping my arms around his chest and awkwardly tackling him to the ground.

The room explodes in noise.

"FIGHT! FIGHT! FIGHT!"

I'm not even sure what my goal is or if Hollywood and I are doing it right. We're just rolling around on the hard tiles, grunting and trying to pound each other on the back.

In the midst of this blur, I hear Darren's cackle again, catch glimpses of his face hovering over us, experiencing pure joy as he screams "Fart Fight!" at the top of his lungs.

I can also hear Beanie shouting for us to stop. Yoo-hoo and Smash too.

Then a shrill whistle cuts through everything, and the world goes quiet.

"Stop it!" Assistant Principal Bachrack says, reaching in a hand to separate me and Hollywood. She's short but incredibly commanding. "You three, my office now!"

"Me?" Darren says. "I wasn't even—"

"Yeah right, Nuggio," Assistant Principal Bachrack says. "Now!"

As we get to our feet and get our stuff, everyone is staring at us, and it all feels horrible. I don't understand how everything got so messed up so fast.

I try to make eye contact with Hollywood as we leave the cafeteria, hoping to convey that I'm sorry, or just have a moment of like, *whoa I can't believe this happened*, but he's not having it, his expression stony, his eyes straight ahead.

"You're gonna pay for this, Fart Talent," Darren mutters from behind me.

I think it's safe to say that Monster Club Battle Royale Semifinals have not been a success.

8

DARK TIMES AT KING'S WONDERLAND

I messed up.

I messed everything up.

And now, not only is Monster Club probably over, but my friends won't even talk to me.

Assistant Principal Bachrack was happy to, though. Darren went into her office first, with Hollywood and me waiting on a bench in the hallway. The whole time Darren was in there—had to be at least ten minutes—Hollywood continued giving me the silent treatment, even after I told him how sorry I was.

When it was my turn, I watched Assistant Principal Bachrack squeeze one of those red stress balls as she lectured me about the importance of solving my problems without resorting to violence. She gave me a full week of detentions, starting tomorrow. My first thought was, *Oh no, I'm gonna have to miss Monster Club.* But then I remembered there might not *be* a Monster Club anymore.

Seeing that Hollywood had already blocked the Monster Club group chat thread didn't help.

At the beginning of English, I tried to apologize to Yoo-hoo, but he just looked at his feet and said "It doesn't matter" before walking to his desk and giving me the same silent treatment as Hollywood.

Now I'm standing outside after school literally hiding behind a tree as I watch Yoo-hoo, Beanie, Smash, and Hollywood talking. It looks like they're reenacting the cafeteria fight, Yoo-hoo laughing as Smash does an impression of Darren pouring soup all over Brickman. I'm too scared to join them. What if literally every single one of my friends gives me the silent treatment? I don't think I could handle that.

The reality is: they seem totally fine without me. Maybe I've been the weak link this whole time.

On the bright side, my best friend brain meld with Yoo-hoo still seems to be intact—I peek out from behind the tree to stare at him as hard as I can, and he eventually looks my way. But then Hollywood sees and says something to the group, and Yoo-hoo stops looking. Seconds later, the four of them hop on their bikes (or, in

Beanie's case, her e-scooter) and peel away down Neptune Avenue without me.

Going straight home on what's going to be my last detention-free afternoon for a while seems like a waste, so I head toward King's Wonderland. As I roll to a stop on the boardwalk, just outside the entrance, I watch Dad struggle with a rusty bolt on one of the cars in the Super Spinner ride. I'm about to announce my presence and offer to help when his wrench slips and he bangs his hand. He swears loudly and hurls the wrench against the side of one of the spinner cars, making an unsettling clang that echoes through the park.

"He curses like my nephew, Vulcan," a hoarse voice says, scaring the bejesus out of me.

It's King Neptune, plastic crown and all, standing next to me.

"Didn't mean to cause alarm," he says.

"Oh," I say. *Then why did you sneak up on me like that?*

"I cannot say I blame your father. It is painful to lose one's kingdom," the old man adds a bit wistfully.

Though it's not surprising that he knows who my dad is—everyone around here knows us—it feels a little creepy. King Neptune probably doesn't have evil intentions, but he's still a stranger. A stranger who walks around in a crown and a dirty toga and thinks he's god of the sea.

"Uh," I say.

"But what can he do? What mortal can hope to triumph over destruction wrought by the gales and zephyrs of the gods?" As he speaks, Neptune turns gleeful, dancing and whipping his hands around as if they're gusts of wind. I notice for the first time that the back of his left hand is scarred and bumpy and discolored. I look away so he doesn't think I'm staring.

"My dad will get King's fixed up," I say.

Neptune laughs, then turns serious.

"I don't think the storms are over for your father, young prince, or that he is the man to stand against them. Now you—you are something else. When I saw your portrait yesterday . . . it stirred up some roiling waves within me as well. You sketch just as your father's father's father did. Isaac. I hadn't seen an image like that since . . . Well, since I was about your age, still wearing mortal skin."

I'm trying to process what King Neptune—with his very weird god-speak—is saying. I never knew anyone in my family drew other than me.

"Isaac?"

"Come on, child! Isaac King? Your great-great-grandfather? The King who started King's?"

"Oh. Yeah." I might have heard the name Isaac thrown around by my dad before, but I honestly can't remember.

"I'm astonished you don't know your own family's history!" He adjusts his crown and scratches the back of his head. "Isaac King founded this place more than a century ago. It was a sideshow then. The best in all of Coney. That shed over there, now a shameful junkheap, within which your father is stomping around? That was Isaac's tattoo parlor."

"Wait . . . seriously?"

"The gods do not jest, young prince! Related to royalty and you don't even know it. And you have his talent. I saw it in your drawing. The same line, the same detail. The same inspired ability to bring the fantastical to life. Doubt me not, for I know of what I speak. Isaac King's tattoos . . . they changed my life. Made me the god I am today."

"Wow," I say. "Thanks." It suddenly occurs to me that maybe the guy standing in front of the Parachute Jump in that photo from the box was Isaac. And maybe that metal device isn't just a random piece of junk. Maybe it's Isaac's tattoo machine. And that nasty stuff in the bottle . . . maybe that was his ink.

"Sadly it appears that great family history is about to end, and the King's castle will soon be stormed," King

Neptune says, which is immediately followed by a horrendous scraping sound, like twenty sets of fingernails trailing down a chalkboard.

I look up, thinking it's Dad's latest questionable way of expressing his anger, but it's actually three bulldozers moving in toward King's Wonderland from the empty lots around it where other rides and games used to be before they got bought out. The bulldozers push up dirt as they press forward.

"No," I say, letting my bike drop to the boardwalk, leaving Neptune behind as I run to help Dad, who's rushing toward the machines.

"STOP!" he's yelling at the top of his lungs, waving his arms in a panic. "STOP!" The bulldozers keep going, forming three massive, ugly piles of dirt on the border of King's.

And then I see them: the Vultures. Mustache is in a hard hat, shouting things into a walkie-talkie, while Beard stands there texting.

"Whaddaya think you're doing?" Dad shouts at the Vultures as I stand behind him, trying to figure out how to be useful.

"Working," Beard says, not even looking up from his phone.

"I have the weekend!" Dad shouts. "This isn't legal!"

"Yeah, this is totally illegal!" I shout. Dad turns to

me, surprised by my presence and too caught up in the moment to even really acknowledge me.

"Look," Beard says, "everything on this side belongs to Pluto Properties. And come Monday, when you're unable to pay up to the bank, everything on *that* side will belong to us too. We're just prepping." Beard twirls a finger in the air, like *keep going*, and the huge trucks do, pushing into the dirt again, this time causing some to trickle off the pile onto our side.

Dad goes ballistic. "HEY! That's my side!" he shouts. "You're dumping dirt onto my ticket line over there!

My customers stand right there!" He picks up a random steel rod from the ground, like he's ready to start smashing some truck parts.

"Dad, no!"

He turns to me again, and the fury in his eyes scares me. "Eric, what're you—Why are you here?"

"I want to . . . I want to help."

"This isn't kid stuff, all right?" He drops the bar onto the ground. "If I don't defend this place right now, we're gonna lose King's, okay? And I'm not gonna be the one to lose it!"

"I know, that's why I want to—"

"Did you hear what I said? You gotta go home."

"But, Dad, I can help—"

"Eric! GO HOME!" he practically roars.

I blink back the tears forming in my eyes. Dad's never yelled at me like that before.

I walk away before he can make me feel worse than he already has, as Beard orders the bulldozers to back up and reminds Dad he's got till Monday before they finish the job.

9

EVERYTHING CHANGES

As I make my way back toward Sea Gate, I can't stop thinking about Dad and the furious look in his eyes.

Eric! GO HOME!

This whole time he's been promising me that King's is going to be fine, that everything's going to be fine. But looks like that's a lie, another lie.

"Dad's in serious trouble," I say seconds after I drop my bike in the garage and step into the house. I know Mom's lawyer brain will be able to figure out how to shoo the Vultures away.

"Here he is," Mom says, phone pressed to the other side of her face. "He's fine. I'll call you back." She puts her cell on the counter. "That was Dad making sure you were safe."

"Did he tell you what was going on over there? They're threatening to—"

"He did, Eric—and unfortunately, they haven't actually done anything illegal. Trust me, I've looked over the documents for Dad at least a hundred times."

"But didn't you once say there was, like, something in Dad's contract with the bank that says he wouldn't have to pay right now because of the hurricane? Like Force Mordor or something?"

"Yes, force majeure," Mom says, sighing. "It's French for 'great force.' Initially I thought that clause might apply—it says you're not responsible for payments during extraordinary circumstances. But unfortunately the bank has an exception for hurricanes."

"That makes no sense. Hurricanes *are* a great force, though!"

"I know, it's frustrating. But, Eric, you need to understand something: King's has been struggling to make ends meet long before the hurricane. So . . ." Mom closes her eyes and rubs her forehead before speaking again, which is never a good sign. "To be quite honest, I'm not interested in talking about your father right now. I want to talk about you fighting at school."

I sort of knew this was coming.

"The school called," she continues. "I was sure there'd been a mix-up, but nope, they said it was unquestionably you. Which is . . . disappointing. What's going on?"

"It wasn't my fault," I say. "I mean . . ."

Mom raises an eyebrow, which is really all she has to do to make me (and, for that matter, probably hundreds of people she's interrogated in the courtroom) crumble.

"I got in a fight with the guys," I say.

"Which guys?"

"Yoo-hoo, Hollywood . . ."

"You got in an actual fight with your *best friends*?" She audibly sighs and shakes her head in a way that makes me want to hide underneath the kitchen table with Pepper and bury my head in my paws. "Why would you do that?"

"We were . . . ," I say, looking at my feet. "We got in an argument about stuff. Like, Monster Club stuff."

"Ohmigod," Mom says, sighing even louder than she did a minute ago. "Eric. You're fighting over a game."

I lean over the counter, grab a napkin and a pen, and start doodling Brickman while Mom talks, in an effort to calm myself down and feel less like a horrible person.

"You're lucky there's no suspension," Mom says.

"I know," I say, outlining Brickman's legs. "I'm sorry."

"Sorry's not good enough. Please look at me when I'm talking to you."

I will my face upward, away from the serenity of my pen.

"You're twelve years old," Mom says, "you need to take responsibility. So you're grounded. For a week."

I don't know how to process this, as I've literally never been grounded in my life. "But I already have a week of detentions. Isn't that—"

"And you're grounded too. No Monster Club. No friends. Straight home after school."

I look down at the napkin and push my pen into it as hard as possible, sketching Brickman with sharp, angry angles, not even realizing that the pen is leaking right through the napkin onto the counter.

"See—you need to pay attention, Eric." Mom pulls the napkin away. "No more drawing at home!"

"But—But what about my art homework?"

"You can use the art app on your iPad this week."

I make some kind of wounded-animal sound. Before I can further plead my case, Mom is marching up the stairs toward my bedroom, plastic bag in hand.

Nooooooo.

"You're going to do some thinking," she says as I follow behind, Pepper hot on our heels. "I know it's hard, Eric. All these changes. But that doesn't mean you get to act out." I try to squeeze past her and get to my room first. It's impossible. Once inside, Mom is ruthless, grabbing every art supply she sees and putting it into the plastic bag—pens, markers, sketchbooks, scissors, pastels, pencils, paper. "You need to grow up. A week without doodling is gonna force you to think about what kind of person you want to be—and it better be the kind of kid who doesn't get into fistfights at school."

The entire time she's packing up my life, I am sobbing and shouting "No" and "Don't" and "Please." Pepper barks right along with me.

"I'm sorry, Eric," Mom says, one hand on my shoulder, the other holding that plastic bag, which looks like it's about to burst, two pens poking out one side. "But this will help you." She heads downstairs.

"It won't!" I shout, one last pathetic plea. "It definitely won't!"

She doesn't respond.

I flop backward onto my bed, landing on my backpack, which I somehow still haven't put down. I wrestle it off now, rolling around like a crab to de-strap, and then knocking it onto the floor with one last surge of energy.

I have nothing left.

I breathe and stare at the ceiling for a few minutes, trying to understand how so much could be lost so quickly.

My parents' marriage.

King's.

My friends.

And now I'm not even allowed to draw!

At least I still have Pepper, who's curled up next to me, the heat of her furry body bringing me some small measure of comfort.

Mom knows that drawing is like therapy for me. I can't help but feel extra pissed that she's taken it away when I need it most.

I roll from my back to my side and find myself staring at my backpack, lying there on the floor.

Duh.

As thorough as Mom was, she wasn't thorough enough.

I surge out of bed, unzip the main pocket, and dig around the bottom, past the lint and bent paper clips. Surely there has to be something. Then I feel it: an old black magic marker.

Victory.

I pull a Mrs. Franklin homework handout about climate patterns from my folder, flip to the blank back, use the folder as a hard surface, and let my marker do its thing. It is an instant relief. But not even five seconds pass before the marker starts to make that terrible squeaky sound. The black ink gets thinner and lighter and then nonexistent.

"Are you kidding me," I say, rubbing the marker back and forth on the paper and creating nothing. I even try licking it, but no dice.

What is happening? Why can absolutely nothing work out for me right now?

I chuck the useless marker across the rug. Pepper bounds off the bed to fetch it, placing it in front of me.

"No, Pepper," I say. "I don't need it. It's done."

She gives me a quizzical look before running it back across the room.

I go into my backpack and, of course, that was the only thing I had in there to write with.

I want to scream.

From the second Dad appeared with that box, everything this week has been awful. Atrocious. Horrific.

I flop back down onto my bed and slam my hand against the mattress three times before closing my eyes and, eventually, just falling asleep.

When I open my eyes again, I'm not sure how much time has gone by, but it definitely looks darker out. As I look around the room, I remember my stupid day and Mom's stupid punishment and feel frustrated all over again.

But then something occurs to me.

I get out of bed, walk to my closet, and open the door.

There's the box. I dig around for a second and pull out the metal device. And the green-tinted mason jar.

I examine the device first, and I quickly see how

it could have been my great-great-grandfather's old-school tattoo machine, though unless I'm going to get all tatted up, it's useless to me now. I put it aside.

That leaves me with the jar of the nasty stuff, which may or may not be ink.

Even if I had something to use it with, do I really want to unleash that horrendous fish smell on my bedroom?

Most definitely not. I put it down as Pepper reappears with something in her mouth. It's that stupid dried-out magic marker again. Pepper places it down in front of me and looks up, panting eagerly.

"Thanks for the thought, buddy," I say, "but this one's out of . . ."

I stare at the marker. I stare at the mason jar of ink.

"Actually, Pepper," I say, "nice work. This could be good." I'm still not loving the idea of my room smelling like ocean trash, but desperate times, right? I struggle for five minutes with the bottom of the magic marker before I figure out how to snap it off. Then I unscrew the lid of the ink, which is way easier than it was the first time. Unfortunately, it doesn't smell any better. Pepper barks.

"I know, girl," I say. "It's pretty heinous, but . . . it's all we got right now. Here goes nothing."

I carefully pour some of the ink into the back of the

marker. It has an unexpected thickness to it, slowly glooping down from the glass jar. It's weirdly beautiful, with this iridescent shine, sparkling with flashes of all the colors of the rainbow.

It is also not lost on me that this probably isn't the right way to refill a magic marker.

I snap the marker's bottom back in, pop its top off.

I grab another Franklin handout from my folder, flip it to its blank side.

I hope this works.

Before I can even try drawing, the paper rises up toward the marker, like it's magnetized or something.

I push the paper down.

Weird.

As soon as I let go, the paper rises again, almost like it's reaching toward the tip of my marker. It's super creepy, not gonna lie.

I push the paper down again.

I'm tempted to let go again, just to see it rise once more, but instead I touch the tip of the marker to the paper and draw a line.

It works! The marker works.

And not only that, but the color of the line isn't black like the ink. It's a reddish orange.

The perfect color for Brickman.

I look around the room to an imaginary audience,

like *Are you seeing this??*

I return to the paper, drawing and coloring in one brick after another—Brickman's head, his chest, his arms, his cement-shooting hand. When it comes time for me to draw his signature wrecking-ball-and-chain, I've made peace with the idea that it will be brick colored.

But it's not.

Somehow the marker knows the exact shade of gray I need.

"What," I say aloud. I have created a literal magic marker.

This might be the best thing that has ever happened to me.

I attack the page, sketching, coloring, shading, and every step of the way, the marker—or, more accurately, the ink inside it—knows what color I need, almost before I do. It's exhilarating, and soon I'm staring at a full-color image of Brickman, maybe my favorite that I've ever done.

"Eric," Mom's voice says, mere seconds from appearing in the door frame. I quickly flip my drawing over, stash the marker, and stare at the homework handout on the front side with narrowed eyes, as if I'm concentrating really hard. "You slept through dinner."

"I'm not hungry," I say, without looking up, trying to

keep my voice level and not giddy with excitement. "Just gonna keep studying."

"I'm sorry if I was harsh before," Mom says. "You know I love you so much."

"Love you too, Mom." I give her a quick, sad smile. "And this is helpful. Like you said."

Mom gives me a suspicious glance, but I hold strong, and eventually she chooses to believe me. "Okay. Good." I can hear the relief in her voice. "I'm glad you think so too. My god, what is that smell?"

"Oh," I say, trying to conceal my panic. "I know. It's . . . Pepper. She farted. Like, really bad."

"Wow. That is just . . . We should probably consider switching up her dog food because . . . Yeah. Anyway. Dinner will be waiting if you change your mind."

"Thanks, Mom."

As she heads down the hallway to her room, I'm about to apologize to Dr Pepper for selling her out when she starts growling, and I notice that my newly created masterpiece is somehow crumpling itself up into a ball in front of my eyes.

"Wait, stop," I say as Pepper begins to bark. I'm reaching my hands forward to uncrumple it when there's a terrifying *POP!* and the paper ball explodes into shreds. Pepper squeals and dives under my bed, and I'm pretty much right there with her.

What. Is. Happening.

"Eric, what was that?" Mom shouts from down the hall. "Are you okay?"

"Sorry!" I shout, half of me under my bed. "I'm fine! Part of my science homework was to, like, explode a bag."

"Oh," Mom says. "Maybe you could do that sometime that isn't right now, okay?"

"Yes, sorry," I call out, proud that my quick thinking has bailed me out for the second time in two minutes.

I crawl cautiously toward the exploded scraps of paper, in case they somehow burst again. I try to put the shreds back together, thinking Brickman can somehow be salvaged with Scotch tape, but I'm shocked to see they're all blank. The backs still have the homework, but the art I created is just . . . gone.

Pepper's barking again, making it even harder for me to process what just happened. "Shhh," I say. "It's okay, girl, it's just paper." I'm trying to calm myself down as much as I am her. Pepper remains uncomforted, for some reason barking her head off in the direction of my bookshelf. I put down the blank scraps and stand up to look, my heart skipping a beat as I see something on top of the bookshelf, maybe some kind of mouse? Before I can identify what it is, the thing leaps from its perch, whizzing through the air to land directly on Pepper's back.

Pepper freaks the hell out, and I don't blame her. She immediately starts yelping wildly and running around my room like a maniac, the red thing on her back. "Don't

panic, Pepper, don't panic," I say, repeatedly trying and failing to shoo the red rat creature thing off her. Pepper runs headfirst into my nightstand, sending a lamp careening toward the floor, then dashes past me back toward the bookshelf, and it is then that I get a good look at the red creature and realize, in one thrilling and horrifying moment, what it is.

Or I should say *who* it is.

Clinging to Pepper's fur, giggling like a lunatic, is my monster.

Brickman.

10

BRICKMAN VS. PEPPER

No. That can't possibly be what I'm seeing.

Can it?

I feel like I'm losing my mind.

But the more I stare, the more I know it's unmistakably him. Body of brick. Wrecking ball. Flexible mortar joints.

A ten-inch-tall version of Brickman, alive in my room, riding my dog like a rodeo horse.

HOW IS THIS HAPPENING???

I try to shake myself out of my shocked state, reaching forward—with both hands this time—to grab Brickman off Pepper's back. His small, solid brick form twists in my hands, which totally weirds me out. I toss him to the side. He does a perfect forward roll on the rug, lands on his feet, and gets into a karate-ready pose.

It's Brickman.

It's really Brickman.

Come to life.

Holy crapoly.

Even as I'm a little terrified, I can't help but grin. He's exactly as I've always imagined him.

Pepper is less impressed, though, growling before charging full speed at him. Brickman reacts instantly, firing cement out of the tips of his left hand, which is even more awesome in real life.

It's less awesome, however, to see those cement globs hit Pepper. They pin her tail to the floor and dry super quick. She tries to move, but it clearly hurts, so she gives up and whimpers instead. Brickman puts his fists on his waist like a superhero and stares at me, his eyes twinkling.

"Wow," I say, my heart thumping wildly.

Brickman gives me a confident nod.

Mom calls from down the hall, and I freeze. "I thought you were saving science homework for another time," she says. "What's happening in there?"

"I am, I am. Sorry! Pepper, um, flipped out. Because of a bug. She's fine now."

"Geez, okay. Between the farting and the freak-outs, maybe we need to take this dog to the vet. Time to start getting ready for bed, sweetie, okay?"

"Yep, will do." I tiptoe to the door and quietly close it, in case anything else beyond my control happens. I can't help but think Mom wouldn't be thrilled to meet Brickman tonight.

He's still standing there, hands on his hips, looking very much the hero, when I plop back down on the rug.

"Are you . . . ," I say. "So you're . . . Like, you're Brickman?"

Just as I've always imagined, he responds with a grunt instead of words, a low crackly noise that kinda sounds like sandpaper rubbing on the sidewalk.

"And you're real?" I ask.

Brickman spreads his arms wide and gives a thumbs-up with the hand that's not holding a wrecking ball.

"This is nuts."

Brickman gives another crackly grunt.

We stare at each other in silence for a moment.

"Um, my name is Eric," I say. "I drew you. And then . . . I mean, somehow you became real. How did that happen?"

Brickman smiles and shrugs, then lets out a series of grunty laughs. He reaches out his right hand.

It takes me a moment to realize what he's waiting for. I put out my hand, and we shake, his tiny hand sandwiched between my thumb and index finger.

I shake hands with the real-life version of my drawing. No biggie.

Pepper whimpers, still cemented to the floor.

"Ah, sorry, girl," I say, feeling like the world's worst dog owner, repeatedly throwing her under the bus and then leaving her glued to the floor. "Brickman, this is Pepper. She's a friend. So maybe you could, like, uncement her?"

Brickman grunts happily and extends his hand to Pepper. She growls, understandably suspicious.

"Paw, Pepper," I say, wanting the two of them to get along.

Pepper reluctantly reaches out a paw and touches Brickman's hand. Brickman's face lights up. He walks over to Pepper's tail, swings his wrecking ball up into the air, and smashes the cement. Pepper spins in a circle, gives two happy barks, then licks Brickman's head and wags her newly liberated tail. Brickman lets out another little laugh-grunt. I laugh too.

This is insane.

"How did this happen?" I ask, more to myself than Brickman. I quickly answer my own question as my eyes land on the magic marker and blank shreds of paper.

The ink.

My great-great-grandpa's ink did this.

I drew Brickman, and he literally popped off the canvas.

I need to tell Yoo-hoo. Immediately. He picks up on the second ring, which is an incredible relief.

"I'm not talking to you," he says.

"I know, I know, but you won't believe this!"

He hangs up.

I try again. If he'll just listen for five seconds, I know his mind will be blown. It goes straight to voice mail.

"Eric!" Mom says, right outside the door. "Teeth. Pajamas. Now."

"On it," I say, knowing if I don't listen this time, I could be looking at an even longer grounding. "In the middle of changing." I slide into pajama pants and a shirt while Pepper sniffs Brickman's butt. Brickman doesn't seem to enjoy it, but, much to my relief, he takes a few steps away instead of engaging her in battle. "You guys stay here. I'll be back in literally forty seconds."

Brickman bows. Pepper continues to examine our new guest.

I open the door a crack, slide out, shut it behind me, and zip across the hall to the bathroom, where I brush my teeth at superhuman speed.

Brickman is real.

He is in my room *right now*.

It feels like a dream.

I'm rinsing off my toothbrush when I see my bedroom door fling open by itself in the mirror. I gasp and spin around to see little Brickman in the door frame, holding a cement crowbar thing that he's created to jimmy open the door. With his free hand, he gives me another thumbs-up.

"Get back in there!" I shout-whisper (even though I'm also impressed by how strong he is) as I scoop him up and step back into my bedroom, closing the door behind me. "Look, Brick, when I tell you to stay somewhere, you have to actually listen. My mom might bag you up with the rest of my art supplies, you know what I mean?"

Brickman shrugs and grunts as I continue to hold him around his waist. He's surprisingly heavy, though I guess I shouldn't be surprised, considering he's made of bricks.

"Are you gonna, like, stay here a while?" I ask, lifting him up to my face so that we can see eye to eye.

Brickman points at me and grunts.

"It's up to me?" I ask.

Brickman grunts and points at me again.

"You're here for me?"

Brickman nods and smiles.

"Oh. Okay. Cool."

I don't even know what that means, but I suddenly

feel the best I have all week. I flip off the lights and put Brickman down on the bed before jumping under the blankets. Pepper hops in too, taking her usual spot next to me. Brickman just stares.

"Do you . . . sleep?" I ask him.

Brickman shrugs and climbs under the blanket, curling up against Pepper.

Within a few minutes, the two of them are snoring in harmony—Brickman making a noise like rocks spun in a blender—as I stare up at the darkness of the ceiling, trying to make sense of the last hour of my life.

My great-great-grandfather sent me a real-life Brickman.

I try to close my eyes, but I don't think I'll be sleeping much tonight.

11

BRICKMAN'S FIRST DAY OF SCHOOL

"You overslept," Mom says, roaming through my room with a laundry basket, picking up dirty clothes.

I wipe my eyes, and for a few seconds, I don't remember the insanity of last night.

Then I see Brickman at the foot of the bed, yawning and scratching his butt. Thank god Mom is too focused on my laundry to notice. I sit up and fling my blue comforter over Brickman. "Well, I'm awake now!" I say. "So you don't have to pick up my stuff. I'll get it."

"Sure you will," Mom says, bending over to grab a sock.

Brickman starts moving around underneath the blanket. I leap over to sit on him. He starts playfully grunting as he wriggles out from beneath me, so I pretend to have a coughing fit to cover the noise.

"Are you okay?" Mom asks.

"I'm good," I say. "Just a little scratchy throat. I'll get some water." Brickman, still below the comforter, gives me a big shove. "Whoa!"

"What was that?"

"Pepper," I say, going once again to my all-purpose excuse magnet. "She's a little feisty this morning."

"Well, hurry up. You'll definitely be late if you're not out soon."

"You got it, Mom!" I say. She looks back at me with her arched eyebrows before walking out of the room.

I quickly close my bedroom door and flip the comforter off Brickman, who's lying on his back giggling and pointing at me, like our shoving match was the most hilarious thing that's ever happened to him. (Considering he hasn't even been alive a day, it probably was.)

I laugh too. "So you weren't just a weird dream, I guess."

Brickman shrugs.

I think about leaving him here for the day, how Mom will react if she encounters a small monster wandering around her kitchen.

"Hey," I say. "Do you want to go somewhere with me?"

Mom is waiting at the bottom of the stairs to hand me a granola bar like it's a relay baton. "Get out of here, sweetie. You're cutting it way too close for someone who already has a week of detentions."

"Yep, on it," I say.

"Love you." Mom gives me a kiss and pushes me into the garage.

Once the door is closed, I take off my backpack, unzip, and look inside. Brickman is sitting in there calmly next to my books and folders, knees to his chest.

"You okay?" I whisper.

He gives me a thumbs-up.

"Great. Actually . . ." I poke a finger in a small hole in the side of my beat-up backpack to make it wider. "So you can enjoy the view."

Brickman nods, grunts, and smiles.

"All right, buddy. Get ready for your first day of school."

I walk my bike across the street like always, hoping desperately that Yoo-hoo will ride with me to school so I can safely introduce him to the utter insanity in my backpack before we get there.

"Yoo-hoo?" I shout up to his bedroom window on the side of the house.

"He left already, Eric," his mom says, popping her head out onto the porch. "Five minutes ago."

"Oh, okay," I say.

"How you doing? You hanging in there?" I'm not sure what she's referring to—my parents' crumbling marriage, my dad's failing business, or the physical assault I perpetrated on her son yesterday (it's probably all three)—but I don't like being reminded about any of it.

"I'm good," I say, knowing that Brickman's in my backpack. "Thanks, Ms. Pai!" I hop on my bike and get moving before she can say anything else.

As I speed down Neptune Avenue to make it to school on time, I occasionally hear some contented little grunts from Brickman, like he's a tourist oohing and aahing. I can't help but wonder what it's like inside his brain, what kinds of thoughts he's having, how much he understands of what he sees. I also can't help but wonder if bringing him to school is a terrible idea.

"So we're about to go in," I say into my backpack as I lock up my bike in front of Mark Twain. "You just can't move, okay? Or make noise. I'll try to find stretch breaks for you when I can, all right?"

Brickman nods and smiles and gives me the double thumbs-up this time. Does he even know what a stretch break is?

The first homeroom bell rings as I step through the front door, which means I still have a little time. I search the lobby for Yoo-hoo, even though I know he's probably

115

in class already. He has to be the first one I show Brickman to. This is nonnegotiable, both because he's the
cofounder of Monster Club and because I've already let
him down so much. It's clear I'll have to catch him later,
though, because—

"Hey, you," Jenni Balloqui says, giving me a big smile.

"Oh, hi," I say. Talking to her means squandering
any small chance I might have of finding Yoo-hoo.

"Can I see it?"

She knows.

Jenni knows about Brickman. I made the hole in my
backpack too big, and she was able to peek in. "Um," I
say.

"I know we said you have till the end of the week,"
Jenni says, her smile fading, "but I just want to see
what you have so far."

"Oh!" I say, exhaling and loosening the iron grip I had
on my backpack straps. "The Parachute Jump drawing.
Is what you're talking about. Right. Yeah. I, uh, have
made some progress. But not a lot of progress."

I've made zero progress. I tried to work on it two
nights ago, but then I drew Brickman instead.

"Okay," Jenni says, her eyebrows furrowed. "So
you're doing most of it tonight?"

Brickman grunts and starts shuffling around in the
backpack, as if protesting on my behalf. I quickly cough

and jump from side to side to try and cover it up.

"Look," I say, "I actually have to go because I'm late."

Jenni stares at me like she's imagining a wrecking ball smashing into my head. "You know what? Forget it. You're the wrong person for this. Can I get my folder back?"

Opening my backpack in front of her is not an option. "Not right now, no."

"What? It's my folder, just give it to me."

"I still want to do the project with you," I say, panicking, "so—"

"Well, it's too late. You clearly don't care, so I want it back. Unless you lost it."

"I didn't lose it—"

Jenni is surprisingly nimble, springing past me and sliding my backpack off my shoulders. "All right! All right!" I say, snatching the bag to my chest before she can. "I'll give you your folder back. Geez."

I spin around and hunch over, trying to unzip the least amount possible and still get the folder out. Brickman's not sitting calmly the way he has been, though. It takes me a moment to understand what I'm looking at—it's Brickman blowing his nose on one of my homework assignments.

Or that's what I think at first, anyway. I realize with horror it's the Parachute Jump page of Jenni's project, which I hadn't bothered putting back into the folder after my false start.

"Do you have it or not?" Jenni asks. "Now we're both gonna be late."

I yank the paper out of Brickman's hands. He grunts apologetically and taps his nose, as if to explain.

"Whoa," Jenni says as we both stare down at her crumpled paper, which is covered with grayish fluid that I can only assume is some kind of cement snot. "What did you—"

"I'm sorry," I say, pulling the folder out with my free hand and quickly zipping the bag up. "I'm so sorry. Here."

"Sorry?" She grabs the purple folder, leaves me holding the snot page. "I gave you this folder to *protect the work*! What even is that?"

"Yeah, I know, right?" I figure agreeing with her might help maybe . . .

"Ugh, you're so clearly not up for this," Jenni says, huffing away down the nearly empty hall.

I can't even argue with her.

I rush the other way toward Mrs. Franklin's class, whispering down into my bag. "Out of everything in there, you seriously had to blow your nose on *that*?"

Brickman grunts and gives a little giggle as the final homeroom bell rings and I break into a full-on sprint.

12

LIFE IN THE BATHROOM

I make it through Mrs. Franklin's class with no problems (she lets me off for being late with just a warning, which is a minor miracle), but Mr. Zendel's class is a different story.

Yoo-hoo's in his usual seat diagonally behind me. He came in right as the bell rang, which I'm sure he did intentionally so he wouldn't have to risk talking to me. When I tried to get his attention as he walked past me to his seat, it looked for a second like he wanted to smile back—but he didn't.

Jenni, sitting up in the first row, is also avoiding eye contact with me, in spite of my best efforts. Super.

I can't even focus on what Mr. Zendel is saying. All I can think is that I need to introduce Yoo-hoo to Brickman. Soon.

Unfortunately, Brickman seems as restless as I am.

Asha Nadkarni is in the desk next to me looking wide-eyed down at my backpack, which I realize is now inching slowly away from me. I reach out and grab it, slide it back toward my feet.

"It's a toy," I whisper to Asha. "For a friend."

Asha gives me a condescending smile.

"Eric, my dude," Mr. Zendel says. "I'd appreciate it if you didn't talk while I did."

"Sorry about that," I say, feeling the strap stretching in my hand as Brickman strains to get away again.

"And why don't you put that bag away? It's a bit distracting."

"Yeah, of course. Sorry. " I give my backpack a sharp tug, desperately sending the message to *stop moving around in there!*

Brickman goes still—thank god—and Mr. Zendel continues on with his lesson. This would usually be the moment when I'd look back to commiserate with Yoo-hoo, and I almost do it out of instinct before catching myself.

When class finally ends, I know what I have to do.

Yoo-hoo is immediately on his feet and out the door, and I sidle up right next to him.

"You have to come with me," I say.

Yoo-hoo shakes his head as he pulls out his pad of

neon-green Post-its and quickly scribbles something. *NO THNX*, the Post-it says, right before it flutters to the ground like an injured bird.

"But I have to show you something amazing," I say.

"Dude," Yoo-hoo says, stopping in the middle of the hall as kids stream by on either side of us. "You know I'm more into Monster Club than Hollywood is, but I get what he's saying about you. Sometimes it feels like it's the only thing you can talk about, and you're so intense, like our lives are at stake or something. They're just creatures we draw, and it's fun, but we can talk about other stuff sometimes too—"

"I know I get intense," I say, ignoring everything he just said because Yoo-hoo *needs* to see this. Even if he hates me forever from now on, he has to meet Brickman first. "But really, you need to—"

"Whatever new amazing thing you drew, I don't need to see it right now, okay?"

"It's not— Just come on . . ." We're passing the boys' bathroom, and as much as shoving Yoo-hoo again is the last thing I want to do, I don't have any other option. I push him through the door.

"Hey!" Yoo-hoo shouts. "Get off me!"

"I'm sorry!" I say as the door swings shut behind us. After a quick scan of the room and underneath all the stalls, I'm delighted and relieved to see we're alone. "I know you're mad, and you have every right to be," I say as fast as I can, "but it's not a drawing I want to show you. It's this." I unzip my bag and hold it open wide.

Brickman looks up and waves.

Yoo-hoo screams.

"Shhh!" I say, terrified that someone's going to hear. I usher Yoo-hoo into one of the stalls, closing and locking the door.

"What was that?" Yoo-hoo asks. "That looked like . . ."

"Brickman," I say. "Yeah. It is. It's Brickman."

"What? How? Did you make him out of clay? Does he run on a motor or something?"

"Uh . . . definitely not." I reach into my bag, offering my hand as a platform for Brickman to step onto and then lifting him up, holding him toward Yoo-hoo.

"Brickman, this is my best friend, Yoo-hoo."

Brickman grunts and extends a hand.

"What the . . . ," Yoo-hoo says, eyes wide.

"He wants to shake your hand."

"Yeah. I see that." Yoo-hoo slowly reaches out his hand and breaks out into a huge smile as he and my monster shake. "This is insane." Yoo-hoo cracks up, which makes Brickman giggle, which makes Yoo-hoo crack up more, which makes me crack up too.

"How is fricking *Brickman* standing here with us?" Yoo-hoo asks.

"I got some magic ink," I say, shifting my hand toward the toilet paper dispenser so that Brickman can leap onto a more solid surface.

"Good one."

"I'm being completely serious!" I say. "My dad had this box of old family stuff, including this super old tattoo ink that was my great-great-grandpa's. I poured some into this."

I pull the magic marker out of my bag.

Yoo-hoo closes his eyes and shakes his head back and forth like a dog drying off after a bath. "What the heck are you saying to me right now? That you drew Brickman with some grandpa ink and he, like, jumped off the page?"

Brickman grunts.

"Well, exploded off the page is more like it," I say, "but yeah, that's what I'm saying. Try it yourself." I offer him the marker.

"Right now? In school?"

"Draw BellyBeast."

Yoo-hoo stares at me for a few seconds. "You sure about this, Doodles?"

"I am totally sure," I say, which isn't true. But I'm *mainly* sure.

Yoo-hoo pulls the marker from my grasp, a skeptical smile on his face. He takes his binder from his backpack and pulls out a blank sheet of lined paper, sits down on the edge of the toilet (which maybe is kind of gross, but the moment is too exciting for either of us to acknowledge that). Yoo-hoo uncaps the marker and instantly starts gagging at the smell.

"I know," I say. "It's the worst, but I promise it's worth it."

"Ugh, this is a nasty fart marker, isn't it? If you're messing with me, I will drop you right in the toilet. I swear."

"No! Just draw, Yoo-hoo!"

Brickman grunts and nods and swings his demolition ball in the air in agreement.

Yoo-hoo sighs and shrugs. He spins the marker on his fingertips like it's one of his drumsticks and starts to draw BellyBeast.

"Whoa," he says, surprised that the marker has drawn in the exactly correct shade of blue for Belly-Beast's fur. "I thought it would draw in black."

"It draws in *everything*," I say. "Keep going."

Yoo-hoo's mouth gapes open as he draws with a steadily building momentum and the marker provides every color he needs for every part of BellyBeast: his four arms, his long fangs, his gigantic belly jutting out from his black AC/DC T-shirt, his cut-off camouflage shorts. Everything about BellyBeast has always been larger than life, but here he's more vivid than ever, and my heart starts beating faster. Because I know what's coming next.

"Wow," Yoo-hoo says, putting the cap back on the marker and admiring his finished work.

"Yeah," I agree. It's beautiful.

"This ink is nuts. So . . . now what?"

The words are barely out of his mouth when the drawing starts to curl in on itself. Yoo-hoo lets go of the binder in a panic. "Shoot!" he says as it falls to the floor, the paper sliding off and under the stall divider.

I drop to the floor to see if I can grab it back, but it's two stalls over. "Get down here!" I say. "You're gonna want to see this."

Yoo-hoo drops down next to me, and we watch as the paper continues rolling into a ball and then—*POP!*—explodes into shreds. Yoo-hoo screams again.

Standing where the paper used to be is a foot-tall version of BellyBeast. Real fur. Real fangs. Real spit in his mouth.

"BellyBeast . . . ?" Yoo-hoo asks.

BellyBeast smiles and holds up four "Let's rock" horn symbols with all four of his hands.

"Holy macaroni," Yoo-hoo whispers.

"Toldja it was real," I say.

There's an echoing click as Brickman leaps down

from the toilet paper dispenser and lands next to us on the tiled floor. His eyes light up when he sees BellyBeast. I instantly understand what's about to happen, and I mentally kick myself for not having realized it sooner. Brickman lets out some kind of joyful-grunt war cry and charges under the stall divider toward BellyBeast.

"Shoot, wait!" I say, but it's too late.

It's on.

Brickman tackles BellyBeast, who makes his own noise, less of a grunt and more of a throaty roar-bark-yelp, like a dog mixed with a parakeet. Soon the two of them are rolling and scuffling across the bathroom floor, slamming each other into toilets, the dividers, any available surface, really.

"Should we separate them?" I say, flailing around

uselessly under the stall divider.

"I mean . . . ," Yoo-hoo says, "I think they're actually enjoying this. Like, a lot."

And it's true. Brickman and BellyBeast seem to be having the time of their lives.

Brickman giggles after firing cement at BellyBeast's wrist, pinning him to the tile floor. BellyBeast struggles for a moment before roar-barking and ripping his arm free, then heaving Brickman up and over his shoulder into the toilet with a triumphant splash.

"Ew," Yoo-hoo and I say at the same time.

A soaking Brickman climbs out, and I'm wondering if soap will work on his brick body when the door to the hallway opens and three sets of feet walk in. Yoo-hoo quickly reaches out and grabs BellyBeast, pulling him back to our stall. I do the same with Brickman, cringing as I try not to think too hard about what his wet body might now be coated with.

"Yeah, but did you look at his ears? They were *huge!*"

I know that voice. And I know the two voices pathetically laughing in response.

The people who just walked into the bathroom are Darren, Cyril, and Buzzy.

13

BOOM

Yoo-hoo and I try to remain still in the stall, both of us holding tightly to our monsters.

"No more fighting right now," I whisper to Brickman.

He and BellyBeast make pouty faces, and Brickman lets out some sad grunts. I quickly cover his mouth, but it's too late.

"Whoever that is in there," Darren says, walking closer, "I can hear you farting. Keep it down!"

Cyril and Buzzy laugh again, even though Brickman's grunts sounded nothing like flatulence.

I don't know what will happen if Darren and his doofus friends discover Brickman and BellyBeast, but I'm quite sure it won't be good. From the look on Yoo-hoo's face, I know he feels the same.

"Ooh la la," Darren says, now right next to the locked stall door. "I didn't even notice there are two of you in there. Farting together, how special."

"That's nasty," Cyril says, chuckling, and I can't help picturing his stupid man bun.

Yoo-hoo and I look to each other with panicked eyes, like *what do we do????* But the only move we have is to wait this one out and hope that the lock on the door holds.

Unfortunately, that's exactly when BellyBeast decides to poke a furry finger right into Brickman's left eye. Brickman yelps and squirms in my hands, and I drop him.

"No!" I shout-whisper.

As he's descending, Brickman accidentally swings his demolition ball right onto Yoo-hoo's foot.

"OW! Oh god!" Yoo-hoo says, skipping around and dropping BellyBeast.

"Wait," Darren says. "Is that Fart Talent and his farty friend in there? I should've known it was you two!"

I'm bending down, determined to grab our monsters, but Brickman and BellyBeast are back at it—tussling on the floor, tumbling and smashing each other. Brickman gets to his feet and swings his demolition ball, but BellyBeast dodges. Then BellyBeast jumps to his feet and growls and prepares to smack his belly—arguably the most effective move he has.

"Whoa!" Yoo-hoo says. "He's gonna use his sonic boom!"

And then BellyBeast unleashes. A tremendous blast of air reverberates through the stall, blowing back our hair and sending Brickman flying into the stall's rear wall. It also flings open the stall door, sending Darren stumbling backward into a urinal.

"Aaagh!" Darren says, struggling to get his wet butt out of the urinal. "You're both dead!"

That shocks us into action. We scoop up our monsters from the floor (praying they haven't been spotted yet), hide them under our shirts, and burn rubber out of there.

Darren tries to grab us but slips and ends up falling back deeper into the urinal. Cyril and Buzzy crack up.

"Help me outta here, you losers!" is the last thing we hear as we burst out into the empty hallway.

"That was insane," Yoo-hoo says. "This is so insane!"

"I know!" I say, transferring Brickman from under my shirt to my backpack as we run toward math. "Going back in here, buddy," I tell him. Brickman makes a disappointed grunt. "We'll find some more battle time later, don't worry." He gives me a thumbs-up as I zip his temporary home shut.

"See ya soon," Yoo-hoo says into his bag, zipping

BellyBeast in. "Don't sonic boom in there, okay?" Belly-Beast gives a low growly purr of understanding.

"Third period's already started," I say as we turn the corner toward class.

"Third period?" Yoo-hoo says. "Who cares about third period! Our monsters are *alive!*"

"Yeah. But I already have a week of detention. So . . ."

"Oh, right." Yoo-hoo looks down as we're both reminded that, until fifteen minutes ago, he wasn't even talking to me.

"That was too close a call with Darren and those guys," I say quietly as we arrive outside Mrs. Gingold's door. "I don't think we should take our monsters out again until after school."

"Agreed," Yoo-hoo says. "Wanna meet out front after?"

"Well, yeah," I say. "But . . ."

"When does detention end? Three thirty? I'll meet you out front when it's over."

"You sure?" I can't describe how good it feels to hear him say that. We're best friends again.

"Are you kidding? Of course I'm sure. I wanna see BellyBeast crush Brickman again!"

"He didn't *crush* him—"

"Uh, he sonic-boomed him *and* toilet-dunked him, that's the very definition of a crushing." Yoo-hoo flashes me a huge smile before opening the door to Mrs. Gingold's classroom and sauntering in.

The rest of the school day feels about a thousand hours long, and I know Brickman feels that way too. By eighth period, I have to full-on hold my backpack in my lap. When I peek inside, he's doing a Krav Maga training exercise, using a pink eraser strung up by a loose thread as a punching bag, uppercutting it over and over again. Can't say I blame him; gotta do *something* to pass the time.

Beanie, Smash, and Hollywood still aren't talking to me beyond a wave or a "hey" in the hallway, which I'm actually glad about because I don't think I'd be able to stop myself from telling them what's been going on. It's just too risky to take our monsters out in school again today. I'm already flirting with a suspension and jerks like Darren are everywhere.

Brickman and I manage to get through detention, which winds up being me, Hollywood, Darren, and three other kids I don't know sitting in a classroom doing homework while Mr. Orsini, the gym teacher, sits up front watching videos on his phone. (I know they must be stupid because of the way he silently cracks up when he watches them.) Darren glares at me most of the time (after Mr. Orsini yelled at him for flicking my ear, he didn't try anything else), while Hollywood still refuses to acknowledge my existence. When detention is over, Darren is the first out the door, briefly pausing to point at me and slide a finger across his throat. Mr. Orsini, Hollywood, and the other kids rush out right after, so by the time I go, Brickman and I have the hallway to ourselves. He's been stuck in my bag so long, I decide to give him some air, holding him with both hands as I walk.

"Good work, buddy," I say. "That was a lot of time in my backpack, sorry about that."

Brickman grunts and looks around, not angry but not exactly happy either.

"Hey, do you need to eat?" I can't believe this didn't occur to me until just now. "Like food? In your mouth?"

Brickman makes a low noise that sounds like an approximation of the word *no*.

"Okay, good. I didn't think so."

Brickman jabs at the air a few times, then looks to me.

"What? Fighting?"

He nods vigorously.

"You want to do some more fighting?"

He grunts and smiles and nods, then rubs his belly.

"Wait, what?" I say, laughing. "Are you saying fighting is like food for you?"

He nods even more vigorously than before.

"Wow. That's hilarious. And amazing. Well, don't worry, you'll chow down soon. Yoo-hoo and BellyBeast are outside waiting for—"

"Whoa! Eric!" a voice says from behind me in the hallway, startling me so much that I almost drop Brickman. "I didn't know you were experimenting with other mediums. Very impressive."

It's Mr. Solomon, my art teacher. "Oh. Yeah, thanks," I say, frantically grabbing Brickman to throw him back into my backpack.

"Hey, wait, don't put it away before I can look at it," Mr. Solomon says, now next to me, decked out in a bright button-down, as always. This one is green.

"Uh, okay," I say, not sure how to say no to this but terrified about what will happen once my secret's out of the bag with a teacher. "It's just a sculpture. It *doesn't move or anything*." I direct the last part at Brickman, praying he'll understand and go along.

"Wow, the detail is incredible," Mr. Solomon says. "Mind if I . . . ?" He puts out his hands.

"Uh, I don't think so," I say. "It's still, like, wet—"

"I promise to be careful. Please, I really want to see what you did here."

Mr. Solomon is so sincerely eager that I'm not sure I have any other choice.

"Um . . . okay." Brickman plays his part, remaining

rigid as I pass him over to Mr. Solomon, who examines him with a look of awe.

"This is that creature you draw all the time, right? The Brick Monster?"

"Brickman, yeah," I say.

"Brickman, right. What did you even make him out of? Is this actual brick?"

"Uh. It is. Yeah."

"How did you whittle it down so precisely? This looks like professional work. And the joints! Man."

"Just, like . . . I used, like, a brick carver thing. My dad has a lot of tools."

"Well, I gotta say, Eric . . . I am seriously blown away by this. I know I've been pushing you to go outside your comfort zone to make something more realistic, and I see you've really taken that to heart."

"Yeah, definitely," I say, feeling a little guilty but mainly wanting him to pass me back my monster already. "Thanks."

Mr. Solomon finally gives back Brickman, who immediately sighs and goes limp in my hand. Remaining that rigid must have taken every bit of energy he had.

"What was that?" Mr. Solomon asks. "Did you create him with a release button or something?

"Totally, yeah," I say, quickly dropping floppy Brickman into my backpack. "There's a release button, and then his limbs are constructed like one of those wood puppet things—"

"A marionette!" Mr. Solomon says, pointing excitedly as if we're playing charades.

"Yes, a marionette. Exactly."

"Brilliant! He looked so lifelike!"

"Anyway, I'm meeting my friend, so—"

"Of course, yeah, do what you gotta do," Mr. Solomon says. "But just know your work totally made my day, Eric. My week!"

"Thanks so much, Mr. Solomon," I say, taking big, quick steps down the hall so that I can get out of his vicinity before Brickman makes another move or sound that makes me seem like a way more talented artist than I actually am.

14

ANSWERS

"This is definitely the best thing that's ever happened to us," Yoo-hoo says as we watch our monsters scuffle in the sand.

"No question," I say. BellyBeast has Brickman in a headlock, one bulging furry blue arm squeezing around his neck. With another hand, BellyBeast picks his nose and shoves it in Brickman's ear, while using his third and fourth hands to tickle Brickman's stomach.

"He might play dirty," Yoo-hoo says as we both laugh hysterically, "but, once again, Belly's absolutely dominating."

"The tables will turn soon, my friend," I say.

"Sure they will."

True to his word, Yoo-hoo was waiting outside for me

when I finally emerged from Mark Twain. It felt unbelievably good to have my best friend back. We decided to hightail it to the Coney boardwalk, where we could find a spot in the shadows under the boardwalk to let Brickman and BellyBeast brawl freely without anybody noticing. We even drew a rectangle in the sand to make them an official battle ring. I feel confident they've gotten all the fight nourishment they need.

Brickman now frees himself from the headlock and knees BellyBeast in the crotch, causing him to let out a barely audible groan before collapsing hard into the sand. "Yeah, Brickman!" I shout. "That's more like it."

"Yeah, yeah, enjoy your brief moment of victory," Yoo-hoo says. "Won't last long."

He's unfortunately correct, as BellyBeast is up within seconds, smacking his belly to let out another tremendous sonic boom that blows Brickman (along with a blast of sand) out from under the boardwalk. He lands facedown about ten feet away.

"You okay, Brick?" I call.

He raises a thumb without raising his head.

"They're, like, weirdly intelligent, right?" Yoo-hoo says.

"It's nuts. They're just like we always imagined them."

Yoo-hoo shakes his head in amazement. "Except real."

"Yeah. Except real."

"But seriously, though, how is this happening? You said you got the magic ink from your dad. Maybe we should ask him about it."

I can't imagine a less convenient moment for us to seek out my dad's wisdom. The events of the past day distracted me from the stress of his situation with King's, of incoming bulldozers and the imminent demise of his life's work, but now it all comes flooding back. "I doubt he'll know anything," I say. "He barely even knows what was in the box I found it in. It's just been sitting in our basement my whole life."

"Hmm. Yeah."

"Besides, he's got a lot on his plate right now. Since they're trying to take King's from him. Turn it into stupid condos."

"Aw man, it's so messed up," Yoo-hoo says.

"I know. That's why I left practice the other day. I saw those condo vultures at Nathan's, and I'm pretty sure they were talking about how King's would be theirs soon."

"No way! They can't do that . . ."

I glance over to see Brickman repeatedly bashing BellyBeast over the head with his demolition ball, like it's a hammer, giggling as he drives him deeper and deeper into the sand.

"Oh geez," Yoo-hoo says. "Don't let him do that to you, BellyBeast!"

"By Zeus's hoary beard!" a voice shouts from above and behind us, startling me and Yoo-hoo.

I peek my head out from the shadows to see King Neptune standing on the boardwalk looking shocked, eyes wide as he covers his mouth with one hand.

"Oh, uh, hey there," I say. This guy is everywhere. I know we should probably grab our monsters back into the shadows, but it's too late for that—Neptune is striding down the wooden stairs toward the sand, watching with rapt attention as BellyBeast finds a way to dig himself out and then tackles Brickman.

Once he's reached us, the old man with the leathery tattooed skin slowly removes his hand from his mouth to reveal a huge childlike smile. He crouches down to the sand in his grimy toga as he watches the battle continue.

"It's an art project," I say, hoping I can somehow sell this lie again.

"Yeah, for school," Yoo-hoo says. He's totally weirded out, especially since I never told him about my earlier Neptune run-ins.

"I never thought I'd lay mine eyes upon beasts like these again," Neptune says, as if he hasn't heard a word we said. There are tears rolling down his cheeks.

Yoo-hoo and I look at each other. "Again?" I say.

King Neptune emits a weird joyful cry-squeal as Belly-Beast spins Brickman by the ankles in a circle three times and hurls him across the beach like a shot-putter.

"They're every bit as spectacular as my remembrances of them," he says. "They're—" He looks up at me, as if he's just snapped out of a trance. "You must have—You found her bloo . . . the ink, didn't you? You found Isaac's ink!"

Now it's my turn to be shocked. "How did you . . . How'd you know about the ink?"

"You must give it unto me!" King Neptune says, staggering toward me in a way that makes me take a couple of steps back.

"What?" I say.

"You must!" he bellows, reaching out a dirty hand. "Fork it over!"

"Why?" I manage to squeak out.

"Because it must be destroyed! Immediately!"

"Uh," I say, finding it hard to imagine a reality in which I would destroy something that is as mind-blowingly cool as this ink.

"Look, young prince." Neptune takes a deep breath. "I understand the siren song of this pigment. It pulls upon you like the tide. But it is not for mortals to trifle with. For just as the tide, its power runs deep and dangerous. It will suck you in! Your father's father's father's father, Isaac—he knew its peril. He was destroyed by it! The least I can do for him would be to rid you of it, annihilate it once and for all, and spare you from its dangers." He reaches out his hand again, more gently this time. "Come, give it unto me so I may dispose of it."

"If we need to, we can dispose of it ourselves, dude," Yoo-hoo says, giving me a look like *Why is this guy talking about your great-great-grandfather?*

"No!" Neptune says, looking at Yoo-hoo for the first time. "You can't just toss it in the wastebin. Some other mortal might stumble upon it! A substance this magical needs magic to undo it. Magic that is specific. And complicated. And can only be undertaken by a god like me." Neptune's nostrils flare in and out. "So have you got it on you or not?"

Yoo-hoo and I exchange a look. "We don't," I say. It feels wrong to lie, but I also don't like this weirdo demanding I give him anything.

"Then where is it? At your abode?"

"Something like that," I say.

Brickman, wrapped up in an old grungy tortilla from a half-eaten burrito, rolls past us at top speed, Belly-Beast howling with laughter as he bounds up a moment later.

"These beasts can't be out here," King Neptune says, looking around wildly. "Hide them hence. Immediately. Others might see—and that mustn't happen."

"Okay, okay," I say. "Time to rest a bit, Bricky." I unwrap him from the burrito and put him into my backpack as Yoo-hoo grabs BellyBeast and puts him away too.

"Now go. Quickly," King Neptune says. "Retrieve the ink and bring it here, so I can destroy it once and for all."

"No offense," I say, deciding to go the honest route, "but I don't know why I'm supposed to trust you. Me and my friend Yoo-hoo here don't even understand why all of this is happening in the first place. What we *do* understand is that this ink is pretty much the best thing we've ever seen, so when you come up and say, like, 'Give it to me, mortal, so I can destroy it because that's what your dead great-great-grandfather wants you to do,' I'm kinda like . . . confused."

King Neptune stares into my eyes for an epically long few seconds, like the gears in his brain are whirring in thought, before he blinks and looks down. "That's fair, kid. That's very fair. You deserve more. If you have a moment for the King of the Seven Seas, let me tell you why all this is happening. Please settle thyself." He gestures to the sand as he lowers himself down.

I'm still not convinced. "How do you know all this about the ink?"

"Because," he says, rubbing a hand over his beard, "I know everything about Isaac King. I may be a god, but you might say I worshipped him. When I was a kid just like you boys, I was in the crowd and saw Isaac's sideshow. A tattoo he drew with the very ink of which we speak, a tattoo depicting none other than a monster in the likeness of King Neptune—it winked at me. It recognized me when I did not yet recognize myself. Showed me my own godhood, if you will. Made me understand who I am. Then—" King Neptune coughs. "Well, then

Isaac died, destroyed, as I said, by the power of that ink. And me, as I got older, I got a bit lost. I had come to understand that I am a god, but I didn't yet know how and where to wield my power. So I made it my life's work to piece together everything I could about Isaac. I spoke to his inner circle, found all who worked with him, traced his every step, researched his family and his past. I wished to honor his legacy. Which is your legacy too, young prince. I'd like to tell you the story I was able to piece together. If you'd permit me to."

I honestly don't know what to make of this guy at this point. But I'm definitely intrigued. I look to Yoohoo. He shrugs at me. I shrug back.

We sit down across from Neptune on the sand, backpacks close by our sides.

King Neptune takes a deep breath, which turns into a mild coughing fit. Then he adjusts his plastic crown and begins.

"This," he says, "is a story about a boy named Isaac."

15

THE STORY OF ISAAC KING

November 1905.

As Isaac Krutonog stepped off the train into Belgium, into the unfamiliar city of Antwerp, he was hungry and bleary-eyed and too overwhelmed to realize his journey to America wasn't even halfway done. He'd been traveling for almost a week, one uncomfortable wooden train bench after another, making it from Kyiv across Europe to get here. And now he had a boat to catch. Considering he was only fourteen years old and the farthest he'd traveled up till then was to a neighboring village, it all felt somewhat impossible.

But he had no choice.

The situation in Kyiv for Jews like him and his mother and his younger sister had tipped over from bad to horrifying, accelerating within months from rules that discriminated against them to murderous mobs that tried to kill them. The most recent pogrom had lasted three days. Furious rioters blamed all their problems on the Jewish people and left a trail of blood and horror in their wake.

Isaac still couldn't believe it—they'd been hearing of pogroms in other territories, other nearby places, but it never seemed possible that kind of cruel violence could happen where *they* lived. The small one-room hut he'd lived in with his mother and twelve-year-old sister, Sarah, had its windows smashed in but had otherwise remained standing. The same could not be said for many neighbors, whose homes had been set on fire or otherwise demolished.

"You have to go," Isaac's mom had said in Yiddish, still in shock from the assault on their existence.

"You come with me," Isaac said, unable to hold back his tears. "We'll all go."

"We can't afford for all of us to make the trip. You'll go ahead, take a ship to America like your cousin Mordecai did, earn enough for us to join you within the year."

"But what will I do there?" Isaac asked.

"You're young, you're strong, there will be plenty of opportunities. Mordecai is there in Brooklyn; he'll help you."

Mordecai, who adapted his name to Morty when he got to the States, was seven years older than Isaac and, even before he'd left a couple of years earlier, had never been particularly nice to Isaac. Morty spoke almost exclusively in the language of sarcasm, always eager to make a joke at Isaac's expense. And he was to be Isaac's only source of support in a country Isaac had never set foot in, where he barely spoke the language (so far he only felt confident in "yes," "no," "hello," and "thank you"). It was not ideal.

Yet here Isaac was—alone in Antwerp, Belgium, with nothing but a small sack of belongings slung over his shoulder. On the third day of his train voyage, someone had gotten into that sack as he slept, stealing the tin lunch box his mother had packed for him, food to be rationed out through the week. Not only did this leave Isaac achingly hungry, but it had made it impossible for him to relax, as he felt compelled to sleep with one eye open and with one hand in his coat, gripping his dead father's pocketknife. So now, as he wandered Antwerp's unknown streets to find the boat that would take him even farther away from his family, he felt out of sorts and out of body.

He nibbled a hard roll he'd purchased from a bakery, hoping it might ease his days-long headache, while approaching anybody who seemed halfway nice to ask for directions in the form of a ridiculous pantomime. (Isaac didn't speak Flemish either.) Eventually, a kind woman pushing a stroller pointed him in a direction with an urgency that seemed to suggest the boat would be leaving shortly.

So Isaac began to run.

He felt clammy and weak, but he kept going. In his woozy state of mind, he began to imagine the world was cheering him on. "You can do this!" the bird winging above him said. "You will make it, Isaac!" a stray cat purred enthusiastically.

And they were right because, somehow, fifteen minutes later, there ahead of him was the name of the ship company—the Red Star Line—and a boat more massive than any Isaac had seen in his life. Its horn blew; departure time was soon. Isaac entered a large warehouse, waited in line, and purchased his ticket for a spot in steerage, belowdecks (even that was barely affordable), then strode out to the dock to board.

He was approaching the ship's ramp when he heard something disturbing: part human scream, part animal howl, part desperate cry for help.

That alone might not have been enough to stop Isaac in his tracks, but there was something else too—he swore he could hear, almost like a melodic ghostly moan, someone singing his name. *Isaac . . .*

He stopped caring about making it onto the ship on time, walking quickly down the edge of the dock toward a spot hidden in the shadows of the warehouse. There he saw the source of the sound, about ten feet out into the water.

It was a woman, splashing and yelping, in some sort of struggle with what appeared to be a large greenish-blue sea monster, its fin repeatedly flipping above the surface.

No, wait. She was fighting a huge fish. Or . . . Finally, Isaac realized the woman wasn't struggling with a monster or a fish but with a fishing net, and what Isaac had thought was an aquatic beast was actually—could Isaac really be seeing this?—*a part* of her.

A mermaid. She was a real-life mermaid—and she was in serious trouble.

Barely thinking about the serious trouble *he* would be in if he missed his boat, Isaac shrugged off his coat, placed his sack down, zipped his ticket inside it, and dove into the water—the bracingly cold water—clumsily paddling his way over to her.

"I can help you," he said in Yiddish, the words barely escaping his mouth as he shivered and treaded water, grateful for the impromptu swim lessons his father had given him during summer visits to the river. The mermaid woman stopped yelping, watching Isaac as he tugged at the ropes of the net, which had gotten so tangled, it was almost impossible to figure out how to unwind it.

Isaac plunged beneath the surface, eyes open, yanking down on the net to little effect. "Hold on," he said after coming up for air. He swam as fast as he could back to the dock, climbing a small rusted ladder and sprinting to his coat to pull out what he needed: his pocketknife.

As he propelled himself forward through the water, his arms starting to tire, the ship's horn blew again and a man standing on the ramp shouted something in Flemish, most likely, "All aboard! Last call!" It didn't bode well for Isaac, but he couldn't let her drown just to make his boat.

Isaac opened up the pocketknife and showed it to the mermaid so she'd know what he was doing. "I'll cut you out," he said.

She nodded vigorously, and as the sun shone down, he was thrown to see that her eyes were bloodred. He began cutting through the net, one link of rope at a time. His feet were getting numb, but he kept treading water. Even as part of him knew how stupid he was to be doing this, he could also see how appreciative the mermaid woman was, and he knew his mother would be proud.

He was just starting on another link, just beginning to think he couldn't do this a second longer, when the mermaid pushed free from the net and swam to the surface, speeding a circle around him like a giddy ice skater before bobbing up to float in place.

Isaac could really see her for the first time, how beautiful she was—her sharp cheekbones and dark hair, those unnaturally red eyes. A shawl of seaweed covered her torso. The mermaid nodded her appreciation to Isaac and gave him a smile, revealing alarmingly pointy teeth. Exhaustion and surprise got the better of Isaac, and his body gave out. He sank, unconscious, below the surface.

When he came to, he was being carried through the

water toward the dock, guided back to that rusty ladder, which he climbed, slowly, in a half-conscious state, as if just waking from a dream.

He turned back to say goodbye, but the mermaid was already disappearing into the water. As soon as she was gone, Isaac snapped back into himself. What was he doing? He had a ship to catch!

The man who'd shouted in Flemish had just put up a rope in front of the ramp to the ship when a soaking Isaac appeared in front of him.

"Please," he said, holding out his ticket.

The man looked at him for a long beat before sighing, rolling his eyes, and moving the rope aside so Isaac could get on board.

From the moment the ship departed to the moment it arrived in America weeks later, Isaac was seasick. He sat in steerage with his back against the wall, metal bucket between his legs, passengers uncomfortably packed on either side of him. The only things that gave him any consolation were his pencil and notebook, which thankfully hadn't been stolen on the train and which allowed him to send his mind somewhere else, to lose himself in his sketches.

Though Isaac's father had never approved of his drawing, the act of doing it still made him feel connected to the man. His father, Abraham (yes, Isaac was well aware of the uncomfortable biblical parallel), had been an artisan and scribe, his main work the painstaking creation of Torahs, the sacred Judaic scrolls that contained all five books of the Hebrew Bible. Isaac had often sat by his father's side and watched the meticulous process, the way his father's feather quill would carefully trace out Hebrew letters along each piece of parchment, the way his tongue would stick out as he focused. There were very specific rules and laws to follow, and if a single mistake were made, he would have to start all over again.

When he was ten, Isaac had been allowed to practice with the quill himself for the first time. He'd been a natural, quickly nailing the curves and angles, the way the feather's tip needed to hit the parchment for the ink to land the way you wanted it to.

"You have a real knack for this, Isaac," his father had said. "You'll join me one day. We'll work side by side."

Though Isaac had loved having his father's approval, he'd always found lettering to be a bit dull. A few times, when his father was otherwise occupied, he'd experimented with the quill, sketching a little duck, a pair of old boots, a sea dragon, whatever came into his head. Now *that* was exciting. Creating something from nothing—it felt like magic to him.

To his father, of course, it was trivial and useless.

A hobby, not an occupation.

But to Isaac, the drawing and the lettering were directly connected to one another, and now, as he sketched to stave off both sea and home sickness, he felt his father's presence with him, lovingly glowering over his shoulder, even though he'd been dead for over a year from tuberculosis.

Isaac had mostly been drawing the mermaid.

He was pretty certain now that he'd imagined the entire encounter, some strange, exhausted fever dream. But he liked thinking about her nonetheless, if only as a reminder that he was capable of saving someone. And maybe that meant he'd be able to save himself too.

"Krutonog," Isaac said, seeing the narrowed, straining eyes of the heavyset man at Ellis Island who was looking at his identification document. "Isaac Krutonog."

"Yes, I see that," the man said. "Isaac is fine, but the last name . . . It's too confusing for here. Looks like King if you squint. Let's go with that."

Isaac, of course, could barely understand any of that. "No?" he asked.

"Isaac King now," the man said, loudly enunciating every syllable as he scratched out Isaac's old name with a pencil and wrote him a new identity. "It's simpler. And it makes you sound important." He stamped the document. "You've passed your tests. You're all cleared. Welcome to America."

"Yes," Isaac said. "Thank you."

As exciting as being in America was, it was also quite stressful. Upon his arrival, Isaac had gone directly to the boardinghouse where his cousin Morty was staying and was relieved to learn they had space for him. Being with family was an immense comfort, even if Morty was exactly as Isaac remembered him: much quicker to mess with Isaac's head than to offer actual help.

"Work?" Morty had asked Isaac in Yiddish. "Why do you want work? You're just a kid."

"I need to make money to send back to my mom and Sarah, so they can get here too."

Morty laughed heartily and gave Isaac a noogie. "I'm playing with you, little Isaac. Of course I can help. I'll ask my boss what he can do."

Morty had been commuting to the Lower East Side to work in a sweatshop adding buttons to shirts and jackets. Isaac would sit around drawing all day and stay up late every night, listening for Morty's footsteps coming down the hall back to his room, which sometimes wasn't until eleven or almost midnight. Morty would stare at Isaac with that half-dead look in his eyes, dark circles beneath them, and say, "Sorry, little guy. Another busy day. I wasn't able to ask about you yet."

After three nights in a row of this, Isaac realized he was going to have to take matters into his own hands. His funds had already dwindled down to sixty cents, and he didn't want to think about what would happen if he could no longer afford to stay in the boardinghouse.

So he spent a long, lonely day aimlessly roaming the streets, as if expecting a job to fall out of thin air and bop him on the head. He had no idea where he was going or what he was doing, how to even figure out which businesses were hiring. He felt lost and ashamed; his mother had spent her savings to send him here, and thus far he'd been utterly useless. He cried as he walked, hiding his face in his hands, hoping it would seem as if he were just deep in thought. Though his father was dead, Isaac for some reason felt he was letting him down most of all.

When Isaac looked up, wiping at his cheeks, he was stunned to find himself staring into an alley at a man sticking his tongue out a little as he drew with a pen. Just like his father used to do. The very father he'd just been thinking of.

The coincidence was enough to propel Isaac a few steps closer.

This man otherwise looked nothing like his father— he had long white hair, eyebrows so light you could barely tell they were there, and extremely pale skin—and his chosen canvas was not a scroll but human skin. The albino man was sitting on a cinder block, using his strange needle pen to draw a picture on the bare shoulder of a legless woman in a wheelchair. Isaac knew his father would have disapproved of this, as tattoos were technically prohibited by the Torah, but he sensed his spirit here nevertheless and couldn't look away.

Behind them in the alley was a child in a suit counting a thick stack of cash. No, wait—it wasn't a child, but rather a small man, counting his bills as a tall, muscular woman in a sequined jumpsuit leaned against a brick wall talking to him. It was a strange assembly of people. Isaac sensed they were outsiders, like him. He couldn't help but feel connected to them.

As he drew a bit closer to the albino man, he saw that the image he was drawing on the woman's shoulder was a sea dragon, not unlike the ones Isaac used to secretly sketch back home in Kyiv.

That sealed it. This was fate. Destiny.

Before giving himself time to second-guess, Isaac walked up to the man. "I work," he said. His English had slightly improved—now he had twenty words instead of four. "I help." He mimed the motion of a pen.

"What?" the man said, his focus shifting from the woman's shoulder for a moment.

"I help," Isaac repeated.

"This guy thinks he can help," the albino man said. He started to laugh, and so did the woman with no legs.

"We don't need your help!" the small man in the suit shouted. "Get outta here!"

"Yeah, scram!" the large woman said. "Before I make ya scram!"

Isaac didn't need to speak English to understand this was a no.

Not fate after all. Just another dead end.

He quickly walked away as their derisive laughter echoed through the alley behind him.

The sun was setting as Isaac kept walking, the cool November air enveloping him, the darkness starting to descend. There was a cold pit in his stomach. He'd never felt like more of a failure.

Soon the cement of the sidewalk turned into the wooden slats of a boardwalk, which was when he understood he was walking on terrain that, in warmer weather, was somewhere people went to have fun. In the fading daylight, he saw a huge sign that read Luna Park, hanging above various inert structures designed to fling people around for their own amusement. He tried to imagine himself and his sister, Sarah, on the rides together, her screaming in joy as he tried to remain stoic. It was too hard—he just couldn't figure out how they could ever get to that reality from this one.

He turned away from the rides, found himself slipping off his old shoes and socks and stepping down the boardwalk steps into the sand. He walked across the empty beach toward the ocean, letting himself get lost in the crash and boom of the waves.

He missed his mom. He missed his sister, Sarah.

Maybe he could dive in, swim back to Europe, use the little money he had left to hop a train back to Kyiv. He wondered if anybody had ever attempted this swim before.

He could be the first.

He was contemplating whether it would be smarter to take off his clothes to eliminate weight or to keep them on to provide warmth when he heard the same melodic ghostly moan he'd heard before boarding the boat back in Antwerp.

Isaac . . .

It couldn't be . . . could it?

Sure enough, there she was—in the shallows of the ocean:

The mermaid.

Isaac didn't have words.

She flashed him a sharp-toothed smile, her red eyes glinting in his direction.

"It's you."

She nodded.

"You made it all the way here?"

She nodded again, her fin flipping back and forth in the water. She waved him to come closer.

Isaac hesitated. It's not that he was scared of the mermaid; he just didn't fully trust that he wasn't imagining all of this. He walked slowly toward her, wading into the tide.

When he was three or so feet away, the mermaid held up a large brownish-white moon snail shell and blew onto it. A swirl of golden sparkles glinted in the air before floating down into the shell's open mouth. Isaac took a step closer to look when suddenly the mermaid opened *her* mouth. There were rows upon rows of teeth, like inside the mouth of a shark, and Isaac realized he'd made a mistake—this was no mermaid at all but a monster, just as he'd first thought, one that was about to lunge forward and bite him.

"Whoa, whoa!" Isaac said.

But instead, she chomped down onto her own hand, her fangs breaking the skin.

Isaac was relieved but mortified. "Don't do that!"

The mermaid ignored him, instead removing the hand from her mouth and holding it above the shell in her other hand.

Isaac watched in confused horror as thick black blood

slowly dripped down the mermaid's hand into the shell, darkening the golden sparkles in its interior.

He could have walked away but for some reason felt it was best to stay.

Minutes later, the mermaid pulled the bleeding hand away and put it into the water. She offered the shell to Isaac.

"No, thank you," he said, trying to hide his disgust.

The mermaid woman gave him a small, genuine smile, extending the shell closer and nodding like, *Take this. Please.*

Finally he did, though he wasn't sure why. Maybe it was the urgency in her eyes, as if she really believed this was what he needed.

The mermaid woman gave him her hugest smile yet, revealing her newly blackened teeth. Then she slipped beneath the water and sped away, just as she had the first time, leaving Isaac alone on the Coney Island beach, a moon snail shell full of mermaid blood in his hands.

The only thing that stopped Isaac from chucking the shell away as soon as the mermaid was gone was the feeling that he'd then be letting her down too, just like he was already letting down his mother and sister.

It seemed so ridiculous, making the long return walk

to the boardinghouse while carefully balancing a snail shell of blood, but it at least gave Isaac something to focus on. When he made it back to his room, he reached for a green-tinted mason jar above the sink to pour the shell's contents into. As he grabbed it, the shell slipped out of his clumsy hand and toppled into the basin.

Isaac watched as the mermaid's blood spilled out and slunk down the drain.

So that was it, then.

He wanted to cry at his own ineptitude. He picked up the empty snail shell, its gold sparkles visible once more.

And then something astonishing happened:

The shell began to refill itself.

It happened so slowly Isaac wasn't sure what he was seeing, but then it was undeniable—the shell was every bit as full as when the mermaid first handed it to him.

He slowly (and carefully!) dumped this new blood into the green-tinted mason jar.

Moments later, the shell again began to self-replenish and, when it was full, Isaac again poured it into the jar before setting the shell aside in the sink.

He stared down into the mason jar.

The dark blood looked every bit as uninviting by the flicker of candlelight as it had on the beach.

It was also clear, now that he was indoors, that it smelled astoundingly bad. Isaac had experienced all sorts of unbearable odors during his time belowdecks, but this was somehow worse. Like rotting fish. Like a smack in the face.

Why had the mermaid given this to him?

He considered that maybe he was supposed to drink it, that it might act as some kind of healing elixir or give his brain enhanced problem-solving abilities, but the smell made that a definite last resort.

On a whim, he dipped his index finger into the blood. It felt slippery but thick, more like a stew. His finger began to tingle with a strange heat. When he lifted it out, he could no longer tell what color the blood was. Black? Brown? Or maybe purple?

He grabbed his notebook from where he'd left it underneath the bed, flipped to a blank sheet. With the blood-soaked finger, he traced a line down the page.

Isaac was stunned.

The mermaid's blood was so vivid on the white background. It seemed to shimmer in the candlelight as he stared, glinting from black to a majestic purple to a deep green to an electric orange.

On a whim, Isaac added two protruding eyes and a little tongue sticking out in concentration. A tiny monster to honor his father.

It was just a small drawing, but it made Isaac feel more content and accomplished than he had in months.

But then the paper began to crumple in front of his eyes. He grabbed it and flapped it in the air, thinking it had caught on fire, but there weren't any flames. As it exploded with a *POP!*, Isaac let go and dove for cover under the small desk.

As he huddled there, terrified, he was shocked to see a tiny shimmering creature inching toward him. He extended his foot and stomped down, exploding it into dust only a second after he noticed how familiar it was.

Isaac slowly stood up. He stared down at the jar of the mermaid's blood, awed and afraid, and filled with a newfound sense of possibility.

"You again," the albino man said the next afternoon, after Isaac had spent way too long trying to retrace his steps to find the alley from the day before.

"Yes," Isaac said.

"Not sure how we can make it any clearer," the small man in the suit said, holding a new thick wad of cash, "but we don't need—"

Isaac stuck out the green-tinted mason jar of shimmering mermaid's blood, his hand slightly shaking.

"I help," he said.

And that was how Isaac's new life in America truly began.

16

SPARK

"Shoot," I say, staring at my phone, looking away from King Neptune for the first time in a while.

"What?" Yoo-hoo asks.

"My mom just texted to make sure I'm at home."

"I see," King Neptune says. "But you aren't. At home."

"Right," I say. Mom's text pulled me out of what felt like a trance, hearing about my great-great-grandfather when he was only a little older than I am now, everything he went through, leaving his whole family to travel across the world, how he came to possess the very ink that, unbeknownst to King Neptune, is in a marker in my backpack right now. "She's still at work, though, so she won't actually know if I'm home or not."

"We should probably head back, dude," Yoo-hoo says. "Also because I think our monsters are getting tired of being cooped up."

BellyBeast growls eagerly from inside Yoo-hoo's backpack. Brickman grunts from inside mine.

"But . . ." Even knowing Yoo-hoo is right, I still want to hear more. I could sit here listening to King Neptune talk about Isaac for hours. "I mean, does that story even explain anything about the ink? You're saying all this is happening because my great-great-grandfather immigrated to America and some mermaid he saved gave him her blood?"

King Neptune coughed into his hand. "Yes. You've listened well. That is precisely what I'm saying."

"Is that, like, a thing with mermaids?" Yoo-hoo asks. "I've never heard of mermaids just offering people their blood. Almost felt like she was a vampire or something."

"No," I say, "vampires drink *other* people's blood. They don't give away their own. Because they don't have any. Because they're dead."

"Good point," Yoo-hoo says, turning to King Neptune. "Do *you* know if this is a common thing that mermaids do? The whole take-my-blood-as-a-thank-you-gift situation?"

"Of course I do, I'm the God of the Sea!" he says, and I worry we've offended him. "A gift like that is rare.

Exceedingly rare." He gazes out into the ocean. "Rare as Isaac's bravery that earned it."

"But what happened next?" I ask. "Isaac started working with those people? They were, like, sideshow freaks, right?"

"Just like a mortal to call anyone more remarkable than yourself a freak," King Neptune says, turning from the ocean back to us. "They were artists. Masters of their craft. So when Isaac revealed to them his magic, they were not just astonished, they were enraptured. A bond was formed, and it wasn't long before Isaac had enlisted them all to perform for him. King's Sideshow Extraordinaire was born. Which expanded to include King's Tattoo Parlor. And, eventually, years later, became King's Wonderland, a mere shadow of its former glory."

"So their tattoos came to life during the sideshow?" Yoo-hoo asks.

"By Olympus's towering heights, no!" King Neptune says. "Isaac insisted the blood remain a secret unto only them. He knew that if mere mortals were to see this power that truly belonged to us gods, it could only end in tragedy. I'm not even sure his wife knew. Eva. Your great-great-grandmother. So when Isaac opened his own tattoo parlor, it was all regular ink. He saved the magic ink for his performers—he'd tattoo them, and the beasts would rise from their skin to fight each other in the back room—"

"Wait, what?" I say.

"Like battles?" Yoo-hoo says.

"Yes," King Neptune says. "Great, prodigious battles. Just like your beasts upon the sand." I can't believe what I'm hearing. "They'd place bets on which tattoo beast would best the other, watch them grapple, see which monster survived."

"That's incredible," I say.

"So it was," King Neptune says, a small smile forming at the corners of his mouth.

"Oh shoot," Yoo-hoo says, leaping to his feet. Belly-Beast somehow escaped the backpack and is sprinting across the sand.

"Get it," King Neptune says with a hushed intensity. "Don't let it be seen!"

"BellyBeast, stop!" Yoo-hoo says, racing after him. He lunges to grab him before he can reach the ocean, but just ends up tripping in the sand. "A little help here!" Yoo-hoo shouts. "Give me Brickman!"

"Why?" I ask.

"Just give him to me!"

I run to Yoo-hoo, pulling Brickman out of my bag as I do.

"Remember," King Neptune shouts from behind me,

his voice pure panic, "do not defy the king! Bring me the ink as soon as you can so it can be destroyed! And do not use any more of it!"

I choose not to respond. Yoo-hoo takes my monster from me, his hand wrapped around Brickman's waist.

"Hey, Brick," Yoo-hoo says. "I need you to tackle Belly-Beast, okay?"

Brickman's face fills up with a huge smile, and he nods vigorously.

"Great," Yoo-hoo says. "Here we go." He rears back and hurls Brickman forward like he's a football. It looks like Brickman's going to land about ten feet from Belly-Beast, but then he swings down his wrecking ball before he hits ground, using it to propel himself an extra distance.

"Letter *P*," I say, mildly stunned.

"Propulsion attack," Yoo-hoo says, equally awed.

Brickman brushes himself off after landing, before launching off the sand and onto his opponent, who growls in delight as he pounds on Brickman's back.

And suddenly it comes to me.

I understand why all of this is happening, why I discovered Isaac's ink right at this moment, and what it is I have to do, no matter what King Neptune might say to the contrary.

We're going to save Dad's park.

Isaac's park.

We're going to save King's Wonderland.

"We need to call a meeting of Monster Club," I say to Yoo-hoo. "At my house. Like, right now."

17

MONSTER CLUB (RE-)ASSEMBLE

"But . . . aren't you grounded?" Yoo-hoo asks.

"This is more important than that," I say, jogging across the sand so we can grab our monsters and go.

"No offense," Yoo-hoo says, following me, "but I think you're neglecting the fact that your mom can be super intense and maybe you don't want to do this."

"Once she understands why I'm doing it, she'll forgive me."

"Why *are* we doing it?"

I stop walking so I can make full eye contact with Yoo-hoo and create as dramatic a moment as possible.

"Monster Club Battle Royale at the opening of King's tomorrow," I say. "Like a modern-day sideshow, except with all our monsters. Isaac did it, and we can too. Who wouldn't pay to see that? A bunch of real-life monsters fighting? I mean, seriously! Even if his rides don't work, Dad will make bank, and it'll fix everything. We'll save King's."

"Wow," Yoo-hoo says, and I can tell he's on board. "But should we worry about what King Neptune said? That other people shouldn't see this?"

We look behind us, but Neptune isn't there anymore, which is odd. "I mean," Yoo-hoo continues, "Isaac kept the stuff a secret except from the sideshow people he trusted, which might have been for a good reason."

"I know, I know," I say, starting to walk through the sand again, our scuffling monsters only ten steps away. "King Neptune wants to destroy the remaining ink and all, but I don't see what other choice we have! Those vultures are out there waiting for Dad to not come through with the money for the bank, waiting to snatch up King's Wonderland—my *family history*—and turn it into ugly condos. I found the ink for a reason, and this has to be it. We have to do this."

"All right," Yoo-hoo says, a giddy smile forming on his face. "Monster Club Battle Royale. The real version. This is gonna be ridiculously awesome."

"It really is," I say.

We make it to our monsters—Brickman has used his cement to create a small fortress around BellyBeast, whose furry blue head pokes out from the top. He growls, while Brickman cracks up.

"Bricky. Belly," I say. "How'd you like to fight some other monsters?"

Both their eyes light up, BellyBeast so psyched he extends his arms and smashes free from his fortress.

Yoo-hoo and I grin at each other.

"So we'll tell the rest of Monster Club to meet us at my house," I say, my grin fading a bit. "Do you think . . . I mean, do you think they'll come? Or do they still hate me?"

"No one hates you, Doodles," Yoo-hoo says, snapping a few quick pics of Brickman and BellyBeast as they excitedly bump chests. "They're just annoyed. But once they see these pics"—he rapidly types into his phone before sliding it back into his pocket—"they'll show up. Oh, they'll show up all right."

Yoo-hoo is right—or at least two-thirds right.

When we bike up to my house, Beanie and Smash are waiting outside, both of them looking kind of irritated, like they don't actually want to be there. I'll take it. At least they showed up.

"No Hollywood, huh?" Yoo-hoo says as we jump off our bikes.

Beanie shrugs, raising her tall shoulders even higher.

"Yeah. He's done with Monster Club."

Hearing that wrecks me all over again, but I know I have to stay focused on the mission. "Well, I'm glad you both came," I say. "I'm . . . I'm sorry about . . . You know, everything."

"We get it," Smash says, running a hand through her short pink hair and biting nervously on her lower lip. "Though I still might be taking some time away. Like not from hanging with you guys, just from the club."

"Same," Beanie says. "We wanted to tell you in person. And also figure out how you made those sick pics. Is that some new app or have you been working on your 3D rendering skills?"

"Neither," I say, noticing a sleek black car idling across the street. There are two people inside, and—

I don't believe it. The Vultures. Beard is behind the wheel, Mustache in the front seat. They're trying to threaten Dad by coming to our *house*?

They must see me noticing them because they suddenly speed away.

"Was that . . . ?" Yoo-hoo asks.

"Doesn't matter," I say. "Let's go inside."

We head up the stairs to my bedroom, Pepper eagerly joining us, me leading the way at a rapid pace. It's 5:20, so we have at least ninety minutes until Mom is back from work.

I shut the door once we're all in.

"Ha," Smash says, pointing to the bulletin board above my desk, where I've tacked up the winning Brickman from last fall, the one that only has a jaw, a neck, and an arm because she mostly obliterated him during the Nail Polish Remover Incident. "Sorry about that again."

"I forgive you," I say. "Mostly. Now are you ready to have your minds blown?"

"Sure," Beanie says with minimal enthusiasm, clearly keeping low expectations and wanting to get this over with.

"True that," Smash agrees with a shrug.

I look to Yoo-hoo. He nods. I nod back.

"Unleash!" I shout as we unzip our backpacks and dump Brickman and BellyBeast onto the middle of my bedroom floor.

They immediately pounce on each other with glee.

"What the—" Beanie shouts, falling back onto the bed as Smash bolts toward the door. Pepper starts barking her brains out.

"It's okay, it's okay!" I say, cuddling Pepper, trying to calm everyone down.

"Really, don't worry," Yoo-hoo says, going to the door to stop Smash from running away.

"What are we even looking at right now?" she says,

hanging back, freaked out.

"Is that . . . ?" Beanie asks, cautiously moving forward on the bed, laser-focused on the entangled clump on my green rug. "Is that what I think it is?"

Yoo-hoo crouches down and crawls forward toward the skirmish. "Hey, guys," he says. Brickman and Belly-Beast continue fighting.

"Guys," I say, bending down to them with Yoo-Hoo. Nothing.

"GUYS!" Yoo-hoo yells. The monsters finally pause. "Can you break it up for a second so you can meet our friends?"

They pull apart from each other and wave at Beanie and Smash.

"What," Smash says, stunned.

"So it wasn't an app," Beanie says, equally awestruck.

"It was not," I say.

"So how . . . ?" she asks.

"Kind of a long story," I say, pulling the marker out of my pocket and holding it up. "But the short version is: magic."

"Told you this would be worth it!" Yoo-hoo says.

"No no no no no," Beanie says, her long braids swaying back and forth as she shakes her head. "You can't reveal that your monsters have come to life and then not explain it any more than 'MAGIC!'"

"Yeah, that doesn't really cut it for me either," Smash says.

"Fair enough," I say. Yoo-hoo and I give them the longer version of the story, and their minds are blown even more.

"Okay," Beanie says. "Still a lot about that explanation I find lacking—"

"He seriously saved a *mermaid*?" Smash asks.

"—but it's a much better start. Next question," Beanie says. "When do *we* get to use that thing?"

"I thought you'd never ask," I say, laughing as I hand her the marker.

"Wait, wait, wait," Smash says, and we all turn to look at her. "Like . . . Is this the best idea? All of us just making our monsters? What if they, like, I don't know, escape or something? Out into the world?"

We all think about this for a moment.

"BellyBeast," Yoo-hoo says. "Do you want to escape?"

BellyBeast emphatically shakes his head no.

"How about you, Brickman?" Yoo-hoo asks.

Brickman grins and shakes his head too.

"See? They don't want to escape."

"Yeah," I say. "They're *our* monsters, so they'll listen to us."

Smash stops chewing on her lower lip. She smiles. "Okay. I can't resist. Let's do this."

Yoo-hoo hands Beanie his sketch pad, which she positions in her lap before quickly outlining DecaSpyder's pointy metallic angles as Smash, Yoo-hoo, and I crowd behind her on the bed, watching over her shoulder. The colors are as vivid and perfect as ever, the ink transforming into the perfect shade of silver for DecaSpyder's titanium exoskeleton and eight spindly legs, the exact right deep pink for her four eyes.

"This is wild," Beanie says.

"It gets wilder," Yoo-hoo says.

As if on cue, the paper crumples into itself and explodes—we all jump, Pepper hating it even more than she did yesterday—leaving a real-life DecaSpyder standing on all eight legs on the rug.

"Yeah," Beanie says, frozen in shock. "This is wilder. What's up, DecaSpyder."

The new monster dips her head to her creator.

Brickman and BellyBeast just stare, seeming both delighted and intimidated, unsure how to go about fighting this big metal spider.

DecaSpyder shows no such hesitation, skittering past a pile of books into the corner of my room, where she starts spinning a web out of her titanium silk.

"Gimme those," Smash says, yanking the marker and sketch pad from Beanie. Minutes later, there's a *POP!*, and hovering in midair is Skelegurl, a skeleton with two swords on her back, two large bony wings, and a single swoop of pink hair coming down over her skull. Like all the monsters, she's even more devastatingly cool here than she is on paper.

"You are so awesome," Smash whispers. Skelegurl flies over and lands on Smash's shoulder. She reaches back, unsheathes both swords, thrusts them into the air, and lets out a raspy triumphant shriek.

"Man, Skelegurl is *intense*," Yoo-hoo says.

"I love it," Smash says, eyes wide, still in disbelief that her monster is literally standing on her shoulder.

Brickman and BellyBeast grunt and roar back at Skelegurl. DecaSpyder fires off a string of titanium silk, as if it's celebratory confetti.

"So," I say. "Shall we get the battles started?"

18

BATTLES AT HOME

We spring into action and, mere minutes later, we've set up a makeshift battle ring in my bedroom using an old fridge box from the garage.

The first meeting of real-life Monster Club begins.

And it's the best thing ever.

First up:

DECASPYDER VS. BELLYBEAST!

DecaSpyder is way faster than BellyBeast, zipping around him while shooting out titanium silk, specifically wrapping it around his belly so that when he goes to sonic boom, nothing happens. She proceeds to ensnare him in a cocoon he can't seem to find his way out of.

"Come on, Belly!" Yoo-hoo says as his blue monster struggles and growls in discomfort. "You got this!"

"Give it up, Yoo-hoo," Beanie says, laughing. "Belly-Beast is cooked."

Yoo-hoo looks in desperation over to Smash, who sighs. She nods to Skelegurl on the sidelines, who unsheathes one sword and, with one swift slice, cuts BellyBeast free.

"Whoa, wait," Beanie says. "We're doing Monster Assists? Doodles, did you say that in the rules up top?"

"I didn't," I say, "but I guess everyone gets one assist . . . ?"

BellyBeast doesn't seem to care what conclusions we

come to about the rules, as he's already smacking his newly freed belly to unleash an epic sonic boom that rattles my entire room, knocking books off shelves and sending all three monsters sprawling to the floor. DecaSpyder is flipped onto her back, her thin metal legs moving uselessly in the air.

BellyBeast throws all four arms up and growls victoriously.

"Woo-hoo!" Yoo-hoo shouts as I scrawl a win tally for him on a Post-it I stole from his pad. Keeping score is beside the point at this moment, but I can't help myself.

"There's no way you can count that as a win," Beanie says. "Deca totally had that. If anything, it's a draw."

BellyBeast helps flip DecaSpyder onto her feet and pats her on the back.

"I mean, Beanie," I say, "if we're counting Monster Assists, then it's fair."

"Oh, I'll show you fair. Deca, engage targeting system!" Beanie points at DecaSpyder, who seems to know exactly what that means, shooting lasers from her eyes at BellyBeast. He wildly dives for cover under the bed, and the lasers burn little holes in my comforter. "Yaaaaaaas!" Beanie shouts.

Next up:

SKELEGURL VS. BRICKMAN!

Skelegurl's ability to fly gives her a distinct advantage over Brickman, who's very much on the defensive at first. He rolls around, attempting to dodge this way and that as Skelegurl swoops down with her swords out.

I, of course, don't want to see Brickman lose, but honestly, it barely matters—this is so insanely fun, I can't believe it's happening.

Monster Club is back together.

And our monsters are living and breathing and inadvertently destroying my bedroom.

It's glorious.

King's is going to make so much money tomorrow, Dad will stay in business forever.

"Bricky, buddy," I say, "you gotta do something!"

Brickman looks at me with panicked eyes as he continues dodging Skelegurl's swords. He flings his wrecking ball above his head, but Skelegurl easily flies out of its reach.

"Nice try," Smash says, laughing.

"Cement!" I shout. "Use your cement!"

Brickman's eyes light up. He shoots cement out of his left hand, repeatedly pelting one of Skelegurl's wings, then the other, until she's so weighted down she can no longer remain aloft.

"Yes!" I say.

As Skelegurl lands on the cardboard, Brickman

starts to charge, the upper hand finally his, but she unleashes her signature move, a massive burp. Death Breath. Brickman gets one whiff and is knocked unconscious, thudding to the mat.

"No!" I say.

"You're my hero, Skelly," Smash says, crouching down to give her monster a high five.

"That was amazing!" Yoo-hoo shouts, putting an arm around Smash's shoulders in his excitement, then quickly pulling it back. "Sorry," he says. "Didn't mean to—"

"No, it's cool," Smash says, and it looks like she's turning a little red.

It suddenly occurs to me: Smash and Yoo-hoo like each other. Like, they are totally crushing on one another. I don't know why I never noticed before. And, even though I would usually find that kind of thing annoying, like they're distracting from our battles, right now I actually maybe don't mind it.

"Okay, yeah," Yoo-hoo says. "Anyway, Skelly killed it."

"Yeah," Smash says.

Skelegurl and BellyBeast walk to Brickman and lightly slap his face until he comes to. He says something in grunts, and the three of them all start making noises. DecaSpyder crawls over and joins in, raising and lowering her head.

"I think they're . . . laughing?" Beanie says.

"Yeah, I think so," I say.

"That's hella weird," Smash says.

We start laughing too, which only makes the monsters laugh even more.

Pepper is confused.

SKELEGURL VS. BELLYBEAST!

As is customary in Monster Club, the winners of each previous battle face off. Smash and Yoo-hoo grin at each other as Skelegurl and BellyBeast get into it. BellyBeast seems to have taken some lessons from Brickman's fight, quickly tackling Skelegurl before she can take to the air.

I lose track of what happens after that because I'm hit with my first pang of disappointment amid all this euphoria:

I wish Hollywood were here.

He was the third official member of Monster Club, and for him not to be witnessing this magic feels wrong somehow. I should probably text him myself, but I doubt he'd even care.

I'm pulled back into the moment by Smash screaming in delight. Skelegurl has defeated BellyBeast by stabbing her blades into the cardboard arena floor, forming a precarious *X* over BellyBeast's chest as he's lying down that he's unable to slide out from.

"Aw man!" Yoo-hoo says, but he's still smiling.

"Skelegurl takes it!" I say.

"Well deserved," Beanie says. "Skelly's got some undeniably sick moves."

"I know," Smash says. She moves her shoulders up and down, doing a little dance.

I hear a sound outside, and my stomach drops.

It's a Toyota pulling into the driveway.

Mom's home early.

19

BEFORE THINGS GET BETTER

"My mom's back!" I shout-whisper. I'm such an idiot; I should have been paying more attention to the time.

Yoo-hoo is the first one to shift into go mode, sprinting to my closet and opening the door wide. "Let's hide the monsters in here!"

"You sure you don't want your mom to see this?" Beanie says in her dry way, picking up DecaSpyder as we all rush across the room. "You never know, she might have a killer monster up her sleeve."

I mean, maybe there *is* a possibility Mom would understand. But more likely she'd freak out, and once that happened, the plan to save King's Wonderland would be dead in the water. Can't risk it.

"She might also have forgotten that I'm grounded," I

say, "but it seems unlikely." I fold up the fridge box and lean it against my bookshelf (which, if anything, only makes the room look messier—it's in total shambles) before depositing Brickman in my closet with the other monsters. "Just don't fight in there, all of you, okay?"

Brickman cracks his knuckles and smiles.

"I'm serious, Bricky! If my mom hears you, it won't be good, okay?"

Brickman nods solemnly as Skelegurl puts a slice in BellyBeast's AC/DC shirt with one of her swords, and they both start doing that monster laugh thing again.

"Chill out, Skelly!" Smash says.

I sigh and shut the door.

I see the marker lying on the floor and race to grab it as I hear Mom coming upstairs. I dash back to the closet, open it a crack, and chuck the marker past our monsters into Dad's box of King's junk where I first found it. No way Mom is looking in there.

Beanie, Smash, and Yoo-hoo have all grabbed books from a lower shelf, so when Mom comes in, they're sitting in various spots of my room pretending to read, and I'm pretending we're in a study session.

"So," I say, "the thing about World War Two that I, personally, find interesting is— Oh, hey, Mom."

She doesn't respond because she's taking in the presence of my friends along with the absolutely heinous state of the room. I follow her eyeline to the comforter, to the small burn holes from DecaSpyder's lasers. Yeesh.

"What in heaven's name . . . ," Mom says.

"Sorry, Mom. We were just studying."

"Sorry?!" Mom says. "What happened in here?" It's possible I've never seen her this angry before. "And you know you're grounded, Eric! All of you, you have one minute to vacate the room. You"—she jabs a finger in my direction—"come with me."

As I follow her downstairs to the kitchen, I'm anxious but also relieved that we're changing locations. At least now the monsters won't be discovered.

Mom, still seething, gestures for me to sit at the kitchen table. She paces over to the small window above the kitchen sink and looks out onto our front lawn.

"Mom," I say.

"Just hush," she says.

I do, waiting as she takes a couple of deep breaths before sitting down across from me.

"I don't even know where to begin," she says, now seeming more sad and defeated than angry. "Maybe you're mad at me? Because of what's going on with me and Dad?"

I look away, thinking that's ridiculous. I'm not doing all this because I'm mad at her—Monster Club came to life! And it's how we're going to save King's! And if we save King's, we save our family!

I hope my friends didn't go home yet.

"Listen, Eric." Mom reaches across the table and takes my hand. "Your dad and I are working through this. And it isn't easy. For any of us. It's horrible, actually. And I'm so sorry."

It's weird to hear her apologizing to me when I thought it was going to be the other way around.

"I know you think I'm the bad guy," Mom says. "'Cause your dad's holding on so hard, all that pressure he's gotten himself into out at King's . . . I see you're hurting, Eric. And I hate it. I really do. But sometimes you have to go through some hurt before things get better. Does that make any sense?"

It . . . doesn't? Because if my plan goes off without a hitch, it's possible we can avoid any more hurt, skip right to the part where everything is okay again. I nod anyway.

"It will make sense," Mom says. "And things will get better. I love you very much, honey."

"I love you too, Mom," I say, and I truly mean it. That's *why* I feel so determined to make this right, why my friends were here battling today.

Of course, Mom picks that moment to glance down at our hands.

"We had a rule," she says, examining the marker ink

she sees on my fingertips. "No drawing!"

"It's from my school," I say. "Mr. Solomon's class."

"I don't believe you." She gets up from her chair and heads back toward the stairs. "I said *no art supplies*, Eric!"

"Mom!" I say. "Please!" I figure I should stall in case they haven't cleared out all the monsters yet, but then I see Yoo-hoo waiting by the bottom of the stairs, his backpack looking particularly stuffed. Good.

"Sorry, Mrs. King," Yoo-hoo says.

"It's okay, Alan."

"Can I at least say bye?" I ask her.

Mom stares at me and sighs. "Two minutes. Then get your butt back here."

"Thanks, Mom!"

She stomps up the steps toward my room, and Yoo-hoo and I head outside, where I'm relieved to see Beanie and Smash are also still waiting, even though it's starting to get dark out.

"Well, that was a fun ending," Beanie says.

"Sorry about that," I say. "Wasn't really supposed to have friends over."

"Worth it," she says.

"True that," Smash agrees.

"You didn't . . . ," Yoo-hoo says quietly. "You didn't tell your mom about . . . ?"

"God no," I say.

"I told Smash and Beanie about the plan," Yoo-hoo says even more quietly. "For tomorrow. And King's."

"We're in," Beanie says.

"True that," Smash agrees again.

"Amazing," I say, relieved they're in and even more relieved it didn't take any convincing. Even after everything, they still have my back.

"I grabbed Brickman," Yoo-hoo says, unzipping his backpack, "so your mom wouldn't find him."

"Good call. You better keep him tonight. She's searching my room right now." I don't want to press my luck.

Brickman pops his head out of the bag and gives a little whimper.

"I know, Bricky," I say. "It's just for tonight, I promise. And, on the bright side, you get to spend the night with BellyBeast."

Brickman grunts and shrugs, like *That's actually not a bad deal.* I grin and pat him on his head, missing the little guy already.

"Should we take our monsters home too?" Smash asks, the sides of her neon-green backpack bulging in and out, Skelegurl jumping and / or flying around.

"Well . . ." I suddenly feel weirdly possessive of all the monsters, even though that makes no sense because only Brickman is really mine.

"We don't have to," Smash says.

"No, no, it's good," I say. "You should. Just make sure you keep them a secret. If the grown-ups find out now, who knows what will happen."

"Oh, I know what will happen," Yoo-hoo says, going into his near-perfect impersonation of his mom: "'We should bring these creatures to the police, Alan. This doesn't seem safe.'"

We all crack up.

"All right," Beanie says, "then we bring 'em all to school tomorrow."

"We were thinking we'll do a big reveal in front of Mark Twain," Yoo-hoo says. "Right after the last bell of the day, as everyone's leaving."

"I'm gonna spray-paint a bunch of signs," Smash says. "Like Monster Club Battle Royale! At King's Wonderland! With lots of glitter and crap all over 'em."

"And we'll put it on TikTok too," Beanie adds. "So word really gets out."

"Wow," I say. "You guys were, like, actually planning." I don't even want to show them how touched I am because it seems kind of embarrassing. But I'm really touched. "That's brilliant. Then we march everyone from school over to my dad's."

"Monster Club saves the fricking day!" Yoo-hoo says.

"Totally," I say as I realize that, right after school

tomorrow, I'm supposed to be at my second day of detention. But the fate of everything hinges on our plan: King's. My family. My future. I have no choice but to skip. This is too important. "It's opening day for all of Coney Island," I add. "First one since Zadie, so everyone will be there to show their support. People will go nuts for our monsters, and King's will have the biggest opening in history. Easy."

"Easy." Everyone nods and agrees, but even as we're saying it, I can tell we're all wondering if it actually will be.

20

SERIOUS BUSINESS

After the insanity of the past couple of days, I crashed hard last night. I think I fell asleep by eight, which may be the first time that's happened since, like, second grade. As I throw on some clothes, I see that I've missed a string of texts and videos to our Monster Club group chat thread.

Yoo-hoo was the first to text: *We are having a gooooood time.*

There's a video of him whaling away on his drum set while Brickman and BellyBeast accompany him with pepper shakers. Even as it makes me laugh, I can't help but feel jealous. Naturally, it isn't long before the monsters begin using the shakers as weapons to bash each other. "Guys, come on!" Yoo-hoo says. "Stop! GUYS!"

He stops drumming and runs toward the screen to turn off the camera.

Can't believe you trusted them with pepper shakers, Smash wrote.

You amateurs can have your fun, Beanie wrote. *Deca and I are conducting some serious business.* She sent a video of her in safety goggles in her bedroom, placing a cardboard box in front of DecaSpyder and timing how long it takes Deca's lasers to slice it in half. "Seven seconds!" Beanie shouted into the screen, allowing for a moment of celebration before grabbing a spatula from the lineup next to her—there's also aluminum foil, a hardcover book, and a block of granite—and placing it in front of DecaSpyder. "Now try this."

We're doing serious business too, Yoo-hoo wrote a little later, this time sending a video of him brushing his teeth as BellyBeast and Brickman pee in the sink. I feel jealous again. I didn't even know Brickman had the ability to pee, even if it is a stream of wet cement. Had he been holding it in this whole time?

We're cooler than all you, Smash wrote, with a video of her and Skelegurl side by side at a mirror combing their pink hair. Smash gasps in awe as Skelegurl literally pops her head off so she can better style the hair in the back.

I agree, Yoo-hoo texts, the last one in the thread.

Then there's one text from Yoo-hoo just to me: *I think Bricky is missing you a lot. He even made you a creepy present.*

It's a relief to read those words (mainly the part about him missing me) because, not gonna lie, I was starting to wonder if Brickman was having so much fun over there that he wouldn't want to come back.

Tell him I miss him too, I write. *Meet in front in 10?*

YEAH BABY, Yoo-hoo texts back immediately. *IT'S ON!*

"Hey, sweetheart," Mom says, popping her head in. "Dad's taking you to school today; he'll be here in ten."

"Today? I thought—Isn't he busy with opening day?"

"Very. But he's making time to take you to school and have a little chat."

A little chat? That can't be a good thing.

"Maybe he and I can chat real fast, and then I can bike over with Yoo—"

"He's taking you, Eric. End of story. There are some eggs waiting for you in the kitchen." Mom leaves before I can argue any further.

I text Yoo-hoo that I won't be going with him after all, that we should meet out in front of Mark Twain. Then I grab the marker from where I'd stashed it in Dad's box yesterday and put it in my backpack. I'm almost out my bedroom door when it occurs to me the marker may need a refill at some point. I know I promised King Neptune I wouldn't use it, and hopefully I won't have to, but just in case, I go back to the closet to grab the jar of ink—also in the box—and head downstairs, ready for my big day to begin.

21

HAPPY MONSTER CLUB DAY

As expected, Dad chews me out on the way to school for fighting, for getting detention, for trashing my room with my friends even though I'm grounded—all of it. He says he knows it's a hard time with him being around so little, but I need to try to keep it together and make things easier on Mom. I want to tell him everything—about the ink and the monsters and the plan I have that's going to make King's more than enough money to stay in business—but he seems really stressed about opening day, so I stay quiet. It'll be easier to talk about after we save King's.

Moments after Dad and his old truck hurtle away from Mark Twain, I spot Yoo-hoo, Beanie, and Smash. "Hey hey!" I shout, sprinting toward them, unbelievably excited to see Brickman again.

"Doodles!" they shout, almost in unison. They're trying to play it cool to avoid attention, but their excitement about what the day ahead has in store is obvious.

"Happy Monster Club Day," Beanie says, grinning.

"Here," Yoo-hoo says to me, "open your bag." As I do, he surreptitiously reaches into his and guides Brickman from one backpack into the other.

"Brickman!" I shout-whisper. "I missed you, dude." My monster gives me a wide smile, then lifts himself out of my bag to wave an arm at Yoo-hoo, like *Hand it over!*

"Oh, right," Yoo-hoo says, reaching back into his bag and handing me some sort of sculpture, roughly the size of a banana. "Here's the weird thing he made you."

"Hmm," I say, examining the cement sculpture. "I love it, Bricky." He can tell I have no idea what to make of it. He gestures and grunts at me, as if to explain, and suddenly I *do* understand, noticing all the iconic details and angles of his work of art. "Oh man, this is the Coney Parachute Jump, isn't it?"

Brickman nods proudly.

"Whoa, that's hella good," Smash says.

"Seriously, it's perfect!" I agree. Brickman must have carefully studied the photo of the Parachute Jump that Jenni had in her folder and committed it to memory, because the likeness is phenomenal. "I can give it to

Jenni as, like, an apology!"

Brickman nods and points at me like *Exactly!*

"Thanks, buddy. Really nice of you." I place it next to him in my bag.

The first homeroom bell rings, and everyone outside—including us—pushes into the building. I zip my backpack shut.

"Remember," I say as we pass through the school lobby, "we have to keep the monsters hidden till the end of the day, when we'll wait out front to reveal them to everybody, then lead 'em all to King's. Try to find a way out of last period a few minutes early if you can."

"You know," Beanie says, "I'm all for keeping this a secret from everybody till later. But I do think there's one person who would want to know sooner. Even though he might not realize that himself."

"Yeah," I say with a smile, of course knowing who she's talking about and of course completely agreeing. "I'm on it."

I feel like a creepy stalker, standing in the shadows of the locker room, waiting for the right opportunity to talk to Hollywood after gym class.

Finally my moment arrives—I intercept him, back in his regular clothes, as he walks toward the urinals.

"Hey, Hollywood," I say, appearing in front of him.

"Whoa!" he says. "Dang, Doodles, you freaked me out. Like you're Michael Myers popping out of a bush in *Halloween* or something. What're you even doing here? This isn't your gym class."

"Yeah, I know, I—"

"Look, if you're here to lay more guilt on me for—"

"No, it's not that at all," I say. "I wanted to apologize, actually. For the fight. For everything." Hollywood had started to walk by me, but this stops him. "I just . . . I wanted it to be the way it was, but of course you don't have to play if you don't want to. I shouldn't have been such a baby about it."

"Aight, that's fair," Hollywood says. "And I should have backed you up with that clown Darren." He extends a hand to me. "We good?"

"Definitely," I say. We shake, and it feels so good to be friends again, it makes me want to apologize to people all the time.

But of course, I didn't only come here to apologize.

"One more thing, Hollywood," I say, unzipping my backpack. "Just want to show you something kind of cool."

"Dude," Hollywood says, looking at me warily.

"Just look!" I open up my bag, revealing a grinning Brickman inside, swinging around his wrecking ball.

Hollywood's scream echoes through the locker room.

✳ ✳ ✳

Lunchtime is the next period, and I am delighted that Hollywood actually chooses to sit with us. Smash, Yoo-hoo, Beanie, and I huddle around his seat, peering down with him into his backpack.

"I still can't believe what I'm seeing," Hollywood says.

After he recovered from the shock of seeing Brickman alive, I of course pulled out the marker and invited him to go to town. Surprisingly, he actually took me up on it, and suddenly there, gleaming under the fluorescent locker room lights, was a real-life RoboKillz, complete with tank treads, shoulder missiles, lethal saw-blade hand, and a series of random R2-D2-esque beeps and crackles.

"I wish DecaSpyder could get in the ring with Robo-Killz right now," Beanie says. "Finally end this question of which robot monster is superior. Because obviously it's Deca."

"Ha!" Hollywood says. "You're living in a fantasy, Beanie. DecaSpyder won't last a minute. Man, I wanna see all your guys' monsters!" Hearing Hollywood excited about Monster Club again is the best feeling.

"They're pretty spectacular," Yoo-hoo says. "Doodles, you sure we can't just do the reveal now?"

"I know," I say. "I wish we could, but we've almost

205

made it through the day. I don't want things to get too out of control, have our monsters get confiscated or something."

"Good point," Yoo-hoo agrees.

I see Jenni Balloqui across the cafeteria heading toward the exit, and I remember the cement sculpture. "Hold on, gotta do something." I grab the sculpture and jog toward her. "Thanks again, Bricky," I say into the backpack. "We'll see how this goes."

I call Jenni's name. She ignores me.

She's obviously still mad about my failure to draw anything. And maybe also about the cement snot I got all over her paper.

"Wait, please!" I say. "I have something for you. To apologize." I hand her the sculpture of the Parachute Jump.

"Uh . . . ," she says, stopping right at the door to the hallway to take it from me. "Okay?"

"It's . . . I mean, you see what it is, right?"

"I . . . Oh. Wow." She takes in all the details. It's an undeniably impressive sculpture. "Where did you—Did you get this at a souvenir shop or something?"

"A friend of mine made it," I say.

"Huh." I can tell she's not quite ready to forgive me yet, which I understand, but she at least seems to appreciate the gesture. "Thank you. It's . . . Like, I wanted you to *draw* it because you can't put a sculpture into a graphic novel, but . . ."

"No, I know," I say. "But this is just . . . I felt really bad about what happened."

"You could have just said you didn't want to do it."

"But I did want to! I tried, but . . . I wanted to do a really good job, you know? And there's been a lot going on. And I messed up, is what I'm saying. I'm sorry."

Jenni stares at me with her deep brown eyes, and I realize my neck is tingling, but like in a good way. "Thanks, Eric," she says.

"Yeah," I say, smiling back. Apologizing is amazing! Who knew?

"Oh, Fart Talent, this is so moving. I think I'm gonna cry."

Of course Darren Nuggio is always nearby to ruin a nice moment. I turn and the redheaded giant is standing behind me, with Cyril and Buzzy by his side as always. "Or maybe," he says, getting up in my face, "I'll make *you* cry instead."

"Back off," Jenni says.

Darren ignores her. "As if landing me a week of detention wasn't bad enough, you had to pull that stunt in the bathroom too. And I can't let that slide." He gives my shoulders a hard shove and I'm thrown back a few steps.

"Stop it!" Jenni says.

Darren glares at her. "Stay out of this. I have no problem making girls cry too." He snatches the Parachute Jump statue out of her hands, as if to prove his point. "What a lovely present this is."

"Give it back," I say.

"I don't think so." Darren lifts the statue up and smashes it to the floor. But it doesn't break. He tries again, harder this time. It remains intact. He puts it on the floor and lifts his sneaker, ready to try one more stomp when I, for some reason, decide to speak.

"Guess you've finally found the one thing thicker than your skull, huh?"

A roar of laughter rises up from kids at nearby tables, and Darren's face turns as red as his hair. He glares at me, and I know this won't end well.

While he's distracted, Jenni grabs the statue back.

I, meanwhile, freeze in panic as Darren charges toward me.

Before I feel any pain, though, I'm jolted left by a strong tug from within my backpack, and Darren completely misses me.

Brickman has my back. Literally.

Darren snarls and turns, lunges for me again, and Brickman yanks me to safety once more, this time to my right.

Darren's rage is only increasing, and I don't think

this dodging routine will work three times in a row, so impulsively I leap onto his back, arms around his chest. He can't hit me if I'm behind him, right?

"Get off me!" Darren shouts, spinning us around and around as shouts of "*FIGHT!*" reverberate through the cafeteria. The only adult in the room is old Mrs. Ovadia, and as I spin, I'm dismayed to see she is snoring in her chair. Buzzy and Cyril rush over to pull me off Darren, but Hollywood intervenes—even as I'm getting nauseous from the circling, it warms my heart to know that this time he's sticking up for me. Smash jumps to my rescue too, and together they put their bodies in the way so Darren's dipstick sidekicks can't get to me. Yoo-hoo and Beanie are also there, but I'm so dizzy, I can't even fully make sense of what's happening. All I'm thinking is *hold on, don't let go, hold on, hold on.*

That becomes impossible, though, once Darren decides to flip me over his shoulder. I land with a thud on my back, thankful that Brickman seems to have had the foresight to shift himself out of the way. I grimace and slide the backpack straps off my shoulders as everyone stares at me.

Darren's totally frozen. Probably worried he broke my spine or something.

"I'm okay," I say, slowly getting to my feet.

But then I realize no one's actually looking at me.

They're looking at the tiny monster who's pushed his way out of my partially zipped backpack.

Brickman smiles and cracks his knuckles.

Well.

Here we go, I guess.

22

THEY'RE MONSTERS

Everyone is understandably dumbfounded by the sight of Brickman, but no one more than Darren Nuggio.

"What the—" he says, seeming like he's about to say a curse word when a clump of cement shoots out of Brickman's hand and seals Darren's mouth shut. The room gasps again when, with a rock-crushing roar unlike anything I've heard from him, Brickman charges forward. He spins his wrecking ball a few times before swinging it directly into Darren's crotch.

Darren crumples silently to his knees, then falls over sideways.

I pick Brickman up before he can injure anybody else, which turns out to be a wise decision because, a second later, mayhem explodes in the cafeteria as I'm swarmed by classmates trying to get a better look at Brickman.

Luckily, the rest of Monster Club is there to try and shield me.

"Back it up!" Beanie shouts. "Back all your butts up!"

"Yeah!" Yoo-hoo agrees as a clump of kids pushes him closer toward me. "Get back!"

I'm overwhelmed but also delighted. People are losing their minds, and I have no doubt they'll want to come to King's to see more. We just need to get everyone quiet enough so we can make our announcement. Mrs. Ovadia, the cafeteria aide, finally awakened by the chaos, is waving her arms and shouting from the back of the crowd. She's trying to get everyone to calm down, with little success.

BellyBeast has somehow gotten out of Yoo-Hoo's bag and is bounding toward us, waving his arms in the air like a hype man. The crowd has parted like the Red Sea to let him through.

And then, sure enough, next comes Skelegurl flying above all of us, slicing her swords through the air, with RoboKillz zipping right behind, followed closely by DecaSpyder.

And then, if they weren't already before, everyone goes absolutely nuts.

Yoo-hoo, Hollywood, and Beanie swoop down to grab their monsters before they're swallowed by the crowd.

Smash jumps in to try to grab Skelegurl, who playfully hovers just out of her reach.

Jenni Balloqui grabs my arm, staring at Brickman. "What are those things?" It's hard to hear amid all the chaos, but I can tell that she's pretty freaked out.

"They're, uh . . ." I'm not sure what exactly to say.

"WHAT ARE THEY?"

I'm thinking I should grab the marker from my backpack—both as a way to further explain the situation

213

to Jenni / everyone and to make sure it stays safe—but then Jenni's grabbing my shoulders and staring into my eyes. She's so close I can smell a whiff of the avocado she must have had for lunch. Somehow even Jenni's bad breath smells good. "ERIC!! WHAT. ARE. THOSE. THINGS?"

"Monsters," I shout over the din, smiling as I hold Brickman up higher so she can get a better look. "They're monsters!"

Brickman smiles and waves at Jenni, who takes a step back.

"What do they do?!" Calvin Chin shouts.

"How do I get one?" some seventh-grade guy I don't know shouts.

"I can tell you everything," I say, realizing it's now or never. "I just need you all to be quiet!"

No one quiets down at all.

"Quiet!" I shout again. Useless.

"We got this," Hollywood says, giving me a quick flick of his head before raising RoboKillz high in the air—the heavily armored, treaded robot sprays a burst of flames from his mini flamethrower.

That shuts everyone up.

"I AM ROBOKILLZ!" Hollywood shouts into the silence, fully embracing his inner nerd right in front of a shocked Jamie Posterman.

"Thanks, Hollywood," I say.

"Floor is yours, Doodles," he says with a grin.

"What is going on here?" Mrs. Ovadia shouts, finally able to be heard. "You better put that fire machine away! And all those other little machines too!"

"It's just a show," Hollywood says. "We're putting on a show for our classmates."

"Sure you are," Mrs. Ovadia says, slowly making her way toward the cafeteria door. "We'll see what the assistant principal has to say about your little show."

Hollywood gives me a nod, and I know time is short.

"So, uh, hey, everyone," I say. I'm suddenly nervous. "This is Brickman." I lift him up so everyone can see. He salutes and bows. "And this is BellyBeast. And DecaSpyder. And RoboKillz." As I point to my friends, each of their monsters does some kind of wave or bow or nod. "And up there, that's Skelegurl." She theatrically swoops through the air while making a joyful noise that sounds like a baby dinosaur.

"This is so rad!" my sort-of friend from Hebrew school, Shane Weissberger, yells, and everyone hoots and shouts in agreement.

"Well, it gets radder," I say, and thankfully everyone quiets down again. "Because today after school, at King's Wonderland over in Coney Island, all these monsters are going to battle! An epic, glorious, mind-bending once-in-a-lifetime affair! Come one, come all! You don't want to miss this, I promise! You'll see a spectacle the likes of which you've only dreamed about!"

"Monster Club Battle Royale!" Yoo-hoo shouts.

"And when these magic marker monsters get to fighting, it's no joke," Beanie says.

"Ahhhh!" Hollywood practically screams. "I can't wait for this! Fight! Fight! Fight!"

Soon all our classmates are chanting along, and Brickman leaps out of my grasp so he can strut across the cafeteria floor like he's a pro wrestler or something. Yoo-hoo, Beanie, and Hollywood put their monsters down too, and they immediately join in, BellyBeast striking ridiculous muscle poses, DecaSpyder doing little flips, RoboKillz spinning his saw-blade hand at top speed, Skelegurl returning to the ground to walk on her bony hands like an old-timey acrobat.

"Magic marker monsters, huh?" Darren Nuggio shouts from behind us, clearly having found a way to remove the cement from his mouth. "You mean like this magic marker right here?"

I spin around, and my stomach drops.

In one hand, Darren is holding a blank piece of paper.

In the other, he's holding my marker.

23

OOPS

Darren must have swiped the marker from my bag. I can't believe I let that happen. I'm such an idiot. Though Beanie was the one who really gave our secret away by calling them "magic marker monsters" in front of everyone.

Darren grins and starts frantically scribbling on the paper.

"Stop!" I shout. "You don't know what you're doing!"

"Oh yes I do!" Darren cackles.

I rush toward him, with Hollywood and Smash following right behind me. Before we can get close enough to grab the marker back, Cyril Sklar and Buzzy Hoffman step in front of us like a couple of bouncers and shove us backward.

Darren's drawing is a messy collection of grayish-black lines and squiggles, with narrow green eyes and what I guess are supposed to be fangs. He adds one final scribble before holding up his work for the entire room to see.

"I present to you," he says, "Noodle Monster!" Only an amateur puts the word *monster* in the name of their monster. But whatever. "Inspired by the noodle soup I wrecked your last drawing with, Fart Talent. And now my monster's gonna wreck—"

He stops speaking as the paper begins to crumple up in his hand.

"You might want to let go of that now," I say.

Before he can get out the word *Why?* he's so startled by the *POP!* that he lets out a high-pitched scream and flings the paper into the air. Cyril and Buzzy run for cover as Darren's artwork explodes into three dimensions.

Noodle Monster splats onto the cafeteria floor, the new focus of everyone's attention. Noodle is the same height as our monsters and gray-black, with narrow green eyes, sharp fangs, and so many tentacle-like arms and legs you can't even tell its top from its bottom. It opens its mouth and lets out this strange growly hiss. Totally weird and, not gonna lie, pretty terrifying.

"Oh baby!" Darren says, high-fiving Buzzy and Cyril

as they return to his side. "Hey, Noodle Monster—go demolish that fat little pile of bricks!"

Noodle Monster's lizard eyes zero in on Brickman, and a chill runs through me.

But Brickman is undaunted. He cartwheels toward his opponent and vaults into fighting stance. Kids all around us back away to give the monsters room to face off. My heart is beating about a million times a minute.

Noodle Monster hisses at Brickman.

Brickman grunts back at him.

Then Noodle Monster charges, an awkward yet speedy lurch. Brickman sprays out two long poles of cement, spinning them like batons before bashing Noodle Monster across the torso.

The creature is split into two, puffing into a burst of black dust and disintegrating before our eyes.

That was surprisingly easy. Thank god.

The lunchroom erupts into cheers.

"You were saying?" I shout to Darren, which inspires a wave of laughter from everyone around us. Once again, Darren's face turns red.

To add insult to injury, Yoo-hoo snatches the marker right out of his hand and tosses it to me.

I put it into my pocket, feeling absolutely triumphant.

But then Darren makes a wild dive for my backpack. I grab a strap and yank it away just in time, but out comes rolling the mason jar of mermaid blood.

It literally bumps into Darren's arm.

I try to play it cool, like it's a random art supply I don't care about, but he's already seen on my face that that's not true.

He snatches it up.

"The ink!" I shout as Darren barrels through the crowd and sprints toward the exit. "He stole the ink!"

"Follow him, follow him!" Hollywood says.

The five of us scoop up our monsters, and I grab my ravaged backpack, and we start pushing through the mass of kids. We need to get the ink back from Darren before he ruins everything more than he already has.

"Calm down!" a voice says from behind us, at the front of the room. It's Assistant Principal Bachrack. "I'm not sure what's happening here, but I want everyone back to their tables NOW!"

Some kids pause where they are, but most don't. I am one of the non-pausers. I definitely don't need any more detention, but Darren needs to be stopped ASAP.

"Evan, stay where you are!" Assistant Principal Bachrack shouts. "I've heard you're the one creating this anarchy, and I need you to stop right this instant."

If she'd gotten my name right, it's possible I would have felt like I had no choice but to listen to her. But since she didn't . . .

We shove through the cafeteria doors out into the

hallway—and when I say *we* I mean almost every kid in school, including Jenni, who's running by my side. "You sure you don't want to stop and explain the deal to Bachrack?" she asks. "Maybe she can help?"

"I appreciate the concern," I say, "but there's really no time."

We're hot on Darren's heels, and I'm relieved to see Mr. Solomon marching down the hall from the other direction.

"Stop running, Darren," my art teacher says. "Whatever you're up to, it's over now."

Darren disagrees, ducking into the nearest room and locking the door behind him.

"Open up, Darren!" I shout, pounding on the door.

It's the copy room, which has two large windows on either side of the door, so we bang on the glass as Darren frantically tries to figure out what to do next.

"Give us the ink back, Carrot Top!" Smash shouts, straight-up trying to break down the door.

"Yeah right!" Darren shouts back as he rifles through several drawers, obviously looking for paper and something to draw with.

"Open the door, Darren! Right now!" Mr. Solomon says before turning to me. "What's going on here?"

"He stole our ink," I explain. "It's, like, very important ink."

"Totally," Yoo-hoo agrees.

Mr. Solomon seems confused by this explanation but doesn't ask any more questions, instead continuing to shout with us.

Darren has found a pen and a piece of paper but can't figure out any way to get the ink into the pen. He appears to have given up, breathing heavy in the middle of the room. Then his eyes land on the copy machine, and it's like we all have the same thought at the exact same time. Darren smiles at us through the window and sprints toward the machine.

"NO!" we shout, all of us pounding on the door as hard as we can.

Darren pulls and pokes at the Xerox machine until he finds a panel in front that flips down. He slides out a big black tube of toner from inside and hefts it on top of the machine, untwisting a cap on the side to reveal a hole in the tube.

"No, Darren!" I scream. "Stop!"

He opens my great-great-grandfather's jar of ink and pours its contents into the hole.

Every last drop.

"Move over," Yoo-hoo says as Darren chucks the empty mason jar to the floor before closing the toner tube and shoving it back into the copy machine. "I have an idea." Yoo-hoo holds BellyBeast up to the doorknob.

"He just wasted all of it," I say, kind of in shock. "All of the ink."

Darren is using a regular pen he found to rapidly scribble another drawing of Noodle Monster. He puts it facedown on the glass of the Xerox machine.

"Get behind me," Yoo-hoo says. "I need you all to brace me!"

We do as he asks, leaning our bodies against his as BellyBeast lifts up his AC/DC T-shirt and exposes his ample belly.

"Oh wow," Mr. Solomon says, "is that another one of Eric's marionette sculptures? It's fantastic!"

"Uh, yeah," Yoo-hoo says. "Everyone, cover your ears!"

As Darren types the number 10 into the Xerox machine, BellyBeast slaps his belly, unleashing a truly insane sonic boom that blasts the door of the copy room into three chunks that fall to the ground with an enormous thud.

"Wow!" Hollywood says. "That sonic boom is no joke!"

"Whoa!" Mr. Solomon says, looking totally shell-shocked. "That was not okay!"

We rush inside, just in time to see Darren dramatically raise his index finger.

He pushes the big green button that says PRINT.

"No!" I scream as copies of his latest disaster-piece start sliding onto the tray and *POP!*-ing into existence, Noodle Monster after Noodle Monster plunking onto the linoleum. One of the copies gets stuck in the machine, and Darren reaches in to clear the jam.

"Unplug the machine!" Smash says, which I'm embarrassed not to have thought of sooner.

"Yes!" I crouch down and reach toward the plug, but suddenly there are four green-eyed Noodle Monsters blocking it, hissing and baring their fangs at me.

"Nice try," Darren says, crumpling up the copy he just pulled out, which was stretched and warped from getting stuck, and chucking it into the trash can. "But the machine stays on, and your little guys are gonna have no choice but to get their butts kicked by my noodle army."

Five more copies *POP!* into existence, so there are

nine freaky little Noodle Monsters surrounding us.

"Wait, these—These aren't sculptures, are they?" Mr. Solomon says, eyes wide as he takes a step away from us.

"'Fraid not," Yoo-hoo says.

"I'm going to get help," Mr. Solomon says, dashing out of there.

"Yo, Darren," Beanie says. "You get that what you're doing is actually dangerous, right? And also: How many times do you have to get your butt whupped before you stop trying?" She shakes her head as she lowers DecaSpyder to the floor.

We do the same, until all five of our Monster Club monsters are in a back-to-back clump in the center of the room, doing some final stretching to ready themselves for combat. BellyBeast farts.

"Gross," Smash says.

"Now *that's* some true fart talent," Yoo-hoo says.

BellyBeast growls an apology before getting back into fighting stance.

"Let's do this," Darren says.

And without another word, the battle begins.

24

COPY ROOM COMBAT ZONE

RoboKillz is the first to jump into action, firing all six missiles directly at a Noodle Monster, who holds its breath and bloats up like a puffer fish, causing the missiles to bounce off harmlessly. They explode like mini firecrackers on the floor. Undeterred, RoboKillz rolls toward it with his gleaming buzzsaw hand, slicing the Noodle in half and disintegrating it into dust.

"Mmm!" Hollywood says, doing a chef's kiss with his hand. "You do me proud, Robo!"

Then Brickman takes on two Noodle Monsters at once, kicking, punching, somersaulting, and ultimately creating a cement belt around the two of them. He shifts to the side, allowing Skelegurl to come in with the Monster Assist, her swords finishing them off, creating two more clouds of black dust that float off into the air as they disappear into nothing.

"Come on!" Darren says. "Why do my Noodles suck so much?"

Brickman and Skelegurl bump fists, and Smash and I do too. I'm starting to feel a little less panicked. We watch Skelegurl dodge and weave her way around two more Noodle Monsters, swiftly dust-exploding them too before a third Noodle Monster catches her off guard and snatches both swords out of her hands.

It thrusts the weapons toward a retreating Skelegurl as it spits and hisses.

"Aw yeah, this is what I been waiting for!" Darren says. "Get her, Noodle!"

But then the Noodle Monster is abruptly yanked toward the ceiling, where DecaSpyder has strategically positioned herself. She wraps the Noodle Monster up in a cocoon of titanium webbing before giving the whole bundle one final tug. Another Noodle bites the dust. Or, I guess, becomes dust.

There are only three Noodle Monsters left, and Belly-Beast looks like he's having the time of his life taking on all of them. They're trying to wrap their stretchy gray-black arms around him, so he grabs all three toward himself, tying their stretchy necks together into a knot. BellyBeast watches and cracks up as the

Noodle Monsters snap and hiss at each other, frustrated at being entangled. He gestures to Skelegurl to do the honors of finishing them off, but she just shrugs because her swords were disintegrated along with the Noodle Monster who stole them. Instead DecaSpyder webs and yanks up these monsters too, giving them the same cocoon treatment.

"Deca, you are a beautiful genius," Beanie calls up to her. "Just like the artist who made you."

"All of you are beautiful geniuses," Yoo-hoo says to our monsters, who are brushing themselves off and patting each other's backs, congratulating each other on a triumphant battle.

"That was seriously so dope," Hollywood agrees.

"No!" Darren shouts. "That wasn't a fair fight. You dip-snots drew your monsters with cooler powers and weapons and stuff."

It's true. I honestly wasn't even expecting our monsters to dominate so completely, but it's gratifying to know that all the time we've put into perfecting their designs over the years has totally paid off.

Not to mention it's a relief that we've put an end to Darren's chaos before it could get any worse.

"Whoa, what is that?" Jenni asks, grabbing my arm again and pointing toward the copy machine. There's a Noodle Monster scurrying up the side of it, but he looks slightly different from the ones who have just been destroyed—he's taller, about two feet high, and even more stretched out, his features slightly malformed and asymmetrical.

"I thought they got all of them," Yoo-hoo says.

"Oh yeah!" Darren says. "That must be the one I crumpled up and threw in the trash when the machine got jammed! Crumple Noodle, baby!"

"What's it doing on the copy machine?" I say, even as I realize with a sinking feeling exactly what it's doing and that this monster's larger head might mean it's more intelligent than its predecessors. We all watch in horror as it enters 999 into the copy machine.

And pushes the green PRINT button.

"No no no no no no," I say, grabbing the Crumple Noodle off the machine. It feels cold and slippery and awful. It digs its fangs into my arm, and I drop it, watching as two dots of blood spring up from my skin.

The photocopies start flying out of the machine, almost instantly crumpling up and transforming into more Noodle Monsters.

"The plug!" I shout as I use the bottom of my T-shirt to put pressure on the spot where Crumple bit me. "Grab the plug. Turn it off!"

The monsters sprint toward the outlet, but Crumple Noodle works fast, barking out some unintelligible commands from his perch on the copy machine to the newly born Noodles. They respond—as if it's their general and they're soldiers in some ever-expanding Noodle Army—rushing to the plug beneath and forming a barrier around it.

We all watch with fear and dismay as more and more Noodle Monsters pop into life around us.

"Now *this* is a fair fight!" Darren shouts with glee. "Your monsters are going down for sure this time!"

"You idiot!" I shout. "We're *all* going down if we don't stop this!"

"That's right," a commanding voice says from the doorway, pushing aside the masses of students still crowded there. "It's time for all this to stop." It's Assistant Principal Bachrack. "Mr. Solomon told me how out of control things are getting. I want Darren and Evan and everyone else who's involved to . . ." She stops mid-sentence as she notices the room is populated by more than just humans. "What is . . . What are . . ."

"We have a bit of a monster problem," Yoo-hoo says.

Crumple Noodle leaps from the copy machine over our heads and lands on Assistant Principal Bachrack's shoulder, hissing in her face. She screams and flails at Crumple Noodle until she knocks it off, then dashes out of the room.

"She just *left*?" Jenni says. "She's not gonna *help*?"

"Oh yeah, baby!" Darren says, cracking up. "Crumple Noodle ain't scared of some assistant principal!"

"We need to unplug the copier!" I say again as the copy machine starts to smoke and shake. "And then we need to make sure we kill all these things before they can get out into the school!"

"Whoa, whoa!" Darren says, getting in my face. "We're not unplugging anything! You're just jealous you didn't think of this yourself."

"We're not jealous, dude!" Smash says. "We're freaking out!"

"Well, that's not my problem." Darren crouches down to the two-foot-tall Crumple Noodle. "Keep up the good work, Crumple. I command you and your troops to take over the school. And if Fart Talent and his farty monsters get in your way, then destroy them!"

Crumple Noodle nods and grins and makes an awful giggling sound, like a shrieking cat stuck in a motorcycle engine.

The copy machine keeps on humming. Brickman forms a cement spear and hurls it at the plug, but a Noodle Monster leaps in front of it and sacrifices itself for the cause, exploding into nothing.

Seconds later, I hear a loud bang.

The machine has cracked in two, a huge cloud of black dust exploding into the air as dozens of Noodle

Monsters pour out at once.

No, scratch that. *Hundreds* of Noodle Monsters at once.

This has gotten bad. Very, very bad.

25

WHAT IT LOOKS LIKE WHEN THINGS ARE VERY BAD

Crumple Noodle screams out orders to his massive horde of new Noodle Monsters, and they start charging across the copy room toward the open doorway.

"Yeah!" Darren shouts. "You tell 'em, Crumple! Time for us to take over!"

We all snap to.

"Block 'em!" Hollywood shouts. "We gotta block 'em!"

BellyBeast hurls Brickman across the room, and he quickly forms a cement barrier in the door frame in the shape of a large X. He stands in front of it, firing cement at various Noodle Monsters, and soon Skele-gurl, DecaSpyder, and RoboKillz are by his side, doing whatever they can to hold back the Noodles—kicking, punching, firing webs and missiles—but there are just too many of them.

One Noodle Monster punctures the cement X with its stretchy arm, then does that puffer fish thing to bloat itself up, which makes the hole even larger. Soon tons of Noodles are doing that and, within a minute, Brickman's cement barrier has crumbled to the ground. Led by Crumple, the river of Noodle Monsters flows into the hallway where they're greeted with panicked screams. Darren gleefully follows as students and teachers run past in blind terror.

This is a nightmare. Now I understand why King Neptune told me to destroy the ink. I never should have brought it to school.

"What are we gonna do?" Yoo-hoo says. "How do we stop this, Doodles?"

"I don't—I'm not sure!" I say.

"We keep fighting!" Beanie says, her eyes fiery. "That's what we do. You saw how easily our monsters took on those first Noodles. We're smarter and stronger than them, we can do this!"

"She's right," Hollywood says. "We can. No one knows monsters better than us."

"But there are so many!" Smash says.

"Let's get to work, then," Beanie says. "See if we can destroy them all before they leave the school and things get even messier. Go, Deca!" DecaSpyder webs up a few nearby Noodles and squeezes them into dust before they speed down the hallway to take down some others.

Three down, only nine hundred ninety-seven more to go.

But Beanie's and Hollywood's words do lift me up. Them believing this isn't a totally impossible situation gives me a little hope.

"Robo and I will take the left flank," Hollywood says.

"Skelly and I will come with," Smash says.

As the four of them race out of sight, BellyBeast takes a flying leap into the hallway, landing on a bunch of Noodle Monsters with a thundering sonic belly flop that obliterates at least a dozen of them at once.

"Boom!" Yoo-hoo says. "Our new secret weapon!"

I can't help but cheer along, even as I'm doing the mental math and realizing it will take BellyBeast doing, like, seventy of those sonic flops to even come close to defeating all these things.

The other problem becomes apparent a second later, as a giant mass of Noodle Monsters that BellyBeast *didn't* destroy pounce on him. Even knowing how powerful Yoo-hoo's monster is, he's no match for thirty of those creatures. They hiss and spit as they grab on to each of his arms, yanking him in two directions at once, as if he's their rope in a game of tug-of-war. Small streams of black dust start leaking out from different spots on BellyBeast's chest, arms, and back.

"Let go of him!" Yoo-hoo screams.

Brickman tries to bash away some of the Noodles, but it makes no difference. BellyBeast lets out a mammoth growl that abruptly cuts into silence as he's stretched beyond his limit and explodes into ink dust.

"Noooooooo!" Yoo-hoo runs into the hallway and immediately trips over the dozens of Noodles in his path. He's quickly back up on his feet, wildly kicking Noodles out of his way until he gets to the spot where BellyBeast was.

But BellyBeast is gone.

"It's okay," I say to Yoo-hoo, sprinting and weaving through the pandemonium to get to him. "It's gonna be okay!"

"They killed him," Yoo-hoo says, his face drenched in tears. "They killed Belly."

"I know," I say, shouting over the madness surrounding us. "But look." I hold up the marker. "You can draw him again, Yoo-hoo. It's all right. You're gonna draw him again."

Yoo-hoo nods, inhales snot, and looks around. "I think we might have messed up, Doodles. Like, seriously messed up."

I look around too, and it's a hard point to argue. The school hallway is utter chaos. Noodle Monsters are everywhere. They're munching on random school

236

supplies—binders, rulers, an iPad—ripping down art talent's work from the walls, and generally terrorizing people. Mr. Zendel sprints past us shrieking, with a Noodle Monster riding on him piggyback. I grab the Noodle off—it's cold, goopy, and gross—and I fling it far down the hallway behind us while it hisses angrily. Zendel looks back for a second, too shocked and terrified to do anything more than nod at me five or six times before booking it down the hallway, awkwardly dodging more Noodles on his way.

"We did mess up," I say to Yoo-hoo. "But we can fix it. We have to. And it starts with you drawing a new BellyBeast." I scramble around in my backpack to find a blank piece of paper, then uncap my marker and hold it out to Yoo-hoo.

His tears start to dry as he takes it from me and begins to re-create his monster.

He's barely sketched any of him, though, when an inky, stretchy arm snatches the marker out of his hand.

Crumple Noodle.

It sniffs at the marker, a look of ecstasy in its green eyes as it licks its lips.

"No!" I shout. I grab the marker back, but Crumple Noodle is surprisingly strong.

Yoo-hoo joins in, both of us pulling as hard as we can, when Crumple suddenly lets go and we crash to the floor, dropping the marker as we fall.

"Oh man," Darren says, appearing next to Crumple, who makes that grating laughter noise again. "You're hilarious like me!"

Brickman appears by my head, checking that Yoo-hoo and I are all right, before he sprints toward the marker. Crumple Noodle scurries over to it first, though, and picks it up. It sniffs the tip, in absolute bliss, then sticks out its gray tongue and licks the marker.

"Mmmm," it says.

As Yoo-hoo and I get to our feet, Crumple Noodle appears to be growing before our eyes, the ink acting as a monster superfood.

"Whoa!" Darren says, his eyes twinkling with delight.

"Are you insane, Darren?" I ask. "We have to stop this! People are gonna get hurt!"

"Okay, so try and stop it," he says. "You seemed so confident before. What happened?"

"This isn't a game!" Yoo-hoo shouts.

Darren's about to respond when a familiar man bun and shaved head show up next to us.

"Uh, dude," Cyril says, a terrified look in his eyes. "We kind of agree with Fart Talent."

"Yeah," Buzzy says. "Those monsters you made are doing some serious damage . . ."

"Oh, shut up!" Darren says. "Crumple! Deal with these two!"

As it continues licking the marker, Crumple Noodle shoots out four of its other arms to yank Cyril's and Buzzy's ankles out from under them. They land hard on their butts, a stunned look on both their faces. Darren giggles like a maniac. Cyril and Buzzy stagger to their feet and dash down the hallway.

A moment later, Crumple finally stops licking the marker. It's grown to roughly the same height as me and Yoo-hoo.

"Well, this isn't good," Yoo-hoo says.

"No, it's not," Darren says. "It's *amazing*."

Crumple Noodle gives us a freaky smile and extends its tongue to lick the marker again, and I know I need to get my marker back, but Crumple is tall and scary and really in need of some monster orthodontia.

"That isn't yours!" Jenni Balloqui suddenly shouts, right before stabbing Crumple Noodle's left eye with the concrete Parachute Jump sculpture Brickman made for her.

"Noooooo!" Darren yells.

Crumple Noodle screams out in pain, something I didn't even know these monsters were capable of feeling, and drops the marker. A thick trail of black dust gushes from its eye like exhaust fumes from an 18-wheeler.

"Whoa!" Yoo-hoo shouts. "Jenni Balloqui for the win!"

"Seriously!" I say.

Crumple Noodle yanks the sculpture out and chucks it to the ground as Jenni dives for the marker. She grabs it right before Crumple charges at her. She tosses the marker toward us.

Yoo-hoo catches it, but seconds later, he's swarmed with Noodle Monsters, so he passes it to me. I want to make a run for it, but then I'm swarmed too. Fifteen cold, spastic Noodles are climbing all over me, so I chuck the marker back to Jenni.

At least I try to. It arcs high in the air, and the Noodles immediately leap off me after it. I've beefed the throw, sending it too far to the right of Jenni, toward Darren Nuggio instead.

Shoot.

But then Smash busts through on her skateboard and flips an ollie right at the perfect moment to catch it!

"Saw you might need a Monster Assist," she says, skillfully threading her way past Darren and Crumple, then speeding in and around the hordes of frenzied Noodles.

"Yeah, Smash!" Yoo-hoo shouts.

She turns to give him a small smile and flick of her chin and immediately crashes into a bank of lockers. I mean, we call her Smash for a reason. Her skateboard rolls out from under her and gets snatched up by a group of Noodles. They make a joyful shrieking noise that sounds like a badly tuned ukulele as they speed past us in the opposite direction.

We run toward Smash, trying to get there before Darren and Crumple Noodle, but we're too late. They're almost to her when suddenly Smash tosses the marker straight up into the air, just in time for Skelegurl to swoop down out of nowhere and grab it!

Darren and Crumple Noodle scream and reach out to try and snatch Skelegurl out of the air, but she's too fast, speeding around Darren's head and in and out of Crumple's many arms before soaring toward the hallway ceiling.

"Fly, Skelly, fly!" Smash shouts from the ground. "Toward the entrance!" Skelegurl buzzes away with the marker.

Crumple Noodle immediately goes to follow, the black dust no longer streaming from its eye. Before it has time to react or defend itself, though, it's hit with six consecutive missiles in a row, courtesy of RoboKillz.

"Eat that, Crumple!" Hollywood shouts.

The missiles aren't enough to disintegrate Crumple

Noodle in its new and improved five-foot-tall form, but it does careen backward onto the ground with a satisfying splat, several new plumes of black dust floating up from its body. "Not fair!" Darren yells at the top of his lungs, rushing over to help Crumple. Noodle Monsters pour in from every direction to make sure their leader is all right.

We don't stick around to see what happens next.

We're immediately burning rubber toward the lobby—me, Yoo-hoo, Jenni, Smash, and Hollywood—our sneakers slapping on the linoleum in rapid-fire rhythm.

"Oh shoot!" I say, panic forming in my stomach as I take stock of our group. "Brickman. Where is Brickman?"

"He's right back there!" Jenni says, and sure enough, there's Brickman, about ten feet behind us, sprinting as fast as he can to keep up. I race toward him, beyond relieved.

"I'm so sorry, Bricky!" I say as I scoop him up.

Brickman grunts and gives me a small smile. His eyes look sad, and it occurs to me why.

"I'm so sorry about BellyBeast too. I know he was a close friend."

Brickman nods and wipes away a gray cement tear.

"Uh-oh," I say as I get a glimpse of the Noodle Army, which seems to have reorganized, coming up quickly behind us. The hundreds of Noodle Monsters have used their bodies to form some kind of chariot, with Crumple Noodle sitting atop them, screaming out commands, as Darren excitedly dances alongside them.

Skelegurl flies back toward us, hovering in front of me with the marker, as if offering it back to me.

I'd honestly prefer for her to keep it since I can't fly and I'm nowhere near as fast as her, but I take it back anyway. "Thanks, Skelegurl."

"We need that marker!" Darren shouts behind us.

"It'll make us even more powerful!"

"You should put the cap back on," Yoo-hoo says. "I think it's the smell that attracted Crumple and the other Noodles."

"Good point," I say.

"Hey, you okay?" Smash asks Yoo-hoo. "Where's BellyBeast?"

Yoo-hoo just looks away, shaking his head.

"He didn't make it," I say.

"Oh geez," Smash says. "I'm sorry."

"Thanks," Yoo-hoo says quietly.

It's hard to wrap a comforting arm around someone while you're both running away from a horde of little beasts, but somehow Smash pulls it off, squeezing Yoo-hoo's shoulder tight.

"Hey," Beanie says, popping out of a classroom with DecaSpyder in her hand and joining our mad dash toward the exit. Her backpack is so full it seems like she's about to embark on a mountain-climbing expedition. "Got some supplies from Franklin's room."

"Nice!" Hollywood says.

"What's the plan?" Beanie asks.

"Yeah, what *is* the plan, Doodles?" Hollywood asks.

Everyone looks to me, which I appreciate, but it's also a little terrifying.

Because I don't have a plan. I desperately wish I did. And then suddenly, I do.

Well, not a full plan, but at least a small sliver of one.

"Let's lead the Noodles to Coney," I say.

"Whoa, you sure?" Hollywood says.

"At this point, these monsters are breaking out of here one way or the other. And if we go to Coney, we can find King Neptune. He's the only one who knows how this ink actually works. He might be able to help us stop this."

"King Neptune?" Hollywood says. "Old Crazy King Neptune? For real? Doodles, no offense, but this is not a good plan."

"He told me to keep the ink a secret, and he was right about that. He knows how to destroy the ink too, so maybe he knows how to destroy the monsters!"

It's a long shot, I know. But Crumple and its Noodle Army are gaining on us, desperate to get the mermaid ink, and it's the only idea I've got.

We push out of the front doors of our school and run toward Surf Avenue. Back to where it all began. Back toward King's Wonderland.

26

NOODLE AVENUE

There are eight police cars waiting outside Mark Twain as we dash out of there, with several more—sirens blaring, lights flashing—racing down Neptune Avenue toward us. Behind them is a fleet of fire trucks and ambulances. Part of me is relieved that the first responders are here to help, though part of me is shocked that things have gotten this bad this quickly.

"Yo, should we grab our bikes?" Hollywood asks.

"No time for that!" I shout.

Seconds later, the army of Noodle Monsters bursts through the school's doors behind us.

We rush down the front steps toward the line of police cars as officers stare in disbelief.

"What the—" the police sergeant yells into her megaphone before she recovers with, "Stop where you are!" Not a single Noodle in the chaotic throng obeys. "I said STOP," the cop yells again, and again, nothing. Crumple Noodle—who's with Darren, right behind the first line of advance guard Noodle Monsters—screams something and then cackles. Darren cackles too. "These streets are ours now!" he yells. "All of Coney is gonna be ours!" Dozens of Noodles join in the cackling, creating an unpleasant wall of sound, like a horrible ukulele orchestra, as they keep pushing forward.

I gasp as some of the police draw their guns, trying to get a clear shot at the Noodles. It's terrifying because there are still so many of us students and faculty running past.

"There's no way this doesn't get ugly," Hollywood says. "We gotta get out of the line of fire."

We dash across the sidewalk, in between two of the police cars, to the other side of Neptune Avenue, and not a moment too soon.

Crumple Noodle screams out some commands, and within seconds, all the Noodles are full-on charging at the police. Almost in unison, they start yanking at the police officers' ankles—the same move Crumple used on Cyril and Buzzy—sending cop after cop sailing onto their butts.

"This is so messed up!" Yoo-hoo says.

"Told ya it was gonna get ugly," Hollywood says.

I watch as the sergeant who I thought was in charge

crawls halfway into her car—in spite of at least a dozen Noodles yanking at her legs—and grabs her radio. "Sergeant Orell here," she says. "We need some serious help over here at Mark Twain Middle School. Please! Send SWAT!"

"Did you say SWAT?" a voice on the radio asks.

"Yes! And the National Guard too! We've got monsters here. Tons of—"

"Monsters?!" laughs the person on the radio.

She isn't able to finish because the Noodle Monsters drag her away from the car, leaving the radio dangling out the open door.

I can't believe this has gotten too big for the NYPD to handle.

One of the Noodles slides its stretchy body underneath a police car, then does that puffer fish thing, making its body so large that it literally *lifts the car off the ground and flips it onto its roof.*

"Wooooooo!!" Darren shouts triumphantly from the middle of the Noodle throng. "Do more, do more!"

Soon a bunch of Noodle Monsters are turning over police vehicle after police vehicle, transforming them into helpless upside-down turtles, stranded on their shells. Darren is laughing maniacally like it's the funniest thing he's seen in his life.

"Holy macaroni," Yoo-hoo says.

We've stopped in place for a moment, both to catch

our breath and to make sure we're actually seeing what we think we're seeing. One of the cop cars is on fire. The fire department is all over it.

"I don't think the police are gonna save us," Beanie says, in a way that manages to be both sarcastic and completely sincere. A pack of Noodles chases away the firefighters and starts using their hoses on the remaining police.

The rest of the Noodle Monsters flood past the police's joke of a barricade, onto the street. There's a series of loud honks and skids as cars are forced to swerve around them. Then the Noodles start leaping onto people's cars—slamming into windshields, hanging off the back bumpers.

It's complete chaos.

From where we're standing on the sidewalk across the street, I witness four car accidents in the span of fifteen seconds. I can't help but feel responsible for every single one.

I slide Brickman under one arm so I can uncap my marker and wave it back and forth in the air.

"Over here, Noodles!" I shout. "This way!" The Noodles all sniff the air, then turn toward me.

"What the heck are you doing?" Yoo-hoo asks in a panic as the Noodles start shrieking.

"We want them to follow us to Coney, right?" I say. "We can't let them spread out all over Brooklyn."

"You are bonkers, Doodles," Hollywood says, already breaking into a sprint. "Truly bonkers."

The Noodles charge toward us, Darren still right there with them. "Follow that fart!" he screams.

We all start running down West 25th Street, the Noodles right on our heels, and I find myself thinking of my great-great-grandfather Isaac. I wonder if his ink ever fell into the wrong hands. If things ever got as wildly out of control as they are right now.

I think about everything he went through, everything he survived, how he made it to America by himself when he was pretty much our age after essentially being chased from his home village by a mob, not of monster drawings come to life, but of actual hate-filled human beings.

If he made it through all that, then I have to believe we can make it through this.

"Yoo-hoo," I say as we turn left onto Surf Avenue. "Got your Post-its?"

He nods and pulls his go-to neon-green Post-it pad out of his pocket, hands it over to me. I slip Brickman into my backpack to free up my hands for a moment and immediately get to work. I sketch as fast as I possibly can while we run, little nondescript stick figures—some holding bombs, some holding hammers, some with base-ball bats—and I wait for them to *POP!* into life to give us extra cover against the rabid front line of Noodles.

For some reason, they don't.

"Try adding horns," Yoo-hoo says. "Or fangs. Or claws. Monster stuff."

I do as he says, not actually thinking it's going to work, but instantly the *POP!*s start coming. Seems it's only monsters that will come to life. "Brilliant, Yoo-hoo!" I give him a smile as I chuck the new two-and-a-half-inch-tall monsters over my shoulder—all slightly glowing green with a solid black interior—and then continue to produce more soldiers for our mini-monster army until I've used up the whole pad. "BellyBeast version 2.0 will be next. As soon as we have a second."

We hear a small explosion from behind us—one of my mini monsters has exploded a couple of Noodles with his magic-marker monster bomb.

Then we watch as five of the mini monsters jump on a Noodle and start gnawing on its limbs with their fangs while simultaneously whacking it with their mini base-ball bats and hammering until it disintegrates.

"That was rad!" Smash says.

For a brief moment, we forget that we're being chased by a mob of almost a thousand monsters, and all of us high-five. Yoo-hoo smiles for the first time since he lost BellyBeast.

But then a couple of Noodle Monsters race up

Yoo-hoo's back and start giddily tugging at his ears.

"Ow!" Yoo-hoo yells.

Beanie runs up holding DecaSpyder toward the Noodles, and Deca promptly shoots lasers, with incredible precision, at each one, exploding them into dust without so much as grazing Yoo-hoo's skin.

"Thanks, Beanie," Yoo-hoo says, rubbing his ear.

"We got you," she says. "Deca's targeting system is accurate to at least three decimal places."

As we approach the amusement parks, I remember that today isn't just the opening day for Dad and King's Wonderland; it's the first day of the new season for all of Coney Island. There's a small crowd of people gathered around a curly-haired woman holding a microphone in front of the big, empty lot where Blazing Comet Amusements used to be. The rides there kinda sucked, but it's still sad that it's gone.

"So today," the woman is saying as we sprint straight toward her and the crowd, "we celebrate what Coney Island has always been—a place for fun, for games, for rides, for great food—but we also celebrate what it is becoming. Behind us is the site of what will be the first beautiful new condo building from Pluto Properties."

The Vultures. This woman is making a speech to celebrate the Vultures.

Doesn't she get that they're *ruining* Coney Island?

And then I see them: Beard and Mustache, standing to the side of the curly-haired woman, smug looks on both their faces.

As we reach the crowd, someone hands the woman a shovel to do the honors of breaking ground for the future condo building as she says, "It is my absolute pleasure to kick off this first day of—" She frowns as she stares right at us. "What are you kids doing? If you want to run around, then head over to the . . ."

She trails off, which is how I know she's spotted the hundreds of Noodle Monsters bouncing off the light posts and parked cars. She understands the real reason we're running like headless chickens.

"Oh my!" the woman says, before turning to run away herself, the shovel still in her hands. A second later, Beard and Mustache are hoofing it out of there too, terrified, followed by us and the rest of the small crowd.

"You should probably cap that thing now," Jenni says, gesturing down to the marker.

I do, reminded that not only is it my fault that these terrible creatures exist, but also that they are moments away from stampeding into my favorite place in the whole world.

I run faster.

27

CONEY ISLAND CHAOS

I'm hoping we can make it to King's Wonderland and take refuge there, but the Noodle Monsters are everywhere, gaining on us fast. We take cover in the Sirens Shooting Gallery, leaping over the counter that Amy Basis usually stands behind. She isn't here now, even though it's opening day. Hopefully, she, Freddie, and all the other Coney regulars have already made a break for it.

I don't think the Noodle Monsters or Darren saw us when we leapt back here; Crumple Noodle definitely didn't, and that's the one I'm most concerned about. Crumple is big. And smart. And so freaking scary.

For at least a minute, we're silent as we finally have a moment to catch our breath. All of Monster Club plus

Jenni Balloqui are here, our backs up against the splintery wooden counter. I pull Brickman out of my bag and set him on the ground. He looks up at me, those expressive eyes of his radiating worry as he shakes his head and grunts in dismay.

"I know, Bricky," I say. "It's not good."

"Understatement of the year," Smash says from the other side of the gallery, where Skelegurl is slicing the air with a pen and a letter opener that have replaced her lost swords. She cuts through the air at different angles, working on her form.

"You still think King Neptune is gonna get us out of this one, Doodles?" Hollywood asks.

"Who's King Neptune?" Jenni asks.

"Um," I say, fully aware that my answer is going to sound ridiculous. "He's that old guy who, uh, walks around the boardwalk, with the long hair and the weird crown."

"*That* guy?" Jenni says. "*That's* your solution to this?"

"No, I know how it sounds, but he knows a lot of stuff, specifically about this ink. He knew that it was actually mermaid's blood and that—"

"Wait, what? Mermaid's blood?" Jenni says.

"Yo, I never heard that part," Hollywood says, laughing. "That's just stupid."

"It's real, though!" Yoo-hoo says. "I was there. Finding King Neptune really is our best hope at stopping all these Noodles."

Beanie sighs. "I don't know when you all are gonna realize that old men are never our best hope for anything."

"Let's go up here," Jenni says, heading up a ladder that leads to the Sirens Shooting Gallery roof. "We can get a better view of everything, see if that old guy with the crown is anywhere."

We grab our monsters and follow her up. I'm hoping maybe I'll also be able to get a glimpse of Dad and King's Wonderland. At the top of the ladder, we follow Jenni as she pushes open a hatch and climbs out onto the roof.

I'm not fully prepared for what I see next, even though I probably should be.

The Noodle Monsters have full-on swarmed Coney Island.

The Noodles chase a kissing couple out of a photo booth, then stay in there as it flashes, posing for pics. They commandeer the El Dorado bumper cars, the Noodles stacked on each other's shoulders to reach the steering wheel, making loud cackling sounds as they crash into one another. They gorge themselves on funnel cake. One Noodle runs by with two corn dogs shoved where its nostrils should be.

"Get 'em off me!" a man shouts to his friend, flailing desperately to get three Noodles off his head, one of them tugging at his facial hair.

I'm shocked and, I'm ashamed to say it, a little delighted to realize it's Mustache.

"I can't!" Beard responds, his arms waving just as wildly at the five Noodles climbing up and down his back and across his shoulders. "Got my own to deal with, numbskull!"

"Oh my god," Yoo-hoo whispers from next to me as I watch the Vultures stumble away. "Look at the Cyclone." I turn my head toward Coney's oldest and most famous roller coaster and, sure enough, all the cars are filled with stacks of Noodle Monsters, screaming in terror as they head down the first hill. One of the top ones in front throws up, and the vomit flies into the face of a Noodle in the back.

"This is a nightmare," I say. And I can't help wondering if Dad is all right. I scan all angles from the roof to try and see what's going on over at King's Wonderland— but no luck.

Suddenly I spy Darren Nuggio skipping through the chaos, overcome with a crazed joy. He stops at a cotton candy machine and shoves his arm in up to the elbow, then stuffs his face with gobs of blue and pink. "Nom

nom nom!" he shouts. Crumple Noodle is in another area viciously tearing the head off a giant stuffed panda from the Shoot the Red Star game.

I think it's safe to say they haven't spotted us yet.

I scan the park for King Neptune. I don't see him anywhere.

A pack of Noodles speeds by us on a go-kart before crashing into a fortune-teller's stand.

"There's just so many of them," Beanie says, Deca-Spyder perched on her shoulder. "How can we get rid of so many of them?"

"For starters," Yoo-hoo says, "hook me up with that marker, Doodles. I'm ready to finish resurrecting Belly-Beast."

"Do it." I pull the marker out of my pocket and chuck it to him. That alone won't solve this, but it's a start.

"Wait," Smash says, putting her hand on Yoo-hoo's. "You can't uncap that. We might as well hold up a huge sign that says *More Ink Here, Come and Get It*."

"Oh, right," Yoo-hoo says.

"Well, let's try to keep the scent contained, then," I say. "Yoo-hoo, crouch down here with the drawing you started. Everyone else stand around him, help block the smell."

"That's not really how fragrances work," Beanie says. "But maybe if we spray something with a powerful scent, it could act as a sort of smell shield around us. I'm lookin' at you, Hollywood."

"Me?" Hollywood says. "What do you . . . Oh. I get it." He sighs. "Aight." Hollywood pulls a huge can of Axe body spray out of his backpack and goes to town, spraying it in a circle around our group, like it's a force field.

"Ugh," Jenni says, ducking her nose under the collar of her blouse. "That's . . . a lot."

It almost smells as bad as the ink. I join Jenni, raising my T-shirt over my nose.

"Y'all wanted a smell shield," Hollywood says. "At least this is a very seductive one."

"Gross," Beanie says. "And good work. Now let's huddle up so Yoo-hoo can get to it."

She, Smash, Hollywood, Jenni, and I create a tight huddle around Yoo-hoo, who pulls the new BellyBeast sketch he started back at school out of his pocket. My stomach leaps as I put my arm around Jenni. Our ears are kind of touching. Brickman, Skelegurl, DecaSpyder, and RoboKillz squeeze their way into the huddle too. I'm about to pass Yoo-hoo the marker when I look at my friends, our arms around each other, our faces pressed together—it's like Yoo-hoo's in a tent made of Monster Club. (And Axe body spray.)

"I know what's going on is scary and bad," I say, "but I'm really glad we're all together during this."

"Love the sentiment," Yoo-hoo says, unfolding his BellyBeast and reaching out a hand for the marker, "but maybe not the time, Doodles. Because of the Noodles. Hey, Doodles and Noodles rhyme! That's kinda weird."

"Here," I say, passing him the marker.

"Oh shoot," Yoo-hoo says. His unfinished BellyBeast drawing has a rip in it from being crumpled in his pocket. "Will this even work on crappy paper? I need a new piece."

"I have one," I say, unzipping my backpack.

"Wait," Smash says, breaking out of the huddle. "I saw something better." She swings down into the hatch, using the ladder more like a firepole, leaving all of us confused.

"Yo," Hollywood says as I dig around for a fresh piece of paper. "I know you said this drawing's unfinished because Crumple stole the marker, but you sure this wasn't the work of Smash? BellyBeast looks a lot like Brickman did after she went ballistic with that bottle of nail polish remover."

"The infamous Nail Polish Remover Incident," I say, laughing. "Poor Bricky."

Brickman looks up at us, confused, and grunts like *Me? Huh?*

"Oh shut up, Hollywood," Smash says, reappearing from the hatch with a large, yellowed piece of paper. "Use this, Yoo." Before I can hand over my piece of paper, Smash passes him what appears to be an old-timey 1949 newspaper prop from the shooting gallery. "It's bigger. So BellyBeast will be too."

"Whoa," Yoo-hoo says, eyeing the large paper, like he's imagining the possibilities. "Thanks, Smash. Brilliant thinking." Smash nods and turns a little red. Yoo-hoo holds up the marker and takes a deep breath. "Okay. Let's do this." He does his classic marker-as-drumstick fingertip spin and pulls the cap off. We tighten our huddle, as if to make sure not a single atom of the ink smell gets by us.

Yoo-hoo sketches faster than I've ever seen him sketch, drawing a BellyBeast big enough to fill the whole page.

"Ohmigod, that's it!" Beanie says.

"Uh . . . *What's* it?" Hollywood asks.

"What you said before. The nail polish remover."

"What about it?" I ask, watching as Yoo-hoo details the mass of tentacles coming from BellyBeast's face.

"The acetone inside it obliterates ink," Beanie says.

"So?" Hollywood says.

"So?" Beanie looks across the huddle right at him. "We're fighting hundreds of monsters made of ink!"

"Oh wow," I say, finally getting her point.

"You think it'll work, though?" Hollywood asks. "I thought you said this stuff was made of mermaid's blood."

"How should I know?" Beanie says. "But I'm not hearing anyone coming up with any better ideas!"

"We need to try it," Smash says. "My mom has a whole closet full of the stuff at her salon. We can load up."

"Annnnd finished," Yoo-hoo says, putting down the marker as Brickman, RoboKillz, and DecaSpyder gather around the drawing of BellyBeast—Skelegurl fluttering just above it—watching with excitement as the paper begins to crumple itself up into a ball. "Might want to give this puppy some spa—"

The *POP!* and explosion are louder and larger than ever, newspaper confetti raining down as we all startle backward out of the huddle.

There on the roof in front of us is the new, improved BellyBeast. He's now green instead of blue (I guess since the paper was yellow), with faded newsprint on his fur. He's also huge, closer to the size of a dog than to that of his foot-high fellow monsters.

"Belly!" Yoo-hoo shouts as BellyBeast leaps into his arms, knocking him over, the rest of the monsters circling to greet their old friend.

"Reunited!" Smash shouts, leaning down to join in the hug.

The joyful moment is short-lived, though, as all around us we start to hear high-pitched shrieks.

"What is that?" Smash asks.

We peer down off the roof, where Noodle after Noodle

is stopping in place, sniffing the air, letting out an ecstatic shriek, and then turning their heads and looking straight at us.

Or, more specifically, looking straight at the roof where the uncapped marker is resting.

28

GO TIME

"Dude, you didn't recap the marker?" Smash asks, in total disbelief.

"I forgot, I forgot!" Yoo-hoo says. "I was excited to see Belly again, and I thought we had a smell shield! I'll recap it . . . I'll do it now!" He scrambles over to the marker on his hands and knees and frantically puts the cap back on.

But of course, it's too late for that.

The Noodles are oozing toward us from every direction, hissing, spitting, and shrieking. Our monsters spread out around the roof, preparing to mount our defense. RoboKillz spins his buzzsaw. Skelegurl hovers and stabs the air with her pen. Brickman swings his wrecking ball. DecaSpyder shoots her webs. BellyBeast growls and pounds his chest.

"We need to get down from here," Jenni says, looking toward the hatch we came up from. "Like, immediately."

"I agree," Beanie says.

"Right," I say, trying to get the shaky sound out of my voice as I watch the Noodles closing in. "Here's the plan." I'm hoping that saying those words will finally give me an idea for one. "I'll go to King's Wonderland, find my dad. Maybe find King Neptune on the way."

"I'll go with you," Jenni says.

Brickman grunts from his position a few feet away. He's in too.

"And I'll run to Mermaid Nails with Skelly," Smash says. "Raid my mom's supply closets for nail polish remover . . ."

"BellyBeast and I will go too," Yoo-hoo says. "If that's all right."

"Of course," Smash says with a tiny smile.

"Deca and I are also coming," Beanie says, patting her massive backpack filled with stuff from the science lab. "I think we might be useful."

"Hate to break it to everybody," Hollywood says, running a hand across the loop shaved into the side of his head, "but nobody's going anywhere if we can't find a way past all these Noodles."

Directed by Crumple Noodle, they've started to

form a moat around Sirens Shooting Gallery, and some of them are already climbing the building toward us. "There you little farts are!" Darren Nuggio shouts up to us from behind Crumple, a wisp of blue cotton candy stuck to his cheek. "We're taking that marker back! We need to make some more Noodles!"

"I really hate that guy," Beanie says, voicing what we're all thinking. DecaSpyder fires lasers down from the roof, disintegrating a few of the Noodles, while RoboKillz does the same on the other side with his missiles, but it's not nearly enough to stop them all.

"I've got an idea," Hollywood says, gesturing to Yoohoo to pass over the marker. "I'll hold up the marker and we'll use it like a magnet. It'll be like *Invasion of the Body Snatchers*! The Donald Sutherland one! I'll show some emotion and the pod people will come screaming."

None of us have any idea what he's talking about.

"What I'm saying is, I'll get these freaky little squiggle monsters off your tail and give everyone a chance to do their thing."

"Ohhh," we all say, nodding our heads now that he's translated from film-nerd speak.

"With RoboKillz's help, of course," Hollywood adds. RoboKillz makes some affirmative beeps and electronic crackles.

"Ahmed," Beanie says, giving him this serious look

267

that—along with using his actual name—hits home how bad our situation has gotten. "You sure you want to do this?"

"Anything for Monster Club," Hollywood says.

I get chills when he says that, not gonna lie.

Beanie shakes her head. "There's a lot of them to outrun."

"That's why I don't plan on running. Check it." Hollywood points down to the go-kart that the Noodles crashed and abandoned earlier. "If I can get down to that thing, I'm good."

"Uh, guys?" Yoo-hoo says. "I think it's time."

The Noodles have made it to the roof.

"Go! Go! Go!" I shout as we wildly race toward the hatch, flipping it open and starting to head down the ladder one by one.

Our monsters give us some cover—Brickman shooting cement, Skelegurl slicing with her makeshift swords, DecaSpyder firing webs and lasers, BellyBeast smashing with his fists, RoboKillz going to town with his saw blade—but some Noodles are still getting past them and crawling all over us. No matter how many we flail away, they just keep coming. As I start climbing down the ladder, a Noodle shrieks and drools right into my ear before Brickman uses a cement ball to knock it off my shoulder.

Our monsters scramble down ahead of us off the roof,

clearing out some of the Noodles waiting at the foot of the ladder. There are still dozens more trying to get at us from above, though.

"We gotta close the hatch!" I shout up to Yoo-hoo, who's the last one down. He tries to pull it shut, but at least ten Noodles have crammed themselves into the gap to keep pushing it open.

"I don't think I can!" Yoo-hoo shouts back.

"Skelly's on it!" Smash says, and Skelegurl flies up to the hatch, using a deft bit of work with her letter opener to disintegrate, in one fell swoop, the Noodles holding the hatch open.

"Yeah!" I shout, but no sooner is the word out of my mouth than a big, splotchy ink-black hand has grabbed Skelegurl out of the air.

Crumple Noodle has made it up onto the roof.

We all scream as it lifts Skelegurl to its mouth like she's a bunless hot dog and chomps her head off.

"SKELLY!" Smash shrieks. Skelegurl's body falls through the air and puffs into nothingness.

"Close the hatch, Yoo-hoo!" the rest of us shout, almost in unison. "Close the hatch!"

Yoo-hoo moves so fast he looks like he's in a time-lapse video, reaching out and slamming the hatch door shut a split second before a snarling Crumple Noodle would've been through it.

It's a victory, but seeing as Crumple can just jump off the roof and get to us that way, it's only a tiny victory. We're so terrified, we tumble the rest of the way down the ladder. Smash has tears running down her face.

"You'll draw a new Skelly soon," I say, though I don't actually know when we'll have a moment to make that happen.

Down below, the gallery is filled with a sea of Noodles; you can barely take a step without encountering one. They smell the marker amid us, but I don't think they know that Hollywood is the one who has it—they seem to be clinging to and tugging at all of us equally.

"How do we get me over there?" Hollywood says, panic entering his voice for the first time as he points to the go-kart twenty feet away, blocked by a thick wall of Noodles.

"Easy," Yoo-hoo says. "BellyBeast, care to do the honors?"

BellyBeast finishes what he's doing—hurling away four Noodles at once—then looks at Yoo-hoo with a huge smile, sticking his tongue out and making rock horns with both hands. He lets out his classic growl war cry as he vaults himself onto the gallery partition, lifts his shirt, and smacks his belly with immense force.

Now that BellyBeast is at least three times larger than he used to be, the sonic boom that results is absolutely massive, rippling forward like a bolt of lightning, parting the ocean of Noodles like they're the Red Sea.

"Yep," Hollywood says, "that works." Hollywood sprints down the path BellyBeast created, holding Robo-Killz under one arm, as Crumple Noodle leaps down from the roof and lands right next to me.

I'm frozen in terror.

Crumple screams in my face, revealing its horrifying fangs, and suddenly its many arms are grabbing me, pulling me closer, searching all over my body, reaching into my jeans pockets. I try to struggle free, but it's no use.

"Hand it over, Fart Talent," Darren says, keeping a safe distance from our monsters. "You're done."

"Hey, Nasty!" Hollywood shouts at the top of his lungs. "You looking for this?" He's sitting in the go-kart, holding up the uncapped marker.

Crumple Noodle releases me and roars in rage, speeding toward him. Darren follows.

Hollywood hits the gas, but the go-kart doesn't move. No.

He tries again. And again.

Crumple Noodle and Darren are almost on him.

"Over here, over here!" we all shout, trying to distract them as whatever scrap of a plan we had evaporates before our eyes.

It doesn't work. Crumple Noodle and Darren are too laser-focused on the marker in Hollywood's hand.

Crumple is reaching out to grab it but then abruptly topples to the ground.

"Huh?" Darren says, moments before he topples too.

I realize DecaSpyder scurried into position and webbed a bunch of Crumple's legs together with Darren's.

"Yeah, Deca!" Yoo-hoo shouts.

Hollywood's go-kart engine springs to life and he burns out of there.

"Go, Hollywood, go!" Beanie shouts.

From his perch on the back of the go-kart, RoboKillz fires missiles at the Noodles chasing them.

Crumple Noodle screams in rage as it gets back to its feet.

"How did you mess that up, dude?" Darren shouts at Crumple.

Crumple hisses back at him. Then, with a terrifying stomp, it crushes DecaSpyder into black dust beneath one of its feet, letting out another furious scream before chasing after Hollywood, with hundreds of other Noodles and Darren following. "Yeah, that's more like it!" Darren shouts.

Beanie is crushed too. "Deca," she says quietly, staring forward into nothing.

"She saved Hollywood," I say, putting a hand on her shoulder. "And Hollywood saved me. We'll draw her again when we get the marker back. But right now we have to move forward with the plan."

Beanie takes a deep breath and nods. "We gotta stop these things."

"I know," I say, taking a look around. Coney Island is a disaster. It's as if Hurricane Zadie has hit all over again: game booths overturned, rides destroyed, a trail of trash and food and chaos everywhere you turn.

"So let's do this," Yoo-hoo says. "We may have lost Skelly and Deca, but we'll still have BellyBeast covering our backs."

"And we'll have Brickman," I say, scooping him up as Jenni gives me a nod.

"Just want to take a quick second to acknowledge that what's happening is absolutely insane," she says.

"Agreed," Smash says, already jogging toward Surf Avenue. "But we gotta get to my mom's place ASAP. Hollywood can only distract the Noodles for so long."

"Good luck, Doodles and Jenni! And Brickman!" Yoo-hoo says as he and Beanie follow Smash away from the boardwalk, BellyBeast running sideways to keep an eye out for any other Noodles on the attack.

"You too!" I say as Jenni, Brickman, and I start jogging toward King's Wonderland, but, to be honest, I think our luck needs to be much better than good if we want to come out of this alive.

29

KING'S NOODLELAND

We're running down the boardwalk, swerving around partying Noodle Monsters (who seem to have missed the memo that they should be chasing down Hollywood and the marker), when my phone buzzes.

I look down and realize I've missed an epic number of calls, voice mails, and texts from Mom.

Saw your school on the news! her first text from a while ago says. *Are you OK??*

Please call me, her next text says. *Hopefully you're home by now.*

Leaving work. Need to know you're ok
Are you OK???

And so on and so on up to the text she just sent:

Just got home and you're not here. If you don't respond

soon, I'm calling the police. Please, I'm so worried

Then there are a couple of recent texts from Dad:

Mom says you're not at home

I hope you're nowhere near King's, bud. It's a bad scene here

I quickly type, *I am ok, don't worry!!* and send it to both of them on the same thread.

Where are you? Mom texts back within seconds, and then she's calling me.

"Hey, Mom," I say. "I'm fine, don't worry. I'm almost at King's, and I'm really fine and safe, but I gotta go. I'll call you as soon as I can, I promise! I love you!"

"Eric, you need to come ho—" I hang up. It feels terrible, but I don't have any other option. She, of course, calls back immediately. I don't pick up.

"Hey, isn't that him?" Jenni asks.

I look up to see King Neptune crouching on the boardwalk in front of two Noodles. He has an open cage made of twigs, seaweed, and pieces of shell.

"Step in here, my beastly friends," he says to the hissing creatures, who take a couple of curious steps toward him. "I am King Neptune, God of the Seven Seas. But I am a benevolent deity. I will take good care of you."

"What—What are you doing?" I ask, running toward him.

King Neptune is startled by my presence, and once

he takes his eyes off the Noodles, they scramble away, cackling as they hop into a nearby popcorn machine.

"What do you think I'm doing, kid?" King Neptune says, not even trying to conceal his anger. "Trying to clean up the mess you've made by not listening to me!"

"But what will . . . what will putting them in a cage do?"

"Did I not tell you to keep them hidden?" he asks. "Did I not tell you to give me the ink so it can be destroyed? A careless mortal kid like you shouldn't be in possession of such a powerful thing."

"You did, yes, and I'm sorry—"

"*Sorry?* You think sorry will fix the destruction raging all around us? Give me the blood now, before things get even worse!" He extends his hands wildly toward me, giving me another glimpse of the ridged scars on the back of his left hand.

"I don't have it!" I say, on the verge of tears. "My friend does, so he could distract the Noodle monsters and give us time to get the help we need. I thought maybe you'd have advice for us on how to stop all this."

King Neptune stares at me and Jenni with a look that's so unhinged, Jenni and I both take a few steps back.

"Do you know how your great-great-grandfather Isaac died?" he asks quietly. It's not what I'm expecting him to say. "In a fire. He died in a fire that I caused. Sure, it was an accident, I made a mistake, but it was a mistake that killed him. You know what it's like to carry something like that your whole life, young prince?"

I can barely process what King Neptune is saying.

"And though it was my hand that caused the fire, it was the power of the ink that drew me where I ought not have been," he continues, his voice getting steadily louder. "That's why I told you to *bring me that ink and don't use it again*. But you . . . you didn't listen! And now look what you have done. So get that ink back and give it to me while you still can. We shall end these horrors once and for all!"

I have no words to respond to any of that.

"All due respect, sir," Jenni says, stepping in front of me, "but you're way out of line. I'm sorry you started a fire a long time ago, but that's not our problem. We *know* we messed up. That's why we're trying to fix this. And we thought you'd be able to help, but instead you're just yelling at my friend, which is supremely *un*helpful. Now if you'll excuse us, we need to go try to make this all right."

I nod at him and follow Jenni as she strides away.

"Hey, young prince," King Neptune shouts. We turn to look back at him. "Which way did your friend go?"

"That way," I say, pointing in the general direction.

"Remember," King Neptune says. "Bring me the ink wh—"

"Yeah, we got it!" Jenni says, taking my hand in hers and pulling us toward King's. "Geez!"

Now, I know this sounds stupid, but, in spite of the absolute Noodle insanity and destruction that continues to go on all around us, in spite of learning that town weirdo King Neptune is responsible for my great-great-grandfather's death, all I can think about at this moment, in the middle of all this craziness, is that Jenni and I are holding hands.

"Thanks for saying that stuff," I say. "That was really cool."

"You kidding?" Jenni says. "He deserved it. Just because he knows how to destroy some magic mermaid ink doesn't mean he gets to be a jerk."

Brickman emphatically grunts his agreement from my hand.

"Yeah," I say as we pass a pack of Noodles wearing child-size Coney Island T-shirts. "I mean, I think he was just upset. This stuff is important to him."

I know Jenni has a point—I definitely didn't like getting yelled at by King Neptune, but part of me also felt bad for him.

Or maybe I'm just seeing the bright side of everything because Jenni is holding my hand. It's weirding me out how much I'm into it.

Soon King's Wonderland comes into view, though—that familiar sign with those big yellow letters and the iconic mermaid resting against the last letter *d*—and there's zero bright side to be found there. The ground looks like someone's vomited up pieces from various rides: the spinning pods from the Tilt-A-Whirl, the metal cages from the Zipper, the Majestic Mermaids and Twisty Turtles from King's popular kiddie rides. A pack of Noodle Monsters is in the process of joyfully tearing apart the Beast Infinity's engine, the same one Dad worked so hard to restore. He's there in the middle of everything, sweaty and exhausted and cursing, swinging a broomstick to try and stop them.

It's not going well.

They grab on to the broom and a tug-of-war ensues before they rip it from his hands. Then the Noodles rush toward him, dozens of them cornering Dad against the shed—the same shed that, once upon a time, was Isaac's tattoo parlor—starting a new tug-of-war, this time with my father's arms. I let go of Jenni's hand and break into a sprint.

"Dad!"

"Eric!" he says in a strained voice, fighting against the Noodles with everything he has left. "Get out of here!"

Brickman leaps from my hand, landing with a killer forward roll that keeps his momentum going as he charges ahead. When he's within ten feet, he fires off a stream of cement cannonballs at the Noodles, blasting them into dust.

"You okay, Dad?" I say as I arrive at his side, putting a hand on his shoulder.

He's panting and holding his chest. And staring down in shock. "Brickman?!" he says. "Is that Brickman?!"

"Yeah. It is." Brickman grunts and salutes. "And this is my friend Jenni," I say as she runs up next to us.

"Nice to meet you, Mr. King," Jenni says.

"Hi," Dad says, not taking his eyes off Brickman. "How did . . . How is Brickman . . . ?"

"I wanted to tell you in the car this morning," I say, feeling like that was five years ago. "I got some ink from your box and—"

We're interrupted by a loud skidding of tires from the boardwalk. We look up and see a go-kart roll over onto its side.

Hollywood.

I hold my breath for a moment, but he emerges from the go-kart unhurt, running toward us at full speed with RoboKillz under his arm. It immediately becomes clear what the rush is: behind him, the wall of Noodles has grown larger than ever, hundreds deep, with Crumple

Noodle leading the charge and Darren right behind.

"Oh god," Dad says.

"Yeah," I say.

"What do they want?"

"This!" Hollywood shouts as he makes it to us at the shed, holding up the marker and passing it to me.

Crumple Noodle sees the exchange and lets out a mammoth roar.

"All this freaking out is because of a magic marker?" Dad asks.

"Pretty much," I say, wishing I could just make the marker temporarily disappear or teleport it to some safe spot or something.

"I'm sorry I couldn't distract them any longer," Hollywood says, still catching his breath.

"You did amazing," I say.

"Can we use any of this stuff?" Jenni asks. She's gone into Dad's shed and come out with his toolbox.

"Might as well," Dad says.

We all grab for something to defend ourselves with—Dad and Jenni pull out hammers, Hollywood takes a large wrench, and I'm left with a stubby Phillips screwdriver.

Hollywood, Jenni, and I step up next to Dad, who pushes us behind him. We're all posed in fighting stance, staring at the approaching wave of Noodles, ready for battle.

Brickman cracks his neck with his hands, turning his mortar head one way, then the other.

RoboKillz gives off three alert beeps as he powers up his missile launchers.

I hold my tiny screwdriver like I'm ready to stake some miniature vampires.

And then:

The Noodles are upon us.

30

MONSTER ASSIST

This screwdriver definitely isn't gonna cut it.

It becomes all too clear all too fast that our meager weapons are no match for the Noodle Army.

We get off some good hits at first, Hollywood slamming two Noodles into the shed wall with his wrench, Jenni using her hammer to splat one that's eagerly heading toward my leg, Brickman working his wrecking ball with the grace and precision of a ballet dancer, me stabbing a Noodle into dust with my Phillips.

But, again: five or six eliminated Noodles when we're talking about a horde of hundreds is just a drop in the bucket. We are surrounded, a blur of rabid, hissing scribble creatures whirling around us like a tornado.

"Eric," Dad says as he madly brushes a few Noodles

off his shoulders. "What are these things?"

"Ink monsters!" I say, stabbing three Noodles to dust in quick succession.

"What? What does that mean?"

"In that box I put in my bedroom, I found tattoo ink. Great-Great-Grandpa Isaac's old tattoo ink."

"Okay . . ."

"Turns out it was magic."

"*What?*"

"Doodles!" Hollywood shouts. "Heads up!"

I frantically look up, unsure what he's talking about.

"I mean heads down!"

Just as I look down, my ankles are pulled out from under me by a bunch of Noodles working together, and I slam to the ground hard, bright splotches of light swirling across my field of vision.

"Get off him!" Dad shouts. He drops his hammer and starts grabbing the Noodles off me, but no matter how many he flings away, there are always more to replace them.

And they want the marker.

I struggle uselessly to get free. I reach for my pocket, so I can protect the marker, but a dozen or so Noodles pin my arms down.

"Finally!" Darren shouts from the nearby boardwalk.

There's nothing I can do.

Crumple Noodle will get the marker. And, just like last time, he will suck on the ink and grow even larger.

And it will still be all my fault.

I shudder and squeeze my eyes tight as I feel one of the Noodles reaching into my pocket.

It's over.

But suddenly, I don't feel the Noodle anymore.

I don't feel any of the Noodles.

What I do feel is wet, covered with some kind of strong-smelling substance.

I wipe my face with my shirt and open my eyes: Smash is standing about fifteen feet away holding a fire extinguisher. There's now a narrow but clear path between us where seconds ago there was a logjam of Noodles.

"Nail Polish Remover Incident: Part Two!" Smash shouts gleefully.

"It worked!" Beanie says from behind her. "It freaking worked!"

"And we've got A LOT more," Yoo-hoo says, Belly-Beast growling triumphantly as Yoo-hoo unzips a giant purple rolling suitcase filled with bottles and bottles of nail polish remover.

"Yes!" I shout, jumping to my feet, even as a new wave of Noodle Monsters swarms toward me.

"Not on my watch!" Smash says, spraying another powerful stream of nail polish remover, which disintegrates at least thirty Noodles into black dust before they can reach me.

"What the hell!" Darren shouts, spit flying out of his mouth as he vaults over the boardwalk railing toward us, looking sweaty and tired.

"That is so dope!" Hollywood says.

"Thank YouTube," Smash says. "Turns out the trick for filling fire extinguishers with paint works for nail polish remover too."

"Science!" Beanie says, both arms in the air. "Just make sure you don't hit any of *our* monsters with that or they'll be goners too."

"Doodles, catch!" Yoo-hoo chucks a bottle of nail polish remover my way, then one to Hollywood, Jenni, and Dad.

"Thanks, Yoo-hoo," Dad says.

"No prob, Mr. King!"

"Should we just, like, pour our bottles on them?" Jenni asks, unscrewing hers as she stares with disgust at the hundreds of remaining Noodles.

"Not quite!" Yoo-hoo says. "We made a pit stop at a souvenir store too." He pulls a huge paper bag from behind the suitcase, out of which he starts throwing us bright yellow water blasters that say *Coney Island* on the side. "Fill 'em up!"

As Smash continues to provide cover with a nonstop

torrent from her fire extinguisher—with Brickman, BellyBeast, RoboKillz standing behind her both to stay out of the stream and to provide *her* cover—we all fill our blasters.

"Um, Monster Club?" Smash says as she sprays. "A little help?" Three crafty Noodles have gotten past our monsters and climbed onto her back, hissing in her ear and pulling her pink spiky hair.

"On it," I say, clutching my newly filled water blaster. "Bricky, Belly, and Robo: get out of the way." They do, and I make quick work of the three Noodles, evaporating them into nothing.

"Thanks," Smash says, wiping away nail polish remover from her neck. "Wanna trade?" She holds out the fire extinguisher.

I stare at it for a moment. "You sure?"

"Seems like you should have it. You're the one with the marker. The one they're all coming for."

I take a moment to look around. There are still at least three hundred Noodles coming at us. And Smash is right: most of them seem to be coming for me.

"All right." I pass her my water blaster, and I'm reaching out for the fire extinguisher when suddenly another set of hands are on it too.

"Gimme that!" Darren says through gritted teeth, a manic look in his eyes, as Smash and I struggle to keep hold of the extinguisher.

"This has to end, Darren!" I shout. "You're acting like a psychopath!"

"My monster is the strongest," he says. "Which means *I* decide when it ends! Crumple, help me grab this thing!"

Crumple Noodle has been hanging back this whole time to let the other Noodles do its dirty work, and

Darren shouting at it doesn't change that. It's clearly terrified of the fire extinguisher.

"I said *help me!*" Darren screams.

Crumple Noodle unleashes a series of hisses back at him, like *Help yourself!*

"Yo," Darren says. "I *drew* you, dude! Which means—" His sentence ends in a high-pitched shriek as RoboKillz fires a barrage of lasers directly at his butt.

"Owwwww!" Darren says as he finally releases the fire extinguisher to hold on to his injured backside. I'm assuming that's the end of it, but then Brickman comes charging toward Darren, swinging the wrecking ball over his head like a lasso before making direct contact yet again with Darren's groin. He falls to the ground.

"Guess he had that coming," I say.

"Uh . . . yeah," Smash agrees. "Definitely."

The Noodle Army has pressed in closer during all this. I put the makeshift strap over my shoulder and grip the fire extinguisher. "Everybody ready?" I ask.

"Ready!" everyone shouts.

"Monster Club assemble!" I shout at the top of my lungs. Technically we're already assembled, but man, it felt good to say anyway.

And it feels even better once we're all delivering a full-on onslaught of nail polish remover. We've formed a tight back-to-back circle, firing our weapons at the

Noodle Army, and it's incredible how quickly we're able to dissolve their ranks.

"We're doing it!" I say. "We're actually doing it!"

"Of *course* we're doing it," Hollywood says, blasting two Noodles. "We're the only ones who could."

As I watch dozens of Noodles disintegrate in the blast from my fire extinguisher, I almost feel as if I'm holding a gigantic eraser, wiping away the horrible mistake I made allowing all these creatures to be brought to life. Some of the Noodles do that puffer fish thing to bloat themselves up, as if that might repel the spray and protect them, but it doesn't. It just makes them bigger targets, and they disintegrate either way.

We are winning.

"This is for what you did to my park!" Dad says, firing his water blaster like a maniac.

During all this, Brickman, RoboKillz, and Belly-Beast stay down at our feet—away from our ink-erasing streams—handling any Noodles that break through so they can't get to the marker in my pocket.

"Thanks, Bricky!" I shout after he wrecking-balls a few Noodles into dust.

He points at me and smiles before using a Krav Maga back kick to send away another one.

Crumple Noodle, meanwhile, continues to hover on the periphery, steering clear of the acetone carnage. As the minutes tick by, I notice everyone steadily refilling their water blasters. Our supply of nail polish remover is rapidly depleting. We have to be more careful and purposeful with our shots—we can't run out of this stuff before we can down Crumple.

"I think there's less than a hundred Noodles left!" Beanie shouts.

"Keep going!" Yoo-hoo shouts back.

We do. The number of Noodles keep thinning, even as, one by one, everyone exhausts their supply of nail polish remover, until it's just me with the fire extinguisher and Yoo-hoo with a blaster.

It's time to go after Crumple.

Right after I have that thought, a bunch of vans and trucks with the word *SWAT* on the side pull up next to the boardwalk behind Crumple Noodle. Literal tanks are coming up Surf Avenue. Helicopters appear overhead.

Help has arrived—finally.

A pack of ten Noodle Monsters seizes on the moment to sneak up behind me, though, and Brickman, RoboKillz, and BellyBeast spring to my defense. RoboKillz is about to fire off some missiles when two of the Noodles shove their arms into his launchers and puff themselves up. The missiles backfire, and RoboKillz explodes into nothing.

"Robo!" Hollywood yells.

BellyBeast immediately leaps into the air to avenge the death of his friend. He does his classic sonic belly flop onto the two Noodles, who are instantly obliterated.

But then Crumple Noodle screams out a command, and suddenly twenty or more Noodles are dogpiling on top of BellyBeast.

"Stop it!" Yoo-hoo shouts.

Before I know what's happening, Crumple Noodle has taken a soaring leap onto the Noodle pile, stomping down on it. More than a few of his minions explode into dust beneath him, but the biggest explosion of all comes last, a horrifying *POP!*—like a scary, twisted version of the sound that marked the beginning of his life—as BellyBeast puffs into a greenish-black dust.

"Noooooooooo!" Yoo-hoo screams for the second time today, unleashing a gush from his blaster that wipes out a bunch of the remaining Noodles before his stream trickles down to nothing. He's all out.

"Don't worry, Yoo-hoo," I say, leaning down toward him. "I'm gonna finish this, and soon you'll draw Belly-Beast version three point—"

Before I even understand what's happening, a slithery arm is in my pocket.

Crumple Noodle has grabbed the marker.

"Shoot!" I shout as Crumple leaps away.

As the five-foot monster lands, it's already got the marker uncapped and is sucking on it. Before our eyes, its body grows to more than ten feet tall.

This can't happen.

I'm about to blast it with my fire extinguisher, praying there's enough nail polish remover left inside, when I see Brickman run up a metal cage from the Zipper ride and spring off it at Crumple.

"Bricky, wait!" I shout, but it's too late. He lands on Crumple Noodle's head and holds on tight. He's the last of our monsters left alive. And he's my monster! I can't fire and risk losing him.

Undeterred, Crumple Noodle sucks on the marker again, a deep pull that gives it the inky nourishment to double in size. It's twenty feet tall now and if we don't stop it soon, the entire remaining supply of Isaac's ink that's inside that marker will be gone forever.

As if he's thinking the same thing, Brickman fires a cement blast over Crumple's mouth. Crumple tries to shake Brickman off while ramming the marker against its mouth. When it realizes the problem, it starts squeezing the cement shield from both sides with what passes for its hands.

Stress fractures appear immediately.

"Blast him already, Eric!" Yoo-hoo shouts.

"You gotta take the shot!" Jenni agrees.

Brickman fires more cement at Crumple's mouth to counteract the pressure, but it's obviously not going to be enough. Soon Crumple will destroy the shield, drink more ink, get even larger and more dangerous.

"What're you waiting for, Doodles?" Smash asks.

"I don't wanna hit Bricky!" I say.

"You won't! Crumple is gigantic! Just aim at the feet!"

Brickman looks down at me, still firing off that steady stream of cement, and I'm almost certain he gives me a nod.

"Now, Doodles!" Beanie shouts. "Now!"

I try to summon all the technique and focus I've developed from years of playing my favorite Coney game, Shoot the Red Star, knowing there's way more at stake this time than a giant stuffed panda. I aim my extinguisher and send a blast straight toward Crumple's legs.

Crumple is too fast, though. It leaps to the side and somehow manages to flick Brickman off its back . . . directly into the path of the spray.

31

GONE

In case you've never had the experience of watching someone you love evaporate into dust, let me tell you:

It's absolutely horrible.

Seconds after Brickman is obliterated, Crumple crushes the cement shield over its mouth and takes another huge sip of the marker, its body lengthening and growing until it's taller than my house. It's closer to the height of a three-story building, at least thirty feet tall, like it's ready to battle Godzilla or something.

The SWAT team advances toward it, dressed in black, wearing face shields and holding scary gear. Crumple lets out an insane scream—a tremendous rumble and buzz like someone taking a chain saw to the strings of a stand-up bass—before bounding away from them, away from us, trailed by the last five remaining Noodle monsters. The SWAT team pursues.

I can't really take in any of that, though.

Because Brickman is dead.

And the only way to bring him back is in the hand of that enormous monster.

I drop my fire extinguisher and run toward the spot just below where Brickman disintegrated. I fall to my knees and curse the sky. Dramatic, I know, but I can't help it.

"Sorry, Doodles," Yoo-hoo says, one hand on my shoulder.

I'm crying too hard to respond, which is embarrassing because I see the rest of Monster Club and Jenni standing and watching from not too far away. I just nod.

Dad crouches on the other side of me. "I'm sorry, bud. I'm so sorry."

This makes me cry harder. I mean, King's Wonderland is right behind us completely demolished, and Dad is focused on making *me* feel better. I throw my arms around him.

"I'm sorry too, Dad," I say. "I destroyed King's."

"The only thing that matters is that you're safe," he says, squeezing me tighter. "Now let's get you and your friends outta here."

I know he's right, even though I also know that if

we go, we'll all be abandoning any hope of seeing our monsters again. Brickman. Skelegurl, BellyBeast, DecaSpyder, RoboKillz. Gone forever.

"I won," a voice says from my left. It's Darren Nuggio, sitting on the ground next to the scrambled remains of the Scrambler ride.

"What?" I say.

"You heard me, Fart Talent," he says, getting to his feet. "My monsters destroyed all your monsters. I won."

Before I even know what's happening, I charge over to Darren and get right up in his face. "First of all, my name is Eric! And second of all: Are you serious right now? Coney's been destroyed. People have been hurt! And all you're worried about is who won?"

"I'm not worried," he says. "Because I know the winner was me."

"You are so pathetic," I say, and I feel Dad and Yoo-hoo trying to pull me away from Darren. "Not to mention useless! We've been trying to stop this thing, and you're over here celebrating. Just go home already! Party alone in your stupid victory."

Darren turns paler than he already is. He's about to open his mouth to respond, but there's a loud *rat-tat-tat*—farther down the boardwalk, the SWAT team is firing automatic weapons at Crumple Noodle as it stomps on an ice man's pushcart, a rainbow of flavor syrups erupting into the air. Crumple puffs itself up, and the SWAT team's bullets bounce away, clattering harmlessly to the ground.

"My god," Dad says, "we gotta get out of here. Like, now."

"True that," Smash says, she and the rest of Monster Club standing nearby, ready to make a run for it. We all watch as Crumple Noodle bounds toward the ocean, down the wooden planks of Steeplechase Pier, the SWAT team in hot pursuit.

"Let's go," Dad says. I bend down to pick up the fire extinguisher as we all start to follow him—well, all of us except Darren, who can't seem to take his eyes off Crumple—toward the cut-through back to Surf Avenue.

"Wait," Beanie says. We all turn to look at her. "Shouldn't we try to help them?"

"No," Dad says. "Those are real bullets being fired. We need to get out of here. Now."

"But we're the only ones who know about the nail polish remover," Beanie says. "Those folks are all gonna be useless against Crumple if we don't tell them what's up."

"They're trained professionals, Yvette," Dad says. "It's out of our—"

There's a scream like the screeching of tires right before a car crash. It's Crumple Noodle doing a U-turn and charging back up the pier at full speed, whipping around its arms and legs as dozens of SWAT officers jump into the ocean to get out of its way. Crumple reaches the start of the pier and begins bounding back down the boardwalk.

Toward us.

"Oh god," Dad says. "Let's go, let's go!"

"You think I'm so useless, Fart Talent?" Darren says, suddenly inches away. "That I should just go home? Nice try, but it's MY monster—if I tell it to stand down, it will! We'll see who's the useless one!"

Before I can get a word in, he's sprinting straight toward Crumple Noodle.

"Darren!" I shout. "Don't!"

"Watch me end this!" he shouts back.

"Dude's gonna get himself killed," Hollywood says.

"Should we—" Yoo-hoo looks to all of us. "I mean, we can't just let him . . ."

Darren screams up at the thirty-foot monster as it approaches. "CRUMPLE! I COMMAND YOU TO STOP! STOP ATTACKING AND DESTROYING! IT'S OVER, DUDE! IT'S OVER!"

"I'll get him," Yoo-hoo says, suddenly bolting away in pursuit of Darren. "You guys get out of here!"

"No, Alan, Eric: let's go!" Dad screams, tugging at my arm. "Come on, everybody!"

"No!" I say, pulling away, running after Yoo-hoo.

Darren is so fast that he's now almost right below Crumple. "CRUMPLE!" he shouts again. "YOU NEED TO STOP. DO YOU UNDERSTAND? IT'S OVER."

And somewhat incredibly, Crumple does stop moving.

"HEY, DUDE!" Darren shouts up at it. "Do you get what I'm saying? We're done now."

Crumple stares down at him, as if it's actually contemplating what he's saying.

Then it slowly nods its head.

"Yes!" Darren says. "Thank you, Crumple!"

"You actually did it!" Yoo-hoo says as he catches up to Darren. "Way to—"

He doesn't get to finish his sentence because Crumple simultaneously snatches him and Darren up from the ground, wrapping them each in a separate tentacle as it lets out that horrible grating laugh.

"NO!" I shout from ten feet away as Yoo-hoo and Darren scream.

I remember I'm holding the fire extinguisher—I let loose the spray and take out a couple of Crumple's legs. It stumbles for a moment and hisses at me before it's bounding at lightning speed back away from me, trailing twin streams of black dust in its wake.

"HOLD YOUR FIRE!" a voice shouts over a megaphone. "I REPEAT: HOLD YOUR FIRE. WE HAVE

TWO KIDS IN THE MONSTER'S ARMS. HOLD ALL FIRE!"

Hollywood, Beanie, Smash, Jenni, and I take off after Crumple, leaving Dad no choice but to race along with us as helicopters buzz overhead in the same direction.

We've been running for at least a minute when I realize with horror where Crumple is headed:

The Parachute Jump.

The same Parachute Jump Jenni wanted me to draw for our graphic novel.

The same Parachute Jump Brickman sculpted for her on my behalf.

The same Parachute Jump my great-great-grandparents Isaac and Eva were standing in front of more than fifty years ago when they posed for the photo I've been keeping in the pocket of my backpack.

I gasp as Crumple Noodle begins to climb the 250-foot iron structure, with Darren Nuggio and my best friend, Alan Yoo, wrapped in its arms.

32

MONSTER CLUB VS. CRUMPLE

Oh no oh no oh no oh no

That's all I can think as I watch Crumple Noodle continue its ascent. All of us within a one-mile radius stare up in the same direction, holding our collective breath.

Yoo-hoo and Darren could die.

And it's my fault.

"What do we do?" Hollywood says. "We gotta do something."

"Maybe the SWAT team will—" Jenni starts to say.

"SWAT team is useless!" Beanie interrupts. We watch from thirty or so feet away as the SWAT officers rush toward the Parachute Jump, forming a human barrier that fully circles around the tower's base. "All they've got are guns that don't work on Crumple, that they can't shoot anyway because Darren and Yoo are in the line of fire."

Crumple is almost to the top of the Parachute Jump, Yoo-hoo and Darren screaming, trapped in its arms.

"So it's on us, then," Smash says. "We'll go tell them about the nail polish remover."

A helicopter buzzes toward Crumple's head, and Crumple shoots out an arm to grab on to its landing gear. The helicopter tries to pull out of its grasp, which is when Crumple abruptly lets go, sending the chopper spinning until the pilot is able to regain control and buzz away.

"It's not on us," I say.

"That's right," Dad says.

"It's on me." I flip the fire extinguisher and its strap to my back and make a mad dash toward the Parachute Jump.

"Eric!" Dad shouts, racing after me.

I crouch down low and skitter between two SWAT officers, catching them off guard enough to slide right past.

"Whoa, whoa!" they shout. "Get back! Get back!"

But I ignore them and keep running, and before they can decide to give chase, Dad and the rest of Monster Club barge forward. SWAT doesn't make the same mistake twice, and they block Dad and the rest of Monster

Club while I run toward Crumple.

"Let me go!" Dad screams. "That's my kid in there! That's my kid!"

I made this mess. It's on me to clean it up.

Not Dad. Not Monster Club.

Me.

I'm climbing the ladder of the Parachute Jump before SWAT can even think what to do.

I'm only ten steps up, the fire extinguisher strung on my back, when it occurs to me that this is the worst idea of all time.

From above, Crumple Noodle lets out another one of those bone-chilling screams.

If Crumple knocks me off the top, there's no way I'll survive.

But Yoo-hoo's had my back my whole life. It's time for me to have his.

I'm probably fifty feet up at this point. I've stopped looking down. I'm just taking it one rung at a time.

I take deep breaths and focus on the rhythm of my hands and legs as I get higher and higher.

One.

Rung.

At.

A.

Time.

About halfway up, though, something funny happens.

I start thinking about my great-great-grandfather Isaac.

I think about the way he dropped everything to save that mermaid's life, even if it meant missing the ship that was going to save his.

That bravery was in him.

So, genetically, it might be in me too.

And then I think about Dad, his courage in standing up to the Vultures time and time again, and Mom, boldly taking down crooks and cheats in the courtroom.

I might also have their bravery.

I move a little faster up the ladder with these realizations, even though the fear is still coursing through every part of me.

When I'm almost at the top, something buzzes right by me.

One look and I instantly recognize it from Robotics Club:

Beanie's flying a drone!

I hear Crumple Noodle screech as Beanie steers it right past Crumple's face like a pesky mosquito. Crumple swats at it, but Beanie is too fast, zipping the drone away. From my spot a few rungs below the top, I take stock of the situation: The top of the tower branches out into a shape that's like an open umbrella if wind blew the fabric off. Or like a sideways wheel, with about ten iron girder spokes branching out from a small pyramid in the center. Crumple's perched on that pyramid, with Yoo-hoo and Darren belly-down on one of the wheel's spokes, holding on for dear life. Darren is behind Yoo-hoo, closer to the center of the wheel, looking especially scared. The five remaining Noodle Monsters bounce from girder to girder. Crumple picks up one of the passing Noodles and hurls it at Beanie's drone. It misses entirely, and the Noodle shrieks as it careens past me down to the ground.

Crumple is still distracted by Beanie's drone, and I know this is my moment.

In case you're wondering how high up in the air 250 feet is, let me put this into context for you: Picture a football field. Now picture that football field rotated to stand up on one end, straight into the sky.

That's about how freaking high up I am right now.

I take one last deep breath.

I think about Yoo-hoo.

I think about Mom.

I think about Dad.

I think about Isaac.

I think about Coney.

I think about Monster Club.

I heft myself up over the edge of the nearest unoc-
cupied iron girder, getting slowly to my feet as I swing
the fire extinguisher from my back to my chest, getting a grip on it as I watch Crumple Noodle, its back
to mine, scream and cackle as it finally makes contact
with Beanie's drone, slapping it out of the sky.

"Hey, Crumple Noodle," I say, the words coming
out more powerfully than I would have thought I was
capable of at this moment. "Time to turn you back into
noodle soup."

As the monster turns to face me, I squeeze the lever
and start to spray.

I watch as the stream from my fire extinguisher
makes contact with one of Crumple's massive inky legs,
disintegrating it into nothing.

Then another.

And another.

And another.

In the mess of its dozens of limbs and the various
curls of black dust coming off its body, I somehow spot
the one limb holding the marker.

I aim my spray at it. Direct hit. The leg vanishes. The
marker falls.

"Holy crap, Doodles!" Yoo-hoo says, his voice qua-
vering as he lifts his head up to see what's happening.
"You're crushing!"

I am. This is working. We are going to win.

At least that's what I think until I watch the fire extinguisher's spray peter out into a mostly harmless stream of air.

Oh no.

By this point, I've disintegrated at least eight or nine of Crumple's legs, and it's fallen face-forward onto the iron girder, losing some of its fangs in the process.

But it also extends two of its arms and yanks my ankles out from under me, which, I gotta say, is about eight bajillion times scarier when it's happening on an iron girder 250 feet up in the air.

"ERIC!" Yoo-hoo screams, reaching out for me.

But too late: I'm already falling.

33

FALLING

So this is how my life ends.

Knocked off Coney Island's iconic Parachute Jump by a monster I inadvertently helped create.

I hope Mom and Dad can forgive me.

I twist my body in the air and blindly reach out my arms, flailing, falling. I somehow wrap an elbow around the edge of an iron girder.

And like that: I'm not falling anymore.

I am, however, dangling dangerously in midair.

I try to block out the aggressive buzz of news and police helicopters circling all around.

"Hold on, Eric!" Yoo-hoo shouts over the noise, from the girder he and Darren are still lying on and desperately clutching.

"You got this, Fart Talent," Darren shouts, his voice even more quavery than Yoo-hoo's.

I think about Isaac again, pulling himself up onto that dock to get his pocketknife from his coat—his heart must have been pumping just like mine is now—and it gives me the strength I need to pull myself up onto the iron girder.

And that's when I spot it. It's about ten feet away on the girder, precariously close to the edge:

My marker.

I slide the fire extinguisher off my back and balance it on the girder behind me, and I start crawling toward the marker. I don't have paper on me, so it's not like I can draw Brickman to come help us or something once I get it, but I know I need to keep the marker away from Crumple Noodle, if nothing else.

I grip the iron girder with my left arm as I reach out my right as far as possible and scooch myself forward. Then I do the same with my left. Then my right again.

The marker is only a few feet away.

I reach out my hand and I'm about to grab it when—

No.

One of the four remaining Noodles bounces over and snatches it first, hissing in my face.

I try to grab the marker, but it's useless—I can't reach without falling again.

"Let it go," Darren shout-whispers from a few girders over.

The Noodle Monster turns its head to look at him.

"Give the marker to Fart Talent!" Darren barks with all the possible gravitas he can muster. "I command you!"

The Noodle turns back to me, steps forward, and extends the marker.

Crumple may no longer be listening to Darren, but clearly, he still has some influence over the Noodles. Bless you, Darren Nuggio.

I grab the marker away.

"Eric, watch out!" Yoo-hoo shouts.

Crumple Noodle is now back to its full height, screaming as it towers above me.

It sees I have the marker. And it isn't pleased.

Yoo-hoo and Darren are behind Crumple, and both of them look terrified.

Still on all fours, I hug the marker to my chest as at least a dozen of Crumple's arms and legs encircle me, poking and prodding and trying to grab it back. The last four Noodles are hopping and hissing on me too.

"Give me space!" I shout in a panic as I feel Crumple going for my ankles again. "I'll drop the marker!" I extend my arm, holding the marker over the emptiness. "I swear I will! It's the only remaining ink!"

Crumple Noodle goes still. Somehow it understands.

"Give me space and call off the little ones!" I shout.

After a long pause, Crumple retracts its limbs and mumbles angrily down to the Noodles, who leap over to the neighboring iron girder.

I know this is my one moment—Crumple wants the marker; I have the marker. I don't have a choice. I know what I have to do.

"I'll give you back this marker if you let me and my friends go!" I shout up to it.

Crumple stares down at me for a moment.

Then it starts laughing hysterically, making that horrific sound. Clearly it's not feeling my offer. I catch Yoo-hoo's eye, then Darren's, the kid who's tortured me since the day we met and who now needs my help more than anything, and suddenly, I know exactly what I have to do.

"Here, boy! Here, boy!" I shout, getting to my feet and lifting the marker high above my head.

Crumple stops laughing, its one eye locked on me.

"You want this marker, right?" I ask. "Then . . . FETCH!"

And I hurl the marker as far as I possibly can toward the beach.

Crumple Noodle and its four remaining minions take the bait, leaping off the Parachute Jump after it.

"Sucker," I say. Because I haven't actually thrown it.

In midair, Crumple realizes that it's been fooled, screeching with rage as it spins around and reaches for me. I crouch down to hold on to the girder, but it turns out not to matter—Crumple's arms are too short to grab me.

I watch it and the four Noodles descend, shocked that the trick actually worked.

"Well played," Darren says from his girder.

Crumple bloats up in midair as the crowd of SWAT, police, and National Guard below scatters like ants.

The four Noodles splat onto the boardwalk and disintegrate into dust, but the bloated Crumple lands with a muffled boom and bounces once, twice, three times.

It's unharmed.

Oh no.

Crumple unbloats itself, and lets out its loudest scream yet.

But then there's another sound, and as I look to my right, there's a new pack of helicopters heading our way, each outfitted with a bucket hanging by cables below it.

"Oh wow," I say quietly to myself.

The first helicopter releases the contents of its giant vat, directly onto Crumple's head, disintegrating at least half its limbs.

Nail polish remover.

"Yeah!" Yoo-hoo shouts as, one by one, each helicopter hovers above Crumple and douses it with our secret weapon until, finally, there's nothing left of Darren's monster at all.

It's over.

From down below, I can hear wild cheers.

I slide the marker back into my pocket as I exhale.

As Yoo-hoo, Darren, and I ride back down in a helicopter, the exhaustion hits me like, well, like a ton of bricks. It's too loud in here to talk, but it feels like the three of us are agreed that we can't believe what just happened and that we're lucky to be alive.

Once we're safely back on the ground, a small crowd is waiting for us and shouting our names. Mom and Dad rush toward me as Yoo-hoo's mom rushes toward him. I don't see anyone there for Darren, and I lose sight of him as Mom wraps me in the hugest hug of all time. Much to my surprise, I instantly start crying.

"That was the stupidest thing you've ever done," Mom says.

"I know," I say through tears.

"I can't even tell you how scared I was. Probably took twenty years off my life."

"Yeah, mine too," Dad says, putting an arm around me while Mom keeps hugging.

"But we're also so proud of you," Mom says, finally pulling out of the hug and looking me in the eyes.

"Got that right," Dad says, taking his turn to hug me. "Didn't know our kid was a hero. What you just did? I could never be brave like that."

It feels so good to hear him say that. And, as I stand there with Mom and Dad, seeing them so happy, I'm struck by how long it's been since I've seen them like this. Maybe it's all that talk of bravery, but suddenly I'm able to see what was right in front of me all along, the thing I was too scared to admit.

"Dad's not coming home again, is he?" I ask.

Mom's face falls. "Oh . . . Well, sweetie, now's not the time to talk about—"

"No," Dad says, giving my shoulder a squeeze. "I'm not, bud." Mom looks to Dad like *You're telling him this now?* and he looks back like *I don't know, I guess so.* She sighs and rubs my back. "We're so sorry, Eric."

"It wouldn't have mattered if we saved the park, would it?" I ask.

She and Dad are quiet for a moment.

"No," Mom says. "It wouldn't have."

I let out a huge sob. This hurts so much.

"Eric. Buddy," Dad says, his eyes a little teary, "your mom and I . . . We were just kids when we met. And man, we loved each other. More than anyone else in the whole world." He looks at Mom, as if seeing a younger version of her. "But things change." He looks back to me. "And people change. And that's what happened with me and Mom. She outgrew this place. But for me? This is who I am, this park, and I ain't leaving till they drag me away."

"Or till a pack of monsters destroy it," I say, my nose filled with snot.

"Right, yeah," Dad says, somehow finding a small laugh in the midst of all this. "We'll see about that one. Point is, you can't stop a thing changing. You might want to keep everything the way it was, and everybody the way they were, but it's not . . . That's not how it works. All you can do is change with it."

I think I get what he's saying. I hate it, but I get it.

"That's why Dad and I have to go our separate ways," Mom says. "But that doesn't mean we'll ever stop loving each other."

"Yeah," Dad says, "that's one thing that'll never change."

I let out one more sob and wipe my eyes.

"And we'll always be in each other's lives and a part of each other," Mom says. "The love between your father and me led to the existence of a person we both love more than anyone else in the world."

I nod, realizing she's talking about me.

"Yeah, you, ya knucklehead," Dad says. "You're our guy. Nothing's gonna change that. Ever."

"Thanks, guys," I say as the two of them hug me again. "I'm sorry I accidentally ruined Coney Island."

"Ruined?" Dad says, pulling out of the hug. "Eric, if there's one thing I've learned spending my whole life at Coney, it's that this place thrives on publicity. And this story's gonna get a *ton* of it." He points up at the news helicopters, at all the vans pulling up to the scene with different network letters emblazoned on their sides. "A real-life monster story with a bunch of kids heroically saving the day? Forget about it! Coney's gonna be fine."

"But what about the Vultures?" I ask. "What about King's?"

"We'll figure it out, buddy," Dad says.

"Force majeure!" Mom blurts out, looking into the distance the way she does when she's deep in thought on a case.

"Huh?" Dad says.

"The force majeure clause that says you're off the hook for payments during extraordinary circumstances—"

"But," I say, "I thought you said that didn't apply because the bank has an exception for hurricanes."

"Right," Mom says. "But their contract says nothing about an exception for monsters!"

"Oh wow," Dad says, genuinely surprised.

"That's brilliant, Mom!" I shout. "Those monsters were totally a 'great force'!"

"I agree that's pretty genius," Dad says, smiling at Mom. She smiles back. It's almost like, now that they've told me they're not getting back together, they can finally talk to each other with respect again. It's weird. But, not gonna lie, it's nice to hear them get along.

"Mind if I cut in here?" Yoo-hoo says, clearly tired of waiting for his turn to hug me.

"Of course not, Alan," Mom says. "So happy you're all right."

"Thanks, Mrs. King. Your son's my hero."

He wraps me in a hug, and the rest of Monster Club piles on too.

"You really crushed it," Yoo-hoo says. "The hands-down winner of the Monster Club Crown of Glory, till the end of time."

"We were flipping out," Hollywood says.

"You are hard-core, Doodles," Smash says.

"Thanks," I say. "Couldn't have done it without all of you."

"We did what we could," Beanie says, unable to conceal the pride on her face.

"I'm so happy we're not dead!" Yoo-hoo shouts, still squeezing me tight.

"Me too," I say, laughing.

Yoo-hoo finally lets go, and so does the rest of Monster Club, and I see that Darren's standing nearby.

"Hey," he says, hands awkwardly in his pockets.

"Hey," I respond.

"Just wanted to say, like . . . thanks. For what you did up there."

"Thank *you* for saving my butt with that Noodle."

Darren nods. I nod back. We stand there for a few seconds. I'm not really sure what else to say.

"All right, this is weird," Darren says, walking away. "Adios, Fart Talent."

"Later, Darren," I say, right before Jenni rushes up out of nowhere and gives me a huge hug.

"You are really nuts but also really impressive," she says into my ear, and it sounds like she's on the verge of tears. "I was so worried."

"Thanks, Jenni," I say, my whole body kind of tingly from hugging her. Somehow after everything that's happened today, she still smells really good.

I notice Yoo-hoo and Smash on the other side of the boardwalk holding hands.

I walk over to them. "Sorry," I say, "but can I talk to you a minute, Yoo-hoo?"

"Oh," Yoo-hoo says, letting go of Smash's hand and looking a little unsure, like he's worried I might yell at him, which makes me feel horrible. "Sure."

We walk to the far side of the boardwalk, not that far from where we took Brickman and BellyBeast to battle that first day. "I, uh, just wanted to say thank you," I say. "For everything."

"Of course, dude," Yoo-hoo says. "But you're the one who saved me."

"No, but . . . I also wanted to say sorry. Like a real sorry. You're, like, always there for me in every way possible, and I feel like I'm not always the best friend to you."

"Oh, well, I mean—"

"You don't have to deny it," I say. "I literally pushed you at school, and I hate that so much. I've been trying to, like, block it out, or make excuses in my head, which is why I haven't even been able to properly apologize since it happened, but it just sucked. And I'm really sorry."

"Thanks, Doodles."

"And I know I always got so annoyed with Hollywood when he started dating Jamie or whatever, but I mean, it's totally okay by me if you have a crush on Smash. Not that you need my permission, but . . ."

Yoo-hoo's face turns red.

"Honestly," I say, "it seems like she totally likes you back."

"Well . . . maybe." Yoo-hoo grins. "We'll see."

"You know she does, dude," I say, grinning back. "And one more thing: if you want to go by Yoo now, I'll totally call you Yoo."

"*You Yoo*," he says, laughing. "Why don't you just call me that? Yoo-Yoo?"

I laugh too. "But for real. I don't know why I was a jerk about it when you didn't want to be Yoo-hoo anymore. We cool, Yoo?" I extend my hand.

"All right," Yoo says, shaking on it. "We cool."

We're silent for a moment, sitting in the glow of this new understanding we have.

"I was thinking," I say, reaching into my pocket. "I want you to use this first." I hand him the marker. "Bring back BellyBeast."

"Whoa," Yoo says, staring down at it. "I mean . . . do you think we should?"

I guess I'd just been assuming that, since I was able to get the marker back, against all odds, of *course* we would bring our monsters back.

But when Yoo says that, I realize that of *course* we shouldn't.

"Or," Yoo says, "maybe we bring our monsters to life one last time and then destroy it?"

"No. You're right. Even that's too risky." I stare out into the Atlantic, the waves crashing down on the shore like they always do, as if they're still going about their daily business, tide in and tide out, unaware of the insanity that's transpired right next to them. "We made a promise to King Neptune. And besides . . . I don't think we need it anymore."

All five of us in Monster Club stand in the sand, facing the ocean.

"Bye, Skelly," Smash says, cradling the marker as if it's her old friend before passing it to Hollywood.

"It's been real, Robo," Hollywood says to the marker. "You killed it every step of the way." He passes it to Beanie.

She holds the marker in front of her and stares at the cap, mesmerized as if it's a lit flame. "Deca," she says. "Your technical capabilities exceeded my wildest dreams. I'll miss you."

Yoo takes the marker next. "I'll always love you, Belly-Beast," he says, a tiny hitch in his voice that inspires Smash to walk over and put her arm around him as he hands the marker to me.

I stare at it for a while, images of my solid pal running through my brain.

"What can I say, Bricky? You got me through so many hard times. You were, like, my rock. Well, my brick. You were my brick. And I'll never forget you."

I look to the rest of Monster Club.

"We're doing the right thing, right?"

They nod at me. I nod back, putting the marker in my pocket before leaving them there on the sand, off to look for the only person in the world who can definitively end this, once and for all.

"Neptune!" I shout. "Mr. Neptune—I mean, King Neptune!"

He's sitting on a bench on the boardwalk when I find him, far from the hubbub of the Parachute Jump, of police and press vans and news helicopters. Surprisingly, he seems glad to see me.

"Young prince," he says. "I'm sorry for my tempestuous outburst earlier because . . . you most assuredly honored your family legacy. You are every bit as brave as Isaac."

"Thanks," I say. "But I am sorry. I didn't listen to you, and I didn't keep my promise and . . . Things got so out of control."

King Neptune nods. "Learn from this. Let today shape you. Change you."

I nod back, unsure how one responds to that. "Okay." He continues to look at me but says nothing. I stand there awkwardly, knowing what I have to do but not wanting to do it.

"Here," I say finally, holding out the marker. "I'm

sorry I didn't do this earlier, but better late than never. You can make things right. Do some complicated magic and get rid of this."

King Neptune stares down at the marker for a long moment before he takes it from me. "From one King to another," he says. "Gotta say, I'm proud of you, kid. Isaac would be too."

I nod and say bye to Brickman once more in my head. "Thanks, King Neptune. See ya around, I guess."

"Farewell, young prince."

I walk away. When I look back, King Neptune is already walking in the opposite direction. As sad as it feels to think that I'll never see Brickman in real life again, it also feels good to know I've done the right thing, that I've finally taken responsibility.

I jog back down the boardwalk, then break into a run, hoping Monster Club hasn't left yet.

34

MONSTER CLUB WONDERLAND

I'm tracing out an *E* and a *K* in spray paint on the side of Dad's shed when my friends show up.

"Whoa, it's done!" Yoo says.

"It's breathtaking," Smash says before pointing down at the fire extinguisher in my hands. "You're really getting the hang of that thing."

"Yeah, man," Hollywood says. "That slaps."

The mural I've been working on for weeks, pretty much since the day after everything went down, is finally finished. And not to brag, but it's pretty phenomenal, easily my proudest achievement as an artist.

"The dimensions of Deca's legs aren't exactly right," Beanie says. Everyone shoots her a look, including me. "But otherwise it's really amazing, Doodles."

The mural depicts all our monsters—Brickman, BellyBeast, DecaSpyder, Skelegurl, and RoboKillz— battling the ten-foot-tall Crumple Noodle, each of them in the act of using their unique powers. Instead of drawing them how we always used to, I modeled them after their three-dimensional selves, which was a lot harder to do, incorporating shadow and depth and proportion in a way that captured reality. I think it actually came out all right, though. Other than DecaSpyder's legs, apparently.

"Now our monsters will live forever," Yoo says.

"Not only that," I say. "Check out the sign."

I point up to the new one Dad just had made as part of the overall repairs and renovations after Crumple's attacks. King's is no more. Now it's Monster Club Wonderland, with Brickman leaning up against the *M*.

I told Dad he didn't have to do that, but he said he wanted to. Felt like it was time for a change. Really, he's just grateful the park still exists at all. Mom was right about force majeure—the bank had no choice but to admit that a monster attack was an extraordinary circumstance, so Dad won't be on the hook for payments for at least six more months. The park is still his, and there's nothing the Vultures at Pluto Properties can do about it. Meanwhile, the place is well on its way to being fully repaired with the money Dad got from his insurance company, and business has never been so good. Mom's a fricking hero. And I guess, in a way, we are too.

"Whoa!" Hollywood says, taking in the new sign. "That's unreal."

"Yep," I say. "So Monster Club will live forever too."

We're all absorbing the power of that when Jenni walks up and my stomach does a little leap.

"Wow," she says, checking out my mural. "That came out insanely well, Eric. Like, really. Wow."

"Thanks," I say as we hug.

"We should probably go find a spot to watch," she says. "It's getting way crowded out there."

"Yeah, definitely," I say as I take her hand, which I've gotten more used to, though I'm still a little shocked by how much I like it. "Let's go, everybody."

We all walk down the boardwalk, the sun beating down on our necks, looking for the right spot to take in the glory that is today, the Mermaid Parade. It's always been my favorite day of the year in Coney Island, partly because it always coincides with the end of the school year, but also because it's awesome.

We find a spot, and Jamie Posterman and some of her friends join up with Hollywood and all of us as the parade begins. Hundreds of people walk past dressed in amazing and ridiculously elaborate costumes mostly as either mermaids or King Neptunes, all of them following the guy in a black top hat who started the Mermaid Parade almost forty years ago, unofficial mayor of Coney (and Dad's good friend), Dick Zigun.

"Holy macaroni," Yoo-hoo whispers, pointing into the crowd.

And then we all see it: there are people dressed as our monsters.

Brickmen and BellyBeasts, Decas and Skelegurls and RoboKillz, even a few Crumple Noodles.

We stare in awe, speechless. We've become a permanent part of Coney history.

After a while, Hollywood and Jamie break off to go ride the Cyclone, and Beanie shifts position to try and get some better shots with the drone camera she's rigged up herself, and Smash takes Yoo to the boardwalk ramp to try and teach him how to skateboard down a rail.

I don't want to leave yet, though. As I stand there watching, Jenni by my side, I can't help but think about history. How Coney's history is *my* history, how this place is in my blood and always will be. I think about the mermaid who my great-great-grandfather saved, the same mermaid who then ended up saving *him*, who indirectly led to my existence.

And, staring at all these fake King Neptunes in flashy, over-the-top costumes, I of course can't help but think about the King Neptune *I* know. The real King Neptune. The one who knew my great-great-grandfather, the one I've been trying to find the past few weeks with no luck whatsoever. I hope that destroying the ink at last finally gave him some peace.

"Hey, can I show you something?" I ask Jenni.

She says sure, and we leave the boardwalk, head down the steps to the beach. I reach into my backpack and nervously slide out my folder.

"Check it out," I say, handing it to her.

She opens it up and smiles as she sees my fully inked and colored drawing of the Parachute Jump on the cover. I was so amped by the lifelike work I was doing on my mural that I started diving into the graphic novel every night once I got home.

"Hey, look at you!" she says, the sea breeze blowing her dark hair all over the place. "You finally got some of it done. It looks so good."

"Open it up," I say.

She flips the cover open and sees that I've filled in artwork for every panel on every page.

"It's just a first pass," I say.

"Whoa," Jenni says. "Eric, this is—You know this isn't due till next year, right?"

"Just getting a head start."

She smiles again. "You dork, are you quoting me to me?"

"I am."

She gives me a little shove, and I shove her back, and we do that for a while, until we're laughing so hard we fall down into the sand.

I stare out at the water, wondering if we're sitting anywhere near where Isaac was when the mermaid gave him her blood.

Or anywhere near where my parents once sat, on one of their early dates at Coney.

Or anywhere near where Brickman tackled Belly-Beast in the sand that first day.

I miss Brickman.

Jenni takes my hand as we stare out at the ocean together, one wave crashing in after the other.

So much has changed in the past month.

So much keeps changing.

But I guess, as long as I keep changing too, maybe that's all right.

"What are you thinking about?" Jenni asks.

"I'm glad I'm sitting here with you," I say.

"Me too," she says, as both of our histories continue to form.

EPILOGUE

Coney Island, Brooklyn. A few weeks ago.

So our story ends not so differently than it began: with the destruction of that same beloved Coney park—King's—followed by its triumphant rebirth. Things go, things come back. Death, life, the constant cycle. The more things change, the more they stay the same, and what have you.

And that boy from the very beginning of our tale, the one at Coney Island in 1949, who fell so deeply in love with those astounding battling tattoos—so much so that he grew up to be someone who understood that he *was* the hero he'd seen battle in ink form, King Neptune—got to experience that devastating magic once more.

When the young prince handed over the marker to King Neptune so that it could be properly destroyed, the god did not take the responsibility lightly. He held the marker close and ducked into an abandoned old bathhouse soon to be demolished by Pluto Properties. But not to perform any complicated magic.

Fifteen minutes later, King Neptune emerged from the building, and he no longer looked the way he had when he went in. He was actually clean, for one thing. For another, he was not wearing a toga, or sandals, or a crown in his now-slicked-back white hair.

He was wearing an Armani suit. And sunglasses.

He wasn't fully comfortable in these clothes—he thought of them more as his "human disguise"—but unfortunately his work demanded it of him. He hadn't asked to inherit his father's commercial real estate business, but he had, and it had turned out to be so very helpful.

And anyway, the god of the sea didn't mind the clothes, considering today had been an Astonishingly Good Day. His decades-long devotion to learning everything he could about Isaac King's life, to finding the green-tinted mason jar of mermaid's blood he so desperately coveted, had finally paid off. And all it took was gaining the trust of Isaac's naive descendant.

As he walked from the Coney Island Mermaid Bathhouse toward the street, King Neptune felt better than he had in quite a long while. A sleek black car pulled up next to him, and he stepped inside.

"You okay, boss?" the bearded man behind the wheel asked. "That was something else out there."

"Total chaos," the man with a mustache sitting in the passenger seat agreed.

"I'm fantastic," the head of Pluto Properties said, running a hand through his white hair. "Got everything I need. Now let's get out of here."

And so the god of the sea drove away, staring down at the magic marker in his leathery hands, finally ready to move on to the next chapter of his history.

ACKNOWLEDGMENTS

Although this book is a work of fiction, it is an emotional shout-out to my old neighborhood and my childhood buddies. I wish to thank those lifelong friends from Papa Leone's: Lipper, Ross, Jesse, Mark, Ariel, Shane, Brandon, and especially Eric (my original partner in Monster Club) and his daughter—my goddaughter—Harper who gave me a thumbs-up and guidance on an early draft. Thank you to all my teachers from PS 195 and Mark Twain JHS who blessed me with their focused patience and attention. Finally, Ari and I would like to thank Hugh, Cat, and the immeasurable contributions of Lance Rubin, for all their ideas, love, work, and magic helping us bring this book to life.

Darren Aronofsky